Playthings

PLAYTHINGS

ALEX PHEBY

BIBLIOASIS

WINDSOR, ONTARIO

Alex Pheby's *Playthings* was first published in 2015 by Galley Beggar Press Limited

Library and Archives Canada Cataloguing in Publication

Pheby, Alex, author
       Playthings / Alex Pheby.

Issued in print and electronic formats.
ISBN 978-1-77196-172-1 (softcover).--ISBN 978-1-77196-173-8 (ebook)

       I. Title.

PR6116.H37P53 2018   823'.92   C2017-907303-6
                                             C2017-907304-4

Readied for the Press by Daniel Wells
Copy-edited by Jessica Faulds
Typeset by Chris Andrechek
Cover designed by Zoe Norvell

PRINTED AND BOUND IN CANADA

For Emma

Disturbed by an unexpected illness, retired Senatspräsident of the High Court of Saxony, Daniel Paul Schreber, last of the great Schreber line, suffers the return of feelings and thoughts he has long kept in check.

I

Coal dropped through the chute, sending a hint of black rising up the stairs into the hall. Schreber stopped. Framed in the archway into the drawing room, he swallowed and took a deep breath. Nothing to be concerned about. Quite the opposite, really. Some coal dust mingling with the scent of fresh flowers. The post laid in a fan on the hall table. Dim light. The opaque mist of bacon fat heated past transparency on to smoking and spitting. Simple matters.

From downstairs in the kitchen came the crack and hiss of a hot iron skillet banged down onto a tabletop. Perfectly ordinary.

He brought himself up straight.

'Sabine!' Schreber called. 'Sabchen?'

Nothing.

He went back and leaned through the doorway to downstairs.

'Cook! My good woman, is it really so important?'

Cook replied in that hard-done-by manner she had, with only half the words spoken clearly so that the other half had to be guessed at. Something about lunch, the club, a promise. Very well…

'Sabine! Cook is asking after you!'

Nothing.

Was she sleeping?

'Sabine!'

Nothing.

He sniffed and walked down the hall to where the parlour door stood closed.

No sound of her in the parlour. Wouldn't she be humming a tune? Or whistling? He didn't hear either thing. Nor any quiet snoring in their place. He turned his head so that his ear was nearer the door and he listened harder.

Thirty seconds passed.

Nothing.

Cook cursed—an unruly pan of boiling stock bubbling over. By the parlour there was only silence.

Should he open the door and go in?

He straightened his waistcoat.

There was a school of thought amongst the men of his acquaintance that the owner of a house had the right to enter any room of his choice. On the other hand, there was a competing school—advocated primarily by the married men—that said that if a husband was allowed anywhere in the home, it was only on sufferance, and that he shouldn't dare go into a room he suspected of being solely occupied by his wife, the reasoning being that if the wife was not already in her husband's company, then she quite probably did not wish to be.

He turned and coughed and listened again.

Nothing.

On the wall in front of him there was a portrait of his grandfather. It was done in browns and greens and muted reds, dingy through decades of hanging, sun-faded, almost lost amongst the jumble of still lives and theatre playbills. He was standing with one hand in his breast pocket and the other resting on his writing table. Schreber reached out and wiped a line of dust from the picture frame. Poor old Grandpapa. He licked a corner of his handkerchief and ran it gently over the gold finished wood. When he was done he looked back at the old man. It seemed as if he had receded from view, into the background of the picture, into the wall, his modesty overwhelmed by the gold frame and the bacon fat and the coal dust. Standing at the old man's feet was Schreber's father.

Schreber lifted his chin and sniffed. A tic. One that an observer might have recalled seeing when Schreber made his way from his chambers to the courtroom, or earlier, when he was brought before his father in knee shorts, pressed, with the backs of his ears rubbed red and stinging with soap.

'Sabine! Have you gone deaf, dearest? You are needed.'

Nothing.

Should he risk it? Knowing precisely her response if she was busy?

He sighed and coughed and did not move.

Beside his grandfather on the wall was Sabine's father—Herr Behr—a totally different type of man altogether: round-faced and smiling. Exuberant. Extravagant. Even in an etching this man gave off an air of life and energy. It was an advertisement from a theatre in this very city, in Dresden, for *Das Gefängnis*, and he, the leading actor, stood mouth open, singing. A little ridiculous? Perhaps.

Schreber turned away from him and there, now, was the door handle.

'Sabchen,' he said.

What was she up to, behind this door?

There was prickling on the back of his neck. There was thickness gathering behind his eyes.

Tiredness.

Nothing more.

Just a normal day, like every other.

She would be taking tea and attending to her affairs, as he had been attending to his, distracted, both of them, by

3

the business of the day, the arrangements for the party, the news. If Cook needed something, then what of it? Always so demanding! Wasn't it her place to wait on them? Anyone would think it was the other way around! He shouldn't even think of disturbing Sabine with the woman's request. Behind this door he would find her, perfectly well, and she would be testy with him. He was thoughtless and inconsiderate. So much she had said many times, and now he was thinking about bothering her? Distracting her from her important business? Very foolish! She would have the table laid out with a hundred things—cards and napkins and napkin rings in bone—and she would be so busy with her decisions about this and that—things husbands have no comprehension of— that to expect a reply, even if she heard him, was ridiculous. Utterly dim-witted! If he turned this handle and opened the door, he would see her, standing, leaning over the table like a general, moving her troops across the map. When he said her name she would wheel around to face him, and her jaw would be clenched and her brow knotted. Yes. He would have to apologise.

But why was it so quiet?

'Sabine!'

Nothing.

He meant to turn the handle, but, when he tried to do it, his hand gripped the metal until his knuckles poked up. It was as if they intended to breach the skin.

What if...?—he caught the thought and moved his hand back from the handle onto his waist, onto his waistcoat, and he smoothed the round, firm curve that the passing years and Cook's facility with pastry had built between them. Don't be an old fool! It was just an ordinary day. Pull yourself together! Too little sleep and too much milk at breakfast. Nothing to be feared from this place. His home. Hadn't every day proved so much to him a thousand times? He blinked and sniffed and smoothed and before he knew it his hand was making progress through the air again, towards the handle.

'Sabine! What are you up to, my dear?'

If the sounds from the street were not convincing—if they seemed theatrical—then what of it? If the walls seemed thin, knocked up from plaster of Paris, then what of it? Wasn't there also the newspaper beside the post? Wasn't there Bülow, carried unconscious from the Reichstag? The twenty excess invitations that the girl had foolishly requested from the printer, useless except for notes, since the date and time was there plain as day on the front? Weren't those things there too? The flowers? The telegraphs from Sabine's friends, agreeing to come? If the pictures were arranged one way or the other then so what? He could hear Cook downstairs working. He could hear her irritation in the banging and clattering of pans. Didn't this offset the strangeness? Of course it did! He sniffed and blinked and stood tall and reached for the door handle.

'Excuse me!' a voice said from close behind him.

Schreber jumped as if he had been stung by a wasp.

It was Cook. She was a short, fat woman with big red hands like an ironmonger's, and she pouted and looked sidelong when she spoke.

'I don't mean to bother you, sir,' she said.

'What is making that noise?'

'Sorry, sir?'

'In the kitchen. If you are up here, what is making that noise down there?'

Cook said nothing for a while. She examined him from the corner of her eye. Looking for what? Had she discovered warning signs? Could she see what he only felt—the uncanny sensations gathering in the house? Had her years in his company attuned her to these things? Or was she simply slow, like other women of her type?

Eventually she answered.

5

'The girl, sir. Sarah.'

Of course. Schreber nodded slowly, and when he saw the edge in Cook's expression he tried his best to smile.

'Of course… the girl. Noisy thing, isn't she? What was it…?'

Cook looked down at her feet.

'I'm very sorry, sir, but I really must know as soon as possible: will you and the missus want lunch today, or will you be taking it out? I wouldn't press, it's only that with the missus not responding to my earlier enquiries, then, well, I don't know quite who else I should ask.'

Over years of anxiety and service, Cook had rubbed the front of her linen apron smooth and shiny, and she was doing it now. Schreber stared at her, smiling, not speaking, and now she stared back—a little impudently Sabine might have thought—a demonstration of cheek and surliness brought on by her husband taking too friendly an attitude with the staff. Too accommodating by half. Too apologetic. If the master had his peculiarities, then what business was it of theirs?

Schreber couldn't for the life of him think of what to say to the woman. He pulled at his cuffs until they came the proper distance out from the sleeves of his jacket. He swallowed. He pinched with the thumb and forefinger of his right hand the exact centre of his moustaches and then moved finger and thumb apart, smoothing. Cook was waiting, and rubbing, and glancing back down the stairs to the kitchen every few seconds, her attention drawn by a clattering lid, or the smell of scorching. Schreber coughed, and sniffed, and drew himself up.

'Yes, Cook, quite right, we'll take our lunch here, thank you,' he said. That should have been the end of it, but the silly woman went on.

'Very good, sir… it's only that the missus said she was going to let me know about it this morning—so I could send out and have plenty of time to prepare and what not—but she never said, and she gave me to believe that you might very well be

6

lunching at the club, so that now if you want something it'll have to be cold cuts and bread because I've got the stove top full for the function tonight what with the extra for the guests, and will last night's chicken be acceptable? Only the mutton has turned on account of the heat from me having to keep the stove burning last night so that I could make an early start what with it only being me and the girl, you having decided it wasn't necessary for me to bring in my sister, like I asked?'

Schreber made a motion with his head that was neither a shake nor a nod, and had he been asked to account for it he wouldn't have been able to. At first, cook hesitated and stared, but in the end, when her words had disappeared away to nothing and Schreber's gesture was fading from memory, it seemed good enough for her, and she turned and went back downstairs.

Schreber let his shoulders drop.

'Sabine?'

Nothing.

Once, Schreber went down into the kitchen on an errand, and there he found Cook busy scrubbing the flagstones on her knees. Her skirts had caught up on themselves at the back and one calf was visible, almost up to the knee. Schreber knew better than to take advantage of her disarrangement, but he couldn't look away. Her skin was snaked with blue veins that rose from near her ankles. Each vein was the thickness of a child's finger and they crept up and around and under her skirts.

As he often did, Schreber remembered those blue snakes now, standing outside the parlour with his hand on the door handle. A noise came into his head—a buzz—as if prompted by the memory, and with it came a thought—that Cook was a mother and that she had given birth to many children. These were the rightful scars carried by such women. Nothing. A little trap? He stepped back from the idea and thought of something else: his bedtime pipe lit and warm in the palm of his hand. The cold brass of the door handle. Something solid. A defence against

7

his old illness, against dreams of motherhood and death and the way of things. Of God and women. Womb-thought. He put his hand on the door handle and pushed it open.

The room—the part of it that he could see—was as it always was: the benched bay window, the broad cherry table with an arrangement of hyacinths in a blue-and-white vase. There was the mirrored side cabinet and glasses. There were those ornaments beloved of his wife, gathered from small shops in the back streets of a hundred Saxon towns on a hundred jolly excursions and hoarded here: the porcelain dogs, the perfectly tiny glass windmills, the silhouettes and cameos. It was Sabine's room. Even Fridoline was told not to come here, and the skivvy was told not to dust. Here Sabine would shut herself up and play quietly on the piano, or rehearse lines for plays she would never perform again. Here she would lean forward and talk in hushed whispers to her gaudy friends and always know, seemingly, when Schreber set foot in the hall, the audibility of their conversation rising with the change of subject to matters of no import.

It was the same as it always was.

A little different…

There was no sound, except that which leaked in through the window. No operetta played one-handed on the piano, the other hand turning the page. No rustling of dried flowers released from books of yellowed paper secured with a vice. Only a man outside and his horse. Shouted orders that were ignored. The reluctant clicking of iron horseshoes on the stone of the street.

He stepped into the room, two firm steps, straight-legged, and when he took in the rest of it he saw Sabine lying on the ground with her head under a side table. Her legs were arranged as if she was running, except that she was still.

Schreber did not move. Instead, he stared and his head tilted over to one side, like a dog's does. In this way he tried to understand what he was seeing. He sniffed, and coughed, and drew himself up.

Sabine lay there, and her dresses rode up as if they had been kicked high like a can-can girl's. Her arms were outstretched, her hands urgent, reaching across the floor. She was reaching for her necklace: her grandmother's emerald brooch. He had taken it to a jeweller, a Slav, who was nonetheless of good reputation, and who had been wonderfully helpful. He had strung it first on a gold chain of large bold links, and then on a smaller one of silver, both by the same fitment, so that now it could be worn on the bosom and also, when desired, around the neck. The mechanism neither affected its placement close to the breast, nor impeded its straight hanging as a pendant, and all for a very reasonable price. It was a gift for their anniversary, among others, a symbol of his love and his appreciation of their marriage, childless though it sadly was. She was burdened with an incompetency, six times failing, but he loved her despite that. He loved her despite her moods, knowing himself to be the worst! He fixed the brooch in appreciation of her struggles and travails, and for the worry he had put her to. He found it in a box of things long forgotten and stored away. She never asked the circumstances of its rediscovery and he thought it more thoughtful to omit the details. It was the fact that the brooch was found that was the important thing, in any event, and that he had taken it to be altered, knowing his wife's preference for hanging jewellery. When he presented it to her she wept, as he had hardly ever seen her do, because it was returned to her, and he had shown such kindness.

Now it rested on the floor in front of her. Her mouth was open, as were her eyes, and, looking closer, Schreber saw that she was conscious down there on the floor. Her gaze flickered about and she made little motions: shakings in the hands and legs. Her lips tightened and went slack.

At last he came forward, knelt in front of her, and placed his hand on her cheek gently.

He said: 'My love…' to which, no matter how long he waited, she did not reply.

There was a scream.

Cook again, standing now in the doorway, in her hands a covered dish: the one with a fruit pattern—plums and apples and hedgerow berries. It fell from her hands, smashing on the floor, spilling a chicken carcass amongst the shards. Rather than clear up the mess, the silly woman stood and stared, one hand over her wide, silent mouth. Then another woman, another girl—the skivvy—she came in at a run, to see what the commotion was. This girl—a bright little thing, fat and lively—she saw at once what was needed, where her elders remained rooted to the spot.

'I'll fetch the doctor. He's only in the next road,' and she ran off.

Schreber picked up his wife, the top of her at least, her body coming up while her legs lay as they were. He held her to his chest, close to his breast, so that her breath ruffled the handkerchief in his jacket pocket, still smudged with dust from a picture frame. Her panting blew a thread that curled from one corner of the handkerchief forward and back, shaking it as she breathed. He smoothed her hair where it had come loose from its pins and he rocked her a little, like one might rock a baby. He hummed a nursery tune, and in his arms she tensed and relaxed, each transition provoking a gentle moan.

Her mouth was pulled up at the cheek on one side; it was somewhat grotesque, he thought. So different from her public mask: her resolute authority about the house, that showed itself clear not only in her face, but in her posture, and her demeanour, and in the particularities of her use of reason.

To lie there grimacing and shaking?

It was not like her. To suffer such a disturbance?

She was not like this.

She would not let herself become like this. She was a rock. A mighty fortress.

Never.

A plaything of the Lower God?

He sniffed.

That was of the past. Gone away. A dream.

But if not, then what was this thing in his arms? If it was not a puppet? If it was a puppet, and not his wife, then where was that woman: calm, even-handed and haughty, dismissive even to him. What was this? This panting thing? Moaning. It was one thing, or the other, this thing cradled in his arms, this grinning mannequin. Its skin was stretched pale and taut over the bones of the skull, taking on the appearance of wax, like a dressmaker's dummy. It was like a sculpture modelled on his wife's form, but without her soul. A representation, miracled up and laid on the ground, half in his arms. One of a thousand? Taking on a strange solidity, so that the pulling of the corner of its mouth was no longer what concerned him, nor even the slight movement of the lips, and even less the bubbles of spittle that gathered; it was that his wife, strong, would not have allowed this. So where was she?

'Sabine!'

Now here was the doctor, barging past Cook like a man who has been separated from his lunch too soon and who is keen to return without delay. He kneeled beside Schreber's wife—not his wife, the replica—and opened his bag. Schreber was moved by unseen hands to a seat on the red settee. There was buzzing in his head, and his ears, and now, suddenly, in his eyes. The doctor snapped his fingers in front of the replica's face, in front of the improvised thing, made up from the dirt, and then over each of its ears. He called for a lit candle, which he held in front of it, illuminating briefly the interior contours of its nostrils, and of the sides of its mouth. Then he marched out of the room.

He returned almost immediately with a passing drayman.

'Sir, your wife has had a seizure. She will require immediate treatment. I have given this gentleman a few marks to take her to my surgery. I will, of course, add his fee to the bill.'

'If I can get the bloody horse moving,' the short scruffy drayman said, smiling, 'I'll take her on the cart. Else it'll be the young 'un and me. One at the tip, the other at the toe. Alright?'

The man expected a reply, but no one offered it, and it seemed like hours before the drayman and his boy did what they had been paid to do. They wiped their noses with the backs of their sleeves, picked the thing up, and took it from the room.

'That is not my wife,' Schreber said to himself.

The doctor pursed his lips and frowned.

'My apologies, I was told by this girl that the wife of Herr Schreber… she will require treatment in any event. Can I assume you will accept the bill?'

He turned to leave, putting on his hat and gloves.

'That is not my wife.'

The doctor turned to the girl and straightened his coat, and he spoke to her, but Schreber did not hear what he said. He marched rather into the hall, and shouted for his wife upstairs.

'Sabchen! Where are you, old girl?'

Nothing.

He stamped up the stairs in that peculiar way that Sabine had always found endearing, putting his foot to either side of the carpeted runner so that the heels of his shoes clicked on the wooden steps. Though the sound could be heard throughout the house, the carpet never became worn. If it was a habit inherited from some Schreber familial commandment, then it was one that might be allowed to continue in Sabine's house, at least for the men, who were heavy and clumsy and therefore more of a strain on the furnishings.

'Sabine!'

Cook came up behind, calling after him in that plaintive, imploring tone that was exactly what Sabine warned him against succumbing to. The staff must learn to take responsibility for their own actions and not come running to him with every trivial matter. He should not indulge them! They had, after all, her written instructions and were employed on the basis that they might be expected to cope with whatever circumstances the day should bring them. If they could not cope, then no doubt there were a hundred others in Dresden that could and would be glad of the opportunity to prove it. The best thing to do was simply to ignore what they said, and if only he could learn to say no to these people then it would be a great boon to her, because they looked to him as the authority in the house, wrongly. For every helpful suggestion he gave, or ruling on this or that matter, she heard it back tenfold if something was done wrong or forgotten. "The master said that it would be better if I did such and such," or "Sir told me it wasn't worth the time and that I should attend to this or that." Didn't he realise it was hard enough as it was, running a house? Couldn't he spend more time at the club, like other women's husbands?

From the bottom of the stair the doctor coughed.

'Will you come with me, sir? Or will you make your own way to the surgery?'

'Sabine!' Schreber shouted.

The doctor tutted and hissed. After looking up the stairs for a while he gave his address to the skivvy on her promise to pass on the information as soon as was practical.

Schreber bowled into every room in turn, and Cook followed him like a shadow, like a ball attached with string to his coat tails, yanked behind him, bouncing on the floor.

'Sir, what'll be done…? Sir, what about the party…? Sir, will she be alright, sir…?'

Schreber went into his wife's bedroom and there was her bed—the blankets and quilts tight as a drum skin. Here he stopped and Cook stopped with him, running into his back. She kept talking and talking. Schreber turned his gaze to where his wife might have been lying, and examined the space, knowing that this was the place she should be. His dearest, his Sabchen, little round face, a damp flannel laid across her eyes and her hands together over her belly. But there was nothing to see and, though he wished there would be, no matter how hard he concentrated on the bed there was nothing. There was no sign or message, and the pattern of the blanket came toward him in ever closer magnification the longer he stared. Grids of red and green entwined like the mesh of the ether, intersections picked out in gold thread, and below that motif the brown webbing around which each fibre was woven. Each individual filament was taken up and down, over each other, in and out. If his eyes hadn't filled with tears—caused not by any emotion, but by his repression of the urge to blink—he would have seen through to the mattress, and then to the bed, and eventually who knows where? Down to the very core of the Earth? But the fluid over his eyes acted like an imperfect lens, bowing and flexing the image before him, disturbing the space on which his wife had lain. The noise in his mind was building so loud and clear now that he could almost hear it speaking of his bad character. It spat parts of words that never quite came together, still obvious in their disgust at his poverty of will. His impotence.

When his nose touched the blanket he drew back in alarm.

Cook put her hand on his back.

'What did you say?' Schreber snapped, turning. She looked down at her shoes.

'I was just asking what it was that I should do about the guests.'

Of course.

'Will the missus be alright? What was it the doctor said? It's only that in the fuss I didn't quite hear it.'

There was a knock at the door downstairs.

'Excuse me,' Schreber said, and he pushed the dumpy woman on the shoulder, too roughly, much too roughly, clumsy brute, knocking vases over, was he a child? Was he incapable of looking where he was going, like all men? And they call themselves civilised, traipsing mud through the house. He ran down the stairs, heels clacking loud, with his hand on the banister and each foot kicking out to the side. They threatened to slip on the varnish, to send him falling back, to crack his skull. Clumsy brute. Silly man.

The skivvy was at the bottom, opening the door. He was sure it would be Sabine, returning from an errand: a small bag with ribbons inside, decorative lace for the table, a new bone napkin ring to replace one yellowed and cracked.

But it was not her. It was a boy.

'Block of ice, Fräulein? Have I got the right place?'

The skivvy turned and looked at Schreber. He was standing one stair from the bottom. In his mind there was something like speech: the odd word, muttering, louder and louder.

'Send him away,' he said, and he took the last step down.

The girl did as she was told and the boy went back down the path, rubbing his neck and checking a grubby piece of paper. Schreber held out both arms and the skivvy, conditioned by daily repetition, slipped his long, grey winter coat over his shoulders and looped his scarf around his neck. She was nothing: a flimsy ripple in the world.

He ran out into the street.

'Sabine! Where are you?'

The day is cold
and windy. Schre-
ber finds the world
has changed. He
drifts away from his
home, and is brought
back by his adopted
daughter, Fridoline.

II

As he rounded the corner of Angelikastrasse, the November
wind bit. The cold air purged the remnants of the house—the
slight persistence of its odour, its lingering warmth on his skin,
the fuggy oiliness of an interior—it all disappeared instantly,
and now he was left at the end of the street not knowing quite
what he was doing. He banged the side of his head with his
palm, hoping to jar himself right.

Where the hell was Sabine?

He pulled his coat tighter around his shoulders and hesitated,
thinking he might turn back and have the girl bring him the
calfskin gloves and perhaps even the Russian fur hat, but when
he looked back down the street it was not there.

His house was not there.

Neither were the trees. No railings. No streetlamps.

In their place were representations of these things. The
objects that he walked past every day after breakfast, lunch
and supper—they were changed. Objects that he counted off
as he took his constitutional—one, two, three, with his chest

17

out and his head back, cane first, slicing up and down, in front and behind, cutting a straight path through the traffic of the street—they were all wrong.

The ornate gate of the Burgenthaler house, the iron post where tradesmen tied their carts so that they did not roll off down the hill and into the Elbe, the grid through which rain made its way down under the street—all those things were there, but when Schreber came close and put his cold fingertips to them they were as smooth as pieces of letter paper and just as thin.

When he craned his neck to see behind them and around them, even though the blasted wind blew up dust from the street and made his eyes water, he could see that they were not real. They were nothing more than stage decorations gaudily painted in primary colours, like those things his father in-law had pressed upon them to store for him in his time of greatest difficulty, as the melodramatic old sot had put it. The garden, so often Schreber's place of small refuge, where he would sit beneath the trees and read of politics and revisions to the law became overrun with fakes, occupied in one corner by a long black locomotive, and in another by a piece of a wall, draped with vines dripping luscious grapes: all utterly false.

He crept back toward his own house—the house that he and Sabine had built together—and that too was nothing. A trick. A painted piece of wood three stories high and supported by what? A balsa scaffold, hidden from view? A single layer of bricks with nothing behind it? An egg shell? His home? So fragile?

'Sabine!'

She was nowhere.

There were other people on the street. A couple. The man raised his eyebrows as he passed and the wife's arm looped tighter around his. She watched Schreber all the way down to the corner, clutching her husband in defence.

At another time, perhaps only a few hours ago, Schreber would have been mortified—on his own street, outside his own house, in Dresden, where he was a man of reputation, respected still, possibly—but now he took no mind of any of them. Because they too were nothing. He might once have nervously glanced down the street, in through the doors of the passing carriages, up at the curtained windows of the other houses—the Burgenthaler house, the Brahe house, the Werninger house—watching for signs that he had been over-looked, but now it was nothing to him, because they were all nothing. Fleeting-improvised-wretched-plaything-human-beings. Puppets, soul-less automata, clicking and whirring and chirruping to each other on a flat street of false houses and dust blown by the perishing cold wind. Now, when he shouted for his wife, he paid no heed to anyone's furrowed brows, or tut-tings, or wide berths given.

If that was Herr Merstenberg's niece taking flowers to her aunt, then that was also nothing. If she held the flowers in the crook of her arm, and put a handkerchief to her mouth, and lifted up her skirts and trotted away from him? These people were nothing, their lives ended the moment they were out of his sight. Marionettes. Demons. Mechanical birds.

'Sabine!'

A girl came toward him, an awkward little thin thing in black crinoline, holding a rectangular paper parcel. She was as insubstantial as tissue paper. When the wind blew, she came with it, skipping on tip-toes across the flagstones until she ran smack into him. She wrapped her arms around his waist and her parcel fell to the ground. Through the ripped paper, the luminous, yellow flesh of a pat of fresh butter.

'Papa!'

Her face was set in a curious expression that Schreber couldn't recognise. Her black eyes were wide and above them arched two oddly thick slugs of hair. Though she was a girl, her forehead was furrowed. Her mouth hung open at the end of a word, waiting, with the bottom row of teeth flashing wetly with each heave of her chest. She was silent, and now Schreber heard, as if through water, a coarse bellowing roar which, quite unexpectedly, seemed to be coming from his own mouth. He shut it, and the sound stopped too.

'What is wrong?' the girl wept.

Schreber felt the urge to reach over and wipe the tears away. He moved his hand, but in the end the tears dropped from her cheek and fell onto her dress without his trying to stop them.

'Papa!'

An imp. A changeling. A black wood sprite, thin-wristed and sharp-nosed, ready to sneak in at night and do whatever mischief its instincts provoked it to: the rearrangement of important papers, or the addition of a purgative to the milk. Small things. Childish things. Spiteful things.

Yet she was familiar.

Her greased back hair was familiar. The ornament she wore on her shawl, too much for her, like an old woman's keepsake, or a medal. Hadn't he given something like that to a thing like this? His own mother's brooch, rusting away in a tin box in a cupboard and now in the world again. On the day of the funeral? One so dead and the other still alive. The cheeky creature! Hadn't he loved something like that? A scamp. There when he returned from Sonnenstein. Arriving fully formed. Her odd way of arranging her cutlery, as if she were from France, and she wouldn't be convinced, no matter how much Sabine chastised her. Hadn't he taken her side? Not her, the thing she represented. Arranging his own cutlery in the same way and calling for *potage* when he meant soup? Fashioning his moustaches into points? Smoothing his hair into a parting? Marching here and there about the room in the manner of a Napoleon? Sabine's face falling and Fridoline's rising, as if in symmetry?

But this couldn't be that girl. Could it?

'Papa!'

She addressed him and expected a reply. Schreber could think of none.

'Sabine!' he cried, but the significance of the word was drifting away from him.

'Mother?' the girl asked.

'I must find her,' Schreber muttered.

'She will be inside. I left her only a few minutes ago. I went to get butter.'

The girl looked down. Somehow, in the confusion, she had trodden in it. She jerked her leg back, leaving her foot swinging in the air, hanging from her upraised knee with the print of her shoe on the paper wrapper.

'I'll be for it now...'

She looked at him.

'I'll be for it now, won't I, Papa?'

Schreber said nothing.

'Papa, please! What has happened?'

'You are Fridoline?'

'Of course! Please... you are frightening me!'

'You are not mine.'

'I don't understand what you are saying. Come inside, please!'

'Don't be ridiculous!'

'I'm getting Mother!'

'She's gone.'

'Where? What about the party?'

'There is nothing. You are nothing. A puppet. A plaything of the Lower God.'

'Please, Papa!'

She looked up at him, and she was such a frail and odd little thing. It occurred to him that he might push her aside, down onto the pavement, and walk past. He reached out, palm first, and when he touched her shoulder he had every intention of forcing her down. But he did not. He touched the smooth, cold surface of the dress and, through it, the flesh and bones of the shoulder.

She was not flat, this thing.

He jerked his hand back as one might from the handle of a kettle left too long on the fire, but his fingers retained the memory of the touch.

She was not simply false.

When he looked her in the face there was, in her eyes and in the quality of her gaze, something. It was plain and innocent and hopeful. Something of a child. Love? Faith? Adoration? He swallowed and coughed and drew a breath. He blinked his eyes, and when they opened, after that infinitesimal break with the continuity of his vision, the world was almost solid again. He banged the side of his head with his palm, hoping to jar himself right. The girl was solid. Fridoline. The girl Sabine had adopted to keep her company while he was away. His daughter.

'Frida?'

'What is it, Papa?'

Her voice. It pained him to hear it, and now, as he did nothing, simply blankly returned her gaze, there was a growing anxiety on her face: a pinching of the muscles at the sides of her nose. Doubt. Then, as he watched, fear—something like fear—creeping into the unconscious movement of the muscles beneath her skin. Then a returning wateriness in her eye.

He looked away from her.

The street was just that: the street.

There was the gate of the Burgenthaler house—an eagle in twisted metal. It was ostentatious, just like Frau Burgenthaler. Despite the mumbled protestations of her mouse of a husband—a clerk in a bank—it was a vulgar display, sniggered at from behind the hands of their neighbours. Their wealth was inherited from her uncle; her every frustrated whim was suddenly released.

There was the iron post, dented and notched where this or that deliveryman would wait, and smoke, and meet one's gaze with impudent assurance. Lashing down his cart. Spitting at his feet. Passing fingers through his greasy hair, and laughing to himself.

The drain. It was all there.

'Papa? Let's go inside.'

He turned to look where she was looking, down the path through the trees and shrubs, up to the door. Part of the music from *Siegfried* was carved into the lintel. Sabine's idea. A wonderful touch, commented on by everyone. Pointed to. Sabine would sing it for them, only a few notes, but instantly recognisable. If her voice was not what it once was, it was still pretty—very pretty. When her friends came it was not uncommon to hear them still whistling those few notes as they were shown through into the drawing room. Schreber coughed, and sniffed, and turned to look at his daughter. The loose shutter on the pantry window clattered in the wind, and Schreber drew his coat closed at the neck.

'Where is your scarf?' he said.

She began to say something, but he cut her off.

'No excuses, girl! You have been told about this. Your mother is very firm on the matter. You don't have the constitution for wandering the streets half dressed.'

He took off his own scarf and put it on her, winding it around her thin, white throat, and laying the ends across her chest. One side of the scarf was longer than the other. He adjusted it so that the ends were even. The girl reached out her hand, timidly, as if offering food to a garden bird. Schreber took it.

'It has been a most unusual morning,' he said. 'I am not sure quite what is happening.'

The girl nodded and said nothing, drawing him away from the street and back to the house. For a while, he came easily, up the path and through the trees, toward the safety of his study, towards his bed. He would take a light meal and then, perhaps, a sleeping draught. Cook was in the doorway, waiting for his coat.

23

But, just as it appeared he might cross the threshold, he stopped and became immovable as a block of granite.

He raised his face to see the sun, risen above the trees, cold and painfully bright.

'Papa! Please come inside. It's only a little further.'

She took him by the wrists and pulled him.

'Sir? Won't you listen to the young miss? You look as pale as a sheet and, besides that, what about the missus? And the party? Come inside, sir, I beg you!'

The sun was so bright that he could barely see. The girl had him by the wrists and she was still talking. She pulled at his wrists, directing his arms, making him move.

Schreber turned abruptly on his heels, and Fridoline had no choice but to release her grip. The moment her fingertips were no longer felt, he was gone, racing down the street, the tails of his coat flapping and gaping.

'Come back! Papa!'

Schreber turns his
back on his home,
and, by virtue of
familiarity, takes the
route he formerly
took to work. The
world disappears,
and Schreber is
accosted by a tinker
and his son.

III

Schreber could still hear the thing shouting after him, the little
one, her high voice carrying an astounding distance: Papa!
Papa! Come back! As he left her further and further behind, all
that remained was the pitch of her cry, as chill and stinging as
the wind blowing in across the river, all the colder now since
his neighbourhood was left behind and the windbreak of the
houses was gone.

His heels clicked as he ran, and soon the clicking was all he
could hear above the sound of the blood hissing in his ears.

When he reached the brewery he stopped and leant heavily
on the brown stone wall. The sickly sweet smell of the place
caught the back of his throat, but he had no choice but to take
it in with every breath, his chest refusing to be calmed by his
earnest attempts to fill it. When he was able to take a brief swallow and wipe his mouth with the back of his hand, he looked
down the way he had come, the very same way he came every
weekday morning, though more often by carriage. The little
thing was gone.

As he waited, his breathing slowly returned. He stood straight and adjusted his clothes. He banged the side of his head with his palm, hoping to jar himself right.

What was the problem?

A man passed him, walking a tall, thin dog. Schreber gave him a smart bow and the man bowed in return, sparing him little more than a glance. The dog turned its head to watch Schreber, a long tongue pinkly steaming out from the corner of its mouth. The dog swallowed and turned away, the tongue returning almost immediately, but on the other side this time.

Schreber looked up and down the street.

Things were much as they usually were.

So what was the problem?

Schiller Strasse was quiet at this time of day, the only persons with any business there being the employees of the brewery, deliverymen, and those who wished to pick up the tram into the city. When he chose, on ordinary days, to make his way to the courts—and that was more often than not and sometimes more often than he wished, deferring as he did to Sabine's understanding of how much a man's presence could be tolerated around the house—he would take this road, but today…

What was the problem?

He looked back the way he had come. Shouldn't he return home? Right away?

From the sun there was a voice.

The feeling is lacking.

With it came a bright light that made Schreber blink and saturated the world, turned his entire neighbourhood, road, houses, people—all of it—bleached and white.

Sabine.

Without thinking to check the traffic, he walked over the road, hands stretched out in front of him as if he was being led. He turned and turned, trying to put the sun behind him, but it was always in his eyes.

Sabine!

A huge, low steamship slid down the river toward him, black smoke buffeted by the wind, the sulphurous tang overtaking even the stench of brewing beer. He blinked again and again, but, though he could hear the ship and smell it and even, he imagined, feel its warmth as it passed no more than fifty feet from his outstretched hands, the world was too bright to see. Even the Elbe herself.

He grit his teeth and walked into the brightness. It could only be a little way home. He had walked it hundreds of times, alighting a tram stop short of the terminus, preferring on dry days to take the air and cut at the timothy grass that sprouted alongside the towpath with his cane. A few minutes at a bracing pace. When he shut his eyes he could see it all—straight back to the house. To Fridoline. To Sabine. He screwed his eyes shut and despite the fact that his cane was left in the stand by the door he made to swing it, here and there, scattering sticky arrowheads and dandelion fluff wherever he walked.

Just as he always did.

Just another day.

The leading idea is missing.

He screwed his eyes shut. No distance at all, for a man in his prime, freed from the burdens of too much work, and at last able to take the proper time to attend to his health: a regime of exercise and abstinence and early nights. Hadn't they paid off? These brisk strolls in the fresh air had done him the world of good, nodding cheerfully to whomever he might pass, trades-man or clerk, sergeant or barrister.

But then for how much longer… (will your defence against the power of the rays still be successful)?

He screwed up his eyes until his cheeks ached. He was a new man! Wasn't he? Trimming the rind and the glossy white fat from his chops. Putting his hand firmly on top of his wine glass when Cook came with the decanter. No more long meals in his chambers with men who would drive themselves to lassitude with their cigars and liqueurs and butter sauces. Rather, he would take the tram halfway and walk the rest, while they rode a carriage to the club and wasted their time with billiards and talk of matters that could scarcely concern them any less. He would sit with Sabine, and watch her at her preparations, an occasional game of patience and an early night, the sun barely having set and the curtains carefully arranged so that the light did not creep into the room. Sabine sometimes choosing to remain in the drawing room while he got his much-needed rest. It had done wonders for him. He would be home in no time. He coughed, and sniffed, and screwed his eyes up tight, and swished the cane from side to side.

Home.

What are you thinking of now?

Just another day like any other.

His foot slipped out from beneath him as he stretched to sever the head of a phantom thistle, sending him pitching forward, so that he had to open his eyes and put out his hands to break his fall. He hit the ground with a thud: elbow and shoulder, and then his head. For a fraction of a second the road returned to him. From where he lay on the flagstones he could follow it all the way back to the corner of Angelikastrasse. It was no distance at all, barely enough to stretch one's legs, as his father would say. Stop your whining, boy! he would say. It's barely enough to stretch one's legs. And he was right. A few hundred steps. Schreber fixed his gaze at the lamppost on the corner of the street, but when he heaved himself up he caught sight of the sun and it was all gone again. First the brewery—burned to its outline, each of the hundred windows picked out faintly in charcoal, but then erased. Briefly the old barracks was visible behind, but then that went too. What of the men inside? The trees—the light desiccated them, making thin black twigs of healthy limbs—they crumbled to dust. All the real things of the world, solid and stable, that marked his journeys through the city, they all blanched away, and lastly the furniture of the street: the lamps, the tramlines, and the smooth stones that made up the floor beneath him.

Home. He must find home! Just walk!

There was something blocking his path, invisible, but substantial. He pushed against it and it went away, but in the corner of his eye there was a thing that adjusted its shirt and thumbed its teeth. Schreber knocked the side of his head with the palm of his hand and there appeared a short, bowlegged tinker with his cap in one hand. The other was holding the hand of a child. It was impossible to tell if it was male or female, it was so ragged.

The tinker came forward, pulling his grubby little tyke with him. He chewed all the time and was muttering something. Brown teeth and stained fingers. The child pulling away.

'What's the matter with you?' the tinker said.

'I...'

'You want to watch where you're going, that's what you want to do.'

Schreber nodded, and tipped his hat, and made to walk away, but the tinker grabbed his arm.

'Reckon yourself do you, sir? Reckon you've the right to push a working man out of the way as you pass? Not this working man, sir. Not I. I'll have an apology, if you've one to give.'

'I'm sorry.' Schreber licked his lips and bowed deeply. 'I couldn't see...'

'I may be filth to *you*, sir, but I've the politeness to keep out of people's road as I walk the street.'

Schreber stepped back, releasing the man's grip, but when he turned away from the tinker there was nothing again. He moved his attention in every direction but there was nothing to see. He blinked and looked back to where he was sure he could hear the dirty little man telling his child, 'That's how you're not to grow up!' but it was too bright.

'Mind that… person… him there. He's the wrong sort! Understand me?'

Schreber shut his eyes and there were the man and child.

'Why's he making that face?'

'Come away, son!'

'Why? It's just an old man.'

The boy's mouth moved in the manner of a puppet's—carved from a piece of wood and strung.

'What's he doing?'

The boy's father pulled him away by the arm. It twisted at an impossible angle, the ligaments stretching like the cat gut that articulates a marionette, the wooden arm dislocating without causing pain. The boy's eyes were painted open in disgust and glee.

They were flat and dead.

Schreber wanders as far
as the Karola Brücke,
which is in the opposite
direction to his home.
The world returns, but
with it come insulting
voices. Schreber is too
distracted to assure his
own safety.

IV

He screwed his eyes tighter. He banged the side of his head with
his palm, hoping to jar himself right, and now when he opened
his eyes again, slowly, he was standing on the Karola Brücke.

The river rushed below, bloated brown with floodwater.
The afternoon traffic was as it always was: carts loaded with
wood and coal, and on the back of them were men in shorts
and braces, perched with their shirts open down to the waist,
exposing their flat and smudged breasts to the cold wind. Men
and women of more or less substance marched briskly to escape
the waft up from the water.

Schreber blinked once or twice, cautiously, expecting the whiteness to return, but it did not. He cleared his throat and sniffed.

So what was the problem?

Just a day, like any other?

Just a day.

To the courts, then? To work? To Pillnitzer Strasse? And
lunch with Sabine? So she could show him all the things she
had bought?

He crossed the bridge with his chest high and out and his head back so that his moustaches bristled in the wind, and he hummed and muttered:

'A mighty fortress is our God,
a bulwark never failing;
our helper he amid the flood
of mortal ills prevailing.'

He walked past the elegant new terrace and down the wide paved boulevard. Deep breaths. Tipping the hat. A mighty fortress. Stick to those things a man knows, those things proper to him, and the world will fall into order. Inevitable. Down onto the Moritz-Allee.

Schreber bit his lip and silently, without moving his arms—perhaps only a little—saluted his father as he always did when he set foot on this road. Moritz Schreber, so long passed and mourned every day!

There was one time, on a noisy flickering night, when the whole family marshalled in the hallway. Torch-light came in from the street and men shouted impatiently.

'There are things that must be done and ills of the world that must be fought,' his father had said, turning at the end of almost every word as if the outside was pulling him toward it. 'We should not take pleasure in it, or pride, but we must apply ourselves with all the more vigour because of that!'

With which he left them at a run. His heels clicked like hooves on the polished tiles, avoiding the good rug.

They rushed to the window and, below, their father mounted his horse and was away down the street, his whip-hand raised high and his boot buckles glittering.

The wind came and Schreber pulled his coat close and he could see Moritz now, high on horseback, coming down the Moritz-Allee, driving Catholics before him, beating down on their backs, setting them to panic while all the time he remained stern and impassive, determined and controlled, routing his enemy. Schreber swished with his free hand as if it was he and not his father who had the whip. He wondered for a second where he had left his cane. In the hallway no doubt. That girl! Something would have to be done. Sabine would have to have words.

Sabine.

Just a day.

Pillnitzer Strasse jutted off Moritz-Allee before it had barely begun and Schreber followed his route to work automatically, without thought, his legs doing the thinking and the phantom cane, the phantom whip, doing its work on the heads of phantom thistles and long-gone Catholics.

He walked into the carriageway without missing a beat, gingerly stepping over the metal rails and threading his way through the traffic.

The Prince of Hell is responsible for the loss of rays.

He stopped.

He should (think) *about the Order of the World.*

Just a day.

Luder!

Like any other.

A deep breath. A cough, and a sniff, and the blowing of the wind ruffling the soft down on the back of his neck that the damned barber never properly attended to. Growing like marram grass, wherever it wished.

Excite yourself!

Nonsense. A sniff, and a cough. He banged the side of his head, hoping to jar himself right, and now the thinking-about-nothing-thought—a progression of notes mapped onto the keys of his piano. Their echoing in the corridor. *Ein' feste Burg.*

The ringing of bells.

He is a soul murderer, like his father.

'You know nothing of my father!'

The ringing of bells.

Fancy a person who was a Senatspräsident allowing himself to be f——d.

Just another.

The ringing of bells.

The leading idea is missing.

Bells rang loud and urgent and there was a rattling below them, like that which announced the arrival of coffee at the club, but deeper. It was as if the trolley was enormous and the cups and saucers and spoons were made for a giant, and if he had put down the paper, and sat up straight he would have been puzzled to see the great thing, trundling across the library floor, even as his mouth watered at the thought of his morning biscuits.

'You must move, sir!'

It was a woman's voice.

Schreber turned and there on the pavement in front of Wertheim's were two women. The older had her hand over her mouth so that her lace handkerchief covered her lips and chin. Her eyes were wide. Her companion was younger, a very pretty girl in yellow, who clutched at the first's arm with both hands so that her fringed parasol fell at her feet. She seemed a modest child, but her lips were very red, as if she had painted them. Her mouth was also open.

'For pity's sake!'

The bells were terribly loud now and the rattling such that something must surely break. Schreber followed the direction of the women's attention—which he realised now was not quite on him—and there was a tram car.

The numerals for "sixteen" were written on a card placed in the slot in front of where the driver sat, and next to that it said: "Fürsten Platz—Streissener Platz—Sacshen Platz—Albert Brücke—Albert Platz," two to a line with the last alone and in larger script and bold.

'Good Lord preserve us!'

The tram was moving at great speed. The driver turned a handle above his head furiously, bobbing up and down with every revolution, and the bells rang out. The wheels sparked and there was a keening, grinding sound.

He was applying the brake.

If Schreber had put his hand out directly in front of him he could have touched the window. Behind it the driver was frozen in anger and, similarly still, the passengers: men and women, faces appalled at the spectacle of what must soon be a man crushed by a tram.

Schreber looked down and saw that he was standing directly in the centre of the metal tracks which had been laid into the stones of the road. When he looked back at the tram he traced the contours of the writing on the card with his finger. Sixteen, in Arabic numerals: one straight line and one fat spiral in heavy black script.

The noise was awful: grinding, clattering, ringing, and there was an iron tang in the air as the metal wheels slid on their metal rails.

Sabine. Sabchen.

The tram hit Schreber in the chest.

'Oh, mercy!'

He was knocked to the ground and his head snapped back so that he felt as if his skull was cracked open. The tram passed him, sparks like Catherine wheels everywhere, faces at the window, dumbstruck.

Schreber meets the
Gerhardt mother and
daughter, and they
take him to the law
courts. Matters come
to a head.

V

'He is done for, surely. I cannot look!'

The girl was all in yellow, her hair gathered up under a simple cotton cap decorated with a butterfly pin. Her eyes were wide and blue and she licked her lips until they glistened like cherries washed and piled in a bowl.

'I'm going to faint! Hold me, girl, for goodness' sake!'

Her mother: clearly of the same species of woman, but thinner, dried out—like a hanging rose—her voice crackling in her throat, swamped by the black widow's ruff at her neck and confused by her nervous fingers fluttering the handkerchief over her mouth.

'He is moving. His eyes are open,' the girl said.

'Impossible! Don't you dare let me go! I will die on the spot!'

'But Mother!'

'Not another word!'

'But Mother, he is alive.'

'Stupid girl…'

But she looked anyway, first one eye and then both, and he looked back at them.

They were framed by the window of Wertheim's and to either side of them were dresses on headless mannequins. The back of his head throbbed, and when he moved to sit up the women appeared very vivid, glistening like the fan of peacock feathers that Sabine put in the fireplace of her parlour in the summer months, and there was a shooting pain that made him freeze.

Schreber tried to sit again, more carefully this time, and when he did not fall straight back to the ground, he nodded gently to the women in turn, the widow first. They appeared unable to understand what they were seeing, any more than the mannequins behind them could, so he reached to tip the brim of his hat, a little reassurance, such as he was used to performing to put a certain type of person at their ease. The hat was lost, however, and Schreber passed his hand through his hair and nodded to them again.

'My apologies. I appear to have given you both something of a fright.'

The widow took a step back and pulled on the girl's arm.

'Impossible!' she shrieked, turning so that her face was more or less concealed by the girl's yellow puffed sleeve. The girl, less easily disconcerted it seemed, came forward and reached out her hand.

Schreber thought about taking it, but instead he put his palms flat on the floor and pushed himself up. He lurched forward, at the last, but soon regained his balance, despite the widow's theatrical horror at his sudden approach. He stepped back, brushed down his coat, smoothed his waistcoat and, when all that was done to his satisfaction, attended to his moustaches.

The tram driver, who had stopped some way ahead and come to the footplate fully expecting to attend to another ruined corpse, spat a curse and returned to the tiller, and the tram continued along the track, the rear window half-filled with faces in expressions of more or less anxious bemusement.

When it was gone, the three of them were nothing more extraordinary than any other three people on the street and for a while there was an uneasy silence.

'Are you in pain?' the girl asked. 'That was a very forceful collision.'

The widow snorted from behind her handkerchief and stared, but said nothing.

Schreber considered the question.

'A little. But otherwise I feel very well. Much better than I have felt all day.'

He filled his lungs and held the air within him so that his chest puffed out, and occupied himself with the dust and grit that stubbornly adhered to his clothes.

'I have had something of a difficult morning,' he said, picking and wiping and patting. 'I think I shall return home. Perhaps you could direct me? Where am I exactly?'

'We are near Pirnaischer Platz. We are shopping for new gloves…'

Schreber nodded.

'In Dresden?'

'Of course in Dresden,' the widow said, 'where else would we be?'

'Mother! Where, sir, do you live? Should I find someone to arrange a carriage?'

'I need only get my bearings,' Schreber said. 'I must find my wife.'

'She is with you? She is inside?' the girl gestured back to the department store. Its canopies rippled in the wind, but the stripes were oddly enervated. Were they becoming transparent?

'No… she is not inside,' Schreber said. She was not inside. 'My wife… Sabine, she is… gone.'

There was itching at the back of Schreber's head. He scratched at it.

'Come away, child,' the widow whispered. 'This man is no concern of yours. It is not your place to tend to unfortunates

39

in the street. Why he is not dead is an absolute mystery…Why you are not dead, sir, is an absolute mystery!'

The widow looked around at the passersby, as if seeking confirmation of her opinion. No one met her gaze, so she addressed herself to Schreber again, hissing.

'My daughter and I do not appreciate mysteries, sir!'

'Mother!'

'Come away, child!'

'Do you know my wife? Frau Sabine Schreber? She is very well known in society. She has many friends. Many parties. She is a wonderful woman. We all say so.' Schreber came closer, reaching for the widow's hand, as if to reassure her. It had the opposite effect, and she jumped back, which made Schreber do the same. There was a sudden and very bad pain in Schreber's head and something strange happened.

Once, Sabine had taken him to a séance—this fad was short-lived, thankfully, it not having the same innate ability to dominate his wife's interest as had the theatre, of which it was a poor cousin in both their opinions—and at this display an image, supposedly provoked by the medium from the afterlife, appeared onto a veil of smoke pumped from a bellows. Now the widow appeared in just this mode, the extent of her existence dictated by the random fluctuations of the air onto which she was projected.

Playthings.

Schreber sniffed and coughed. He blinked and blinked and his hand balled into a fist, which knocked against his hip. The back of his head itched.

'She is a marvellous woman. Marvellous voice,' Schreber said.

The widow's face represented a series of expressions, beginning with derision and ending at annoyance, very convincingly.

'I'm sure she must be,' she said, although it sounded as if the opposite was the case.

'No children, sadly,' Schreber went on, picking at the back of his head. 'They wouldn't move, even when I grabbed them by the wrists.'

In the window the mannequins stood firm, but the woman in front of him was as thin as tissue paper. Her daughter was only a little better. They both regarded him as if *he* was the anomaly: the girl with a kindly eye, but nonetheless critical.

The leading idea is missing.

'The leading idea is missing.'

The widow tutted and turned, pulling her daughter by the arm.

'The man is a fool. He is babbling. Come, child! We have our own affairs to attend to.'

'Mother!'

'Don't "Mother!" me, girl! He is a vagrant. There are the gloves and after that we must consider lunch and after *that* we have the Dutch émigrée and her family, and it is already too much. Leave him where he is! The authorities will attend to him in due course.'

The girl flickered briefly like a candle in the breeze, but she stood her ground.

'Forgive me, sir. You say you are well, but you have difficulty standing up straight. You sway a little, and I see that your eyes trouble you. Won't you allow us to see you to your wife? Or to a doctor?'

Schreber looked at himself up in the window of Wertheim's. He moved from foot to foot, sometimes forward and backward, and sometimes from side to side. It was very peculiar. It reminded him of the movements made by those men who consider taking their wives onto the floor for a waltz, but for one reason or other lack the will to do so and remain on the periphery, allowing themselves to be touched only a little by the music.

'My apologies. I fear the accident has rattled me. I am not, perhaps, my usual self.'

'And who are you, sir,' the girl said.

He bowed.

'I am Daniel Paul Schreber, presiding judge of the Third Civil Court of the Supreme Court of Appeals of the Kingdom of Saxony. Retired.'

This announcement, as it often did, seemed to impress. At least it impressed the girl, who even curtseyed. It may have had the opposite effect on her mother, who acted as if his position was insufficient to overturn the opinion she had already formed of him.

'Then you will want the courthouse,' she snapped. 'It is no great distance.'

She turned and began to walk away as if the matter was settled. Her daughter grabbed her elbow and now both were so flimsy that Schreber was surprised there was enough of them to grab, or be grabbed.

'He will want a doctor! Mightn't we walk with him, please? And if, by the mercy of God, he finds himself well, then we will have satisfied ourselves that we have done our duty.'

'I am already perfectly satisfied, thank you.'

Schreber coughed and sniffed.

'You are so thin. The moment I turn away, you will dissolve into nothing…'

'We most certainly will not. Hester, come away! That is an order!'

'Nonsense, Mother. Where is your charity? Would you leave him when he is clearly unwell?'

'I would. I do not care to be insulted.'

'I do not mean to insult you, madam. It is no fault of yours.'

'Let us at least make some progress toward the courts,' the girl said.

'Why do you concern yourself with him? Ignore him!'

'Mother! Pay her no attention. We will go to the courthouse. She will follow.'

'It is of no importance. She is a puppet. She moves at the will of another.'

'I see,' the girl replied.

She took his arm and gently applied pressure to his elbow.

'Am I a puppet, too?'

Schreber observed her carefully.

'I worry, Fräulein, that you are.'

'And you?'

Schreber frowned, but said nothing.

'Might I see…?' she motioned toward the back of his neck. 'There is quite a lump there… and some blood.'

'It is nothing…' Schreber twisted away from her.

'Quite. Then, will you escort me to the courthouse? I have business there that I have just remembered.'

'What are you babbling about, girl?'

Now the widow seemed determined to separate the two. She came and stood so that she was between them, and every time the girl tried to catch Schreber's eye, the widow moved to block her.

'A little matter,' she continued, bobbing around, 'something that a judge might be able to help me with.'

'Perhaps. I am well respected. What is your business there?'

'Matters I would prefer not to speak of in the street. Mother! Stop! Herr Schreber will take us to the courts, and then we will attend to our business.'

Her mother sighed and gritted her teeth, but the girl was so stubborn!

'I am still a man of high standing there. I am allowed to dine in the private restaurant. The clerks will give you whatever help you require.' Schreber drew himself up.

'The clerks, at least, are not puppets?' the widow sneered.

'Well…' Schreber began. Were they?

'The courts are on Pirnaische Strasse, are they not?' the girl said.

'They are on Pillnitzer Strasse.'

'Of course. Will you take us across the road?'

'It would be my pleasure, Fräulein.'

Her mother frowned, but she followed when Schreber stepped out, having first checked in both directions.

The girl put her hand on Schreber's back, patting him gently—a friendly gesture with which a granddaughter might express affection for her grandfather—two taps between the shoulder blades, but when she brought her hand away she rubbed her fingers together and then wiped her gloves into her handkerchief. When Schreber began to walk, the girl showed the contents of the handkerchief, now stained red, to her mother. She considered it for a while, sighed, and, eventually, nodded.

The three walked on, and it was not long before they reached Pillnitzer Strasse. On their right they passed a school. Rows of schoolboys waited with their hands by their sides for a signal. When one or other of them moved an arm, or scratched at their bare knees, a prefect would race along the line and correct them with his cane until order was restored.

'They, too, are puppets, I suppose,' the widow said from the corner of her mouth.

Schreber watched the boys in silence for a while, and it appeared as if he was listening to something that the other two could not hear.

'I fear they are temporary things made up from the dirt,' he said after a long time. 'Like you, they are soulless. God makes them and unmakes them for the purpose of deceiving me. Like Sabine, like Fridoline, like the little ones—you are playthings of Ariman, the Lower God.'

This was too much.

'The Lower God now is it? If a Gerhardt is the plaything of any god, sir, it is of the highest possible God, and I'll ask you not to forget it!'

'Mother!'

Someone blew a whistle and half of the boys marched off into the school buildings.

'I can see the steps of the courthouse,' Schreber said.

There was blood now on the flagstones beneath where he was standing. As he swayed, feet planted wide apart like a man on board a ship in a storm, drops of blood hit the stones in an irregular pattern. Over the school the sun appeared through the clouds. The sunlight streamed down onto the remaining boys, making them blink and raise their hands to their eyes. The prefects corrected them.

'Do you see the sun? Do you see how the rays join with the nerves of those boys? Like puppet strings? I had thought it was all nothing… But first Sabine, and then Fridoline, and now…'

'Let us make our way to the courts.'

'Do you hear them calling to each other?'

'I hear nothing.'

Schreber nodded as if his suspicions were confirmed.

The girl tried to lead him forward but he stumbled, leaning hard on her so that her mother, despite her disgust, came and took his other arm. Schreber looked up close at her, so that his breath moved her hair.

'They come to me, drawn by the excitability of my nerves. I had thought it was all a dream.'

'We must get you to a doctor right away,' she said, and she linked her arm with her daughter's behind his back and the two walked forward, slowly but steadily, toward the courts.

'He is incapable of understanding how he has wronged me. I can hear him now. He insists that I am at fault. He demands things. He calls me vile names. Directly. Through the nerve-speech.'

'Not far now!'

'I am sorry! He demands things of me. He makes me move. I must obey. I had thought this was all nonsense. Sabine promises me it was all nonsense!'

'A few more steps.'

'I cannot deny him. I cannot.'

Schreber stopped and pulled away from them, standing like a boxer to whom a decisive blow has been delivered, but who will not fall.

'He shows me,' he croaked, becoming suddenly short of breath, 'what lies beneath your clothes. Beneath your skin. The nodes where the feminine nerves meet. The places which animate you.'

He grabbed for the girl, put one hand behind her neck and with the other he pointed—like Adam anticipating the touch of his maker—until the tip of his finger was no more than an inch from her dress at the breast.

'He moves my arms. He grips my wrists. He threatens me with miracles.'

His finger described an erratic circle in the air, like the path a bluebottle takes around a chandelier.

'He promises me heirs.'

Schreber touched her.

When it was done, he withdrew the finger in shame, grabbing it with his other hand and pulling it back. It left a blood stain on the yellow cotton. He screwed his eyes shut and knocked the side of his head, but despite the pain, when he opened his eyes, things remained as they were.

'How dare you, sir!' the widow said, but the girl was silent.

'I am sorry, please believe me! I had thought myself mistaken in all this. Sabine… she told me it was all nonsense, a passing storm. Nerves. You see? Just like anyone else. A little worse. We take the waters, she and I, at Baden. Once in the spring and again in the autumn. Sabine knows a gentleman there, a doctor… not quite, he mixes powders… very efficacious. He is the talk of the town. I take them religiously. I had thought this all a dream, but now she is gone and God has returned. It was not a dream. Everything else—that was the dream…'

The girl's mother dragged her and she stumbled away, toward the courthouse. Schreber came after them, equally unsteady, up the steps, drops of blood falling. The building loomed up in front of him solid and dark, but now he saw the sun, risen above it.

Innumerable fine white filaments radiated from it, like the spokes of a wheel, like hair: a tracery that extended from one side of the horizon to the other and down from the sun in a direct path straight into Schreber. They flowed into his body, a hundred thousand or more attracted by the energy of his nerves, joining with them, entering him wherever there was sensation, hundreds on his fingertips, hundreds on his lips, thousands on his breast and down, below his belt, these nerves, these sun rays, penetrated the fabric and burned everything away from him.

'Sabine!'

In response to the commotion there came running several clerks in tall hats and black tails.

'Sabine!'

He was taken away.

Schreber is sedated, and his thoughts turn to memories of an early morning in the orthopaedic institute run by his father.

VI

When he was a boy, Paul lived in Leipzig, a mile or so from Dösen. He played in the garden with his brother and sisters. He played with the children of the Institute. When it was cold he skated on the lake and in the summer he took off his shirt and swam in the same water that was frozen in winter. He exercised on the lawn, bending and turning, with his toes digging into the earth and his fingers stretched and straight. His father stretched him up, his grip around Paul's wrists like iron, and showed him the way to move. He reached up into the sky and down toward the earth, and on rainy days the worms would rise from the soil and lie fat and pink here and there on the grass. When the sun came out the worms would lose their shine and sink back below.

One morning, before rising, it was summer, and the boy was seven. The children's room was painted white—the floor, the furniture, the walls, the ceiling. The shutters at the window were white. The sheets on his bed were white. His nightshirt was white. On this day he was woken, as he often was, by the crying of his sister in the nursery. She would have been a year or so old. The same thing must have happened dozens of times: little Klara crying from behind the closed door, like a lamb—soft and sad.

Klara went on crying for a while and no one came for her. Paul lay straight as an arrow in his bed, and the others in the children's room paid her no attention. The sound did not get through to them. Gustav might have curled slightly to the left under his covers; Anna's mouth might have fallen further open, spit wetting her cheek and then her pillow. Her eyes might have darted under the lids. These things may have happened and they may not. Who knows?

In any event, it was too early.

The sky in the gap between the shutters was barely blue, and the birds singing in the garden were lonely and shrill. Paul slipped out of his bed without squeaking the springs and rubbed his eyes. He walked barefoot to the door, and the floorboards were cold and smooth. When one creaked, he stopped dead and listened for a noise from above over the sound of his breathing. When he heard nothing, he followed the gaps in the floorboards with his toes until he found one he could put his weight on. He crept on until he reached Klara's door.

When he opened it, he stood there, not in one room or the other, both feet on the frame, shifting from heel to heel, and he yawned. He held a breath and there was no sound for the time until he had to take another. He wondered if his sister had gone back to sleep on her own. Her crib was white and high-sided with little carved curves, and it was quite still. He watched it closely for a minute or so, looking for the rocking that would start up if she kicked her legs, or waved her arms.

There was nothing. He turned to go back to bed, but as he did she started crying again, as if she knew he was leaving. The crib rocked and he tiptoed over to her. She looked at him and, for a moment, went quiet. He smiled and reached down to stroke her cheek—she was warm from sleeping. When he moved his hand away she kicked and cried, this time louder, so that Paul looked up at the ceiling and, without waiting, put his hand under her back. He lifted her up and she was over his shoulder. She cried for a second, but when he bounced at the knee she went quiet.

He hummed a tune, very quietly, all the while looking up at the ceiling, and he bounced her. With his free hand he scratched himself. After a minute or two she fell asleep, so he put her in the crib as softly as he could and went back to his own bed.

Schreber comes back to awareness. The orderly, Müller, is introduced. Schreber demands to see his doctor.

VII

He came to, and he was lying in a garden. It was a simple rectangle of grass surrounded by trees to every side with a part given over to the cultivation of flowers and small shrubs. A shallow bank had been carved in the earth and a wooden ramp was set into it. All around were trees and the scent of irises and hyacinths and lavender and the rustling of leaves in the wind. Schreber could feel the short-cropped grass of a lawn tickling the backs of his ears.

It was all very agreeable.

His first uttered sound, as he came to, was a laugh. It was a boyish laugh, as one might hear from a child who sees his sister smile in her crib, or who catches sight of a cat earnestly chasing a bird, only for cat and boy to watch the bird fly away at the very last moment.

He stretched his back against the ground. On the warm earth between the blades of grass, the tips of his fingers pressed into soft clay.

He left his eyes shut for a while and lay still, listening.

He could hear nothing.

The leaves and the breeze.

Perhaps a bird.

Nothing.

He opened his eyes slowly. Above him was the sky.

Nothing.

He looked at the sun.

Nothing.

His shirt was open to the waist, and mother of pearl buttons lay scattered here and there around him. One rested on the tweed of his trousers, another between the hairs on his belly, another off at a distance.

He picked up the pearl button and turned it around in his fingers, observing it as if through a microscope, down to the irregularities of manufacture in the two holes, tracing the turns of a piece of cotton that still wound in and out. It seemed he could see down to the weft of the cotton thread, to the braiding of ever smaller filaments.

Nothing.

Schreber pulled the thread from the centre of the button and rubbed it between his fingertips. It picked up particles of clay and balled together in a pellet which he brought up to his eye. He flicked it high into the air, and it arced over the lawn.

A bird sang—sparse, shrill birdsong—one note and another, separate, clear, with no import or intent other than that proper to birds: one empty note after another, run together to no purpose other than that hidden intention claimed by the bird itself, a purpose closed to the ears of man, like the striking of random keys on a piano.

He closed his eyes again and lay on the grass, turning the button with his fingers.

Nothing.

An orderly stood in the doorway of the observatory—an ape of a man dressed in a white frock coat—peering from under heavy brows down the gentle slope to where Schreber's Bath chair lay overturned.

He appeared to sigh, then he wiped his mouth with the back of his hand and glanced over his shoulder toward the doctors' quarters. When he turned back he spat brown onto the flagstones of the patio and came over to Schreber.

'We can't have you lying there in the dirt can we?' he said with his knuckles on his hips.

Schreber blinked. The man was close enough to smell: disinfectant soap on his skin, tobacco on his breath. There was a halo around his edges, and as he breathed, the sunlight came directly over his shoulder and into Schreber's eyes, making them water. When he put up his hand to wipe out the tears, he dropped his button. With the other hand, now blind, he patted over the bunched fabric at his groin.

'And none of that either,' the orderly said, and he put Schreber over his shoulder, bending as if it was easier for him to be stooped, and only straining when he needed to stand straight.

Schreber pushed up too, planting his hands on the orderly's broad, rounded back, and he pushed until he was horizontal. There was the house in front of him, and it came to him suddenly that he was not at home. He was not in his garden, dozing off lunch between the flowers. Sabine was not with him. He put one hand to the back of his head—the marram grass was cleared, shaved back to the skin and where it had grown there was a long thin cut, stitched and recently healed.

'Where am I?'

The orderly shrugged. 'You are where you always are,' he said, and he coughed, hefted Schreber over a little, and took a half step forward.

'Why are you carrying me?' Schreber dug his fingers into the flesh of the man's back.

'I'm putting you back in your chair.'

'Who are you?'

Müller stopped and craned his neck round, almost enough to look Schreber in the face. He took his free hand and ran it through his hair, sweeping it back and over, behind his ear.

'I'm Müller,' he said, as if the answer should have been redundant.

'I don't understand.'

'No, I don't reckon you do.'

The orderly's hair fell loose again, half obscuring his face, only kept in check by the broken bulge in the man's nose bone.

They were in front of the chair now, and Müller squared his shoulders, set his knees, and prepared to put Schreber down.

'I want to go home... Where is my wife?'

Müller grunted under the old man's weight, but said nothing.

Schreber spoke louder, as he always did with this class of man. His eyes blinked rapidly, as if he was clearing out dust.

'Do you hear me? I want to go home. It is very important. My wife is ill. Sabine!'

Müller roughly shifted Schreber about, as if he still hadn't heard. Schreber lost his balance and slipped until he was bent double, his face in the small of Müller's back. In a second he was back up, pushing against the orderly again, and lifting his head as far as it would go so that he could see the house.

'Please. I demand to be taken home! Angelikastrasse. Put me down immediately and take me there. Send for a carriage!'

Müller edged forward toward the chair.

'You'll have to talk to the doctor about that.'

'Get him!'

'Dr. Rössler?' Müller said, smirking where he could not be seen.

'If that is the man's name, then certainly, you must go and get him. Immediately! It is very important!'

'I'm sure it is,' the orderly said, and he hefted Schreber forward hard, back into his chair. Then he stepped away, smoothed his hair, mopped the sweat from his brow with his sleeve, and looked Schreber up and down. Schreber stared at him, waiting.

Müller's hand went to his chest—to that place where a man wearing a jacket has his breast pocket—but the hand, not finding what it expected, returned empty.

Müller licked his lips and coughed. He looked off around the garden. He looked off across the fields, up the hill, to where his father lived. He thought of his brother, Karl. Then he turned and spat again, this time onto the grass.

'Let's tidy you up, old man.'

'What are you doing? Get your hands off me!'

'He won't see you dressed like that now, will he?'

'The doctor? Are you tidying me up to see the doctor? I am more than capable of doing that for myself.'

Müller pushed Schreber's hands away and pulled the old man's shirt together. He wiped the grass from his shoulders and rearranged the rug. All the while the muscles of his jaw worked.

When Müller spoke it was through wide, tight lips.

'We'll see,' he said.

'See? What will we see? It is I who must see the doctor. Can you understand me? Am I making myself clear? I must see him, this… Rössler. It's a matter of enormous importance. My wife, I must see my wife! She is very ill.'

'She looked alright a minute ago.'

'What? What did you say?'

Müller smiled, but said nothing more.

Schreber frowned. The man was a fool. He tried a different tack. He said, slowly and clearly:

'Take me to the doctor, now, please. I can pay you.' Schreber searched his pockets. 'I have money. I should have it… I must have a few marks… surely… I can get you money! I don't have my purse, but I can get money for you. Anything. I must see my wife!'

Müller went behind Schreber and put his big hands on the handles of the Bath chair, and soon they were inside, wheels rattling on the parquet, making for Dr Rössler's room.

After a long while wait-
ing on his doctor's con-
venience, Schreber is
taken in to see Rössler.
A mysterious Jewish
gentleman appears at
the window, mouthing
insults. Sabine has been
to visit. To Schreber's
disappointment, she has
already left.

VIII

'So you are awake at last,' the man, the doctor—Rössler?—said
from behind his desk, pulling his glasses down a little from
where they pinched the bridge of his nose. He leant forward
in his chair for a second before creaking back, returning his
glasses to their original place. He muttered something under
his breath—"intransigent"? "inconvenient"? Something—and
pulled together papers from here and there, making a pile.

Inside, the light was weak and grainy, blurring the edges
of the heavy leather furniture. Objects—a potted palm, an
unwound ornamental wall clock, a hanging chandelier decorated
with vines—they seemed part of the dark, patterned wallpaper.
The dominating light came from beneath a green, glass-shaded
lamp on a side cabinet. The air was milky, and smelt strongly
of pipe smoke.

'I demand to see my wife.'

The doctor tutted and frowned, reaching across the desk
for an object that turned out not to be the one he required, but
Schreber went on.

'You are Dr. Rössler?' he said.

The man paused and seemed to ponder for a second, then he rubbed the back of his neck and nodded slowly. At last he found what he was looking for and made a chirruping sound. He moved back in his chair, where he was almost completely overtaken by the shadow of a huge shelved bureau.

In his hands was a book. That much at least Schreber was able to make out.

'*The Great Words of a Nerve-Case*. I knew it was here somewhere.'

The book was opened. Pages turned.

'This room is very dark…' Schreber muttered.

Seedy. Like a Turkish brothel. He shuffled forward so that he was perched on the edge of his chair and the doctor and the book were more or less visible.

Rössler was old, too, his knuckles bulbed with rheumatism, but the pages of the book flicked forward and backward like the wings of a butterfly in flight. He was too small for the room, with its palm and bookcase and chandelier. He resembled nothing more than a homunculus escaped from its jar, making mischief while its master was elsewhere.

Schreber made an impatient sniff, and the doctor turned to him, inclined his head a little, and smiled as if to express his regret. The loose skin of his neck, his jowls, his long ear-lobes, they kept their orientation to the ground, hanging down straight.

With a hand that was thin to the point of brittleness—like a twig one finds on the forest floor late into the autumn—he made a sign that Schreber should bear with him for only a moment or two longer. Clean white sleeves swamped his thin wrists. His skin was brown and mottled.

He laid the book down on the table, stood up, and went to stand directly in front of Schreber. Out from behind his desk, at large among the things of the room, his stature was even more exaggerated. Like a child, or a goblin. He groaned as he bent over to get a better view of his patient, with his hands on his knees. When he peered over the top of his glasses, Schreber peered back.

'Now, sir,' Rössler said, surprisingly deeply, 'can we assume you are feeling a little better today?'

Schreber made no effort to answer.

'This place has the atmosphere of a Turkish brothel,' he snapped. 'Would it be asking too much to have a window open and the blinds drawn? It's a very clear day, yet one would never know it in this hole.'

On the table the *Great Words* sat.

Schreber looked back at the doctor.

Rössler smiled and almost nodded—it might even have been his breathing making him nod, very slightly, as he drew air in and out.

'Like a Turkish brothel,' Schreber repeated, this time louder.

He watched the doctor and the doctor watched him, smiling. Unpleasant little man.

When Schreber looked away, his focus failed to settle anywhere in the murk and he received the nauseating impression that the objects of his attention were either very close at hand or at a great distance, and that he couldn't properly distinguish which.

'It is good to hear you speak,' Rössler said, at last.

His voice really was quite sonorous. Was there an accent?

'I suppose,' he went on, 'if nothing else, it's given me time to read your book. I know Dr. Flechsig, by the way. I should probably make that clear. And Weber. Very good doctors. You've been very lucky.'

None of this was relevant. Old words. Dead names. The population of a former era, long passed away.

'Where is my wife?' Schreber asked.

Rössler pursed his lips.

'Yes… I suppose I should have qualified that earlier statement… It is good to hear you speak about something else.' A touch of French? An Alsatian then? An Alsatian dwarf, wittering on and making faces. 'It has been a quite a while since you expressed an interest in anything other than the disposition of your wife.'

Rössler returned to his chair and gathered in the piles of paper. Schreber's notes?

The glasses were pulled down again, then up. Schreber swallowed. Did this man ever intend to answer him?

'Well?'

'Well what?'

'Where is she, man?'

Rössler raised an eyebrow.

'Do you feel well?' he asked.

'That is not an answer to my question, sir.'

'I am aware of that, Herr Schreber, but the question stands.'

'Answer mine first!'

Rössler removed his glasses altogether and placed them in front of him on the desk. Without them, he seemed to become smaller still, his eyes in particular. He compensated for this by exuding an air of intense concentration. Schreber shifted uncomfortably in his chair.

'Are you aware,' Rössler asked, 'that it is a doctor's privilege, in his own office, to expect an answer from his patients?'

'I suppose…'

'Then the question stands. Do you feel well today?'

Schreber stared at him for some time, but, despite his size, the man would not be intimidated.

'I feel very well, thank you,' Schreber said, when it was absolutely clear that there would be no progress until he did.

'And the voices?'

Schreber stared blankly and did not reply, but Rössler stared back. The doctor drew the book towards him and opened it randomly. With a finger he followed the lines and read parts out.

'"In my case... since my nervous illness took the above mentioned... my nerves have been set in motion from without incessantly...," da...da...da..., "incessant voices...," "nerve-speech...," "the rays," da...da...da..., "falsifying my thoughts...," da...da...da... All this—you remember? You wrote this book in hospital last time... These symptoms, have they eased somewhat?'

'That book is irrelevant. I was ill. There is nothing more to say on the matter.'

Rössler smiled.

'Excellent, excellent...' He flicked through the book again. 'Chosen by God to bear a new race of men? Subject of miracles? Unmanning.'

Schreber shook his head. 'That was years ago. I was mistaken in all of it. A nightmare, nothing more. Do not even speak of it. I am perfectly well. I must return home immediately.'

'Your insides?' Rössler enquired. 'Have the miracles ceased?'

'Please... There are no miracles. I am utterly fine. Those things were dreams, tedious dreams, and no one wants to hear about them.'

'Wonderful... The sleep seems to have done you good.'

Schreber frowned and, seeing this, Rössler smiled.

'You have been inaccessible for some time as we gave you a sleeping draught,' Rössler added, by way of clarification, 'and then, as you slept, Müller gave you more. For two weeks. It can be effective...'

'I see.'

'It is a little too early to tell, yet, but at last there does seem to have been some improvement.'

Rössler returned the book to the centre of the table and shuffled his papers until they were tidied.

'May, then, I be allowed to return home?'

'Well, perhaps, Herr Schreber, perhaps.'

Rössler picked up his silver letter opener, intending, it seemed, to use it as a paperweight. He held it above the arrangement of papers as if he was about to lay it down on top of them, but then, at the last moment, he took it between the finger and thumb of his right hand and let it swing back and forward.

'Your wife,' he said, 'she is now well after her stroke. You will be pleased to hear this?'

Schreber came out of his chair and took the few steps over to Rössler's desk.

'A stroke? Good God! I must see her! Please! Is she well?'

'I have told you that she is.'

'Good Lord! And Fridoline? I must see them!'

'All in good time, Herr Schreber! Please return to your chair. Do not make it necessary for me to call an orderly.'

'I must see her!' He leaned forward so that his belly rested on the doctor's desk. Rössler reached for the bell.

'Should we continue this conversation on another occasion, Herr Schreber? I cannot guarantee it will be soon…'

Schreber stepped away. A stroke? And now well? No longer grimacing and shaking down there on the floor… No longer flat and soulless? He took his seat and his hands were shaking.

'Very good. She was here today,' Rössler continued when Schreber was back in his chair, 'until very recently—in fact, moments ago—asking after your health. This was immediately before your… awakening.' Rössler slapped the hilt of the letter opener into the palm of the opposite hand. 'How does that strike you?'

'She was here? Where is she now?'

'She is returning home to Dresden, Herr Schreber. She was very concerned for your physical health.' Rössler remembered something—something written down—and he began to search for it. 'She was very firm in this regard. She worries you will have lost weight. I need to examine you. Ah!' He held a sheet of paper in his hand, sparsely decorated with an untidy hand. He read it for a while, and nodded as he did so. 'I almost let it slip my mind. Would you open your shirt for me, please?'

Rössler came round to stand beside him. Though Schreber was sitting and Rössler standing, they were approximately at the same height. The silver disc of a stethoscope hovered between them.

'And then can I see her?' Schreber asked. 'She will want to see me.'

'I understand your desire to see her, but I'm sure that's not possible. She has already left for home.'

'But you said she was here moments ago. Send someone for her. She will not mind the inconvenience.'

'Herr Schreber, there will be plenty of time for that. For now, let us proceed with the business in hand. Your shirt?'

Schreber moved to leave the chair again, thinking perhaps to run to the door, or the window, and shout after her, but the doctor's hand on his shoulder, brittle-seeming though it was, was enough to keep him in his place.

'Might we open the blinds, at least?'

'Why not?'

Rössler walked over and twisted the sash.

'Now... the shirt?'

Schreber stared at the window hoping that by some accident he might catch sight of his wife, and she of him...

But, in her place, he saw something else.

The window was large, a single pane starting up quite high in the wall, but very wide. A man at the window was blocking the view through the middle. He was a Jewish gentleman of moderate size, with neatly cropped and greased black hair. He stared into the room intently, searching for something. Schreber watched him, and when the man caught sight of the judge, he smiled and spoke. His lips parted and moved together, sculpting words that Schreber could not read. Schreber made the same shapes with his own lips. Ball crusher?

Rössler, catching the direction of Schreber's attention, marched to the window and twisted the blinds shut again so that the gentleman disappeared with the sunlight, and the only illumination was the greasy green-yellow wash of the single oil lamp.

'She is not out there. That window opens onto the gardens. Open your shirt to the waist, please.'

'There was a Jew…'

'Your shirt!'

'But there is nothing the matter with me.'

Rössler removed his glasses and sighed.

'I am perfectly fine. Please call a carriage,' Schreber went on, talking as much to himself as to the doctor. 'I want to go home!'

'If you'll forgive me, I will work around you.'

Rössler slipped the cold metal of the stethoscope under Schreber's shirt.

'The confusion has gone. I am back to my usual self. Do you see?'

Rössler held up his hand for the quiet he needed, and moved the disc here and there over Schreber's chest, listening. When he was finished and Schreber's hands moved to button his shirt—to make himself decent—he was surprised to find every one of his buttons was gone, and broken threads twisted uselessly where the buttons should have been. He tried to put the fabric from one side through the hole in the other, using his little finger to poke it in, but it slipped back out when he breathed. He had no choice but to hold the two sides of the shirt shut with both his hands, one by his throat and the other by his waist. When he looked down he saw that he had no hands free to rearrange his trousers, which gaped open at the lap.

Rössler stood by the desk and said nothing. He appeared to be thinking.

'On the scale, please.'

Sabine… how far would she be away? With one word from this little man…

Schreber returned to his chair, hands clutching his clothes closed, and watched the doctor thinking. His hand moved

66

to rest on the back of his neck, only leaving it to push up his glasses periodically.

The room fell further into silence the longer Schreber waited for the doctor to speak. When his father retired to their private quarters with his head, and the other rooms of the Institute became heavy in the absence of his presence, the children slid here and there through the building in their stocking feet and played softly in corners, their wooden toys removed and replaced with stuffed cotton dolls that they were much too old for. If so much as a chair was scraped on the wooden floor, they froze like statues and stayed that way for thirty seconds or a minute, until it felt to them as if their thoughts must have been too loud, and their heartbeats too. When Paul thought something, he flinched, wondering if his father had been disturbed by the thinking, and if his heart beat faster, then he tried to stop it by squeezing his chest with his arms wrapped tight around him.

Schreber's arms were around his chest now, and he was waiting, and there was that same cacophony of rushing blood.

Rössler turned to him.

Schreber tried to uncross his arms and grip the supports of his chair, but his chest was unwilling to become uncovered. As Paul had waited—to see if his father would thunder red-faced down the stairs with his mother a few steps behind, thin and white like a ghost, eyes red and crying aloud, begging for the days that were gone, the days they had all loved, before the accident, when things were good—so Schreber waited.

Silence.

'Now, Herr Schreber,' Rössler said, breaking the atmosphere as if he was cracking an egg, 'first accept my apologies.' He slid his glasses down his nose and rubbed his eyes through the gap behind them. 'Accept my apologies for my unfortunate oversight in not coming to see whether you had regained consciousness before your wife left. I should have checked first, and I am sorry that I did not. I suppose I have grown used to the *status quo*, and that something might have changed did not occur to me.'

Schreber nodded mutely and blinked.

'I have your notes here along with my own recent observations and, I am sorry to say, they are not encouraging. Quite the opposite. And with your history… The picture is that of an incurable case.' Rössler paused. To see what effect his words were having? Schreber did not react. Where was the verdict?

'That said, the primary resource of the doctor must always be the presentation of the patient himself, and, providing there are no obvious confusions, that patient's opinion as to his own condition. Who would know better, after all, whether he was well or not?'

'I feel well,' Schreber offered.

'This is very good, Herr Schreber. I had almost given up on you. You presented, until today, very much in the manner of many of our patients here—the other hopeless cases—fixed and unreachable. But this, your reaction to the sleep, is very promising. It had been my intention to send you home. I asked your wife to come here to discuss just that. I had given up on the idea that you might be cured and hoped that a return to a familiar environment might trigger some minor recuperation, or at least provide you a pleasant environment in which to live out…'

'I utterly agree. It is home I need and the comforts and routines I have grown used to and which keep these matters under check.'

'Please, let me finish my train of thought before I lose it. That had been my intention. I made this argument strenuously to your wife…'

'Then let us do just as you suggest. Can someone be sent to bring her here?'

'She is already returning home.'

'Send someone to bring her back.'

'She is already in transit. Please remain seated. If you will let me finish. When I thought that you might not respond to any treatment I had to offer, the only option was to return you home. But now, when there is hope of a full recovery, of eventually getting you well, I think we owe it to everyone to make our best attempt at a cure. Don't you agree?'

'I can come here for treatment, certainly. Can I see Sabine? I'm sure we can arrange a course of treatment. She is a wonderfully practical woman, more so than I… She will draw up a schedule and ensure I stick with it.'

'It is felt that your treatment might be best carried out under close observation.'

'Who feels it? I do not feel it.'

'I feel it, Herr Schreber. A week. Ten days. And then, when you are sent home, you might never fear these problems again, and you can live a happy family life.'

'We have our trials, but our family life is already happy, thank you.'

'Two weeks, at most a month. Is that not the reasonable path to take?'

'Might I at least speak to her?'

'She will be away by now.'

'How can you be sure?'

'Very well…' Rössler sighed. 'Müller!'

Schreber looked at his knees and, as time passed, stared at the window blinds.

'Müller! Where is the man?'

Schreber watched the light come in from the garden, illuminating remnants of pipe smoke. She might be near—just outside the precincts of this place. At arm's length.

Rössler marched to the door, and for a little while he left the room. Schreber turned to look for him, but the door was closed. He might take her dancing. She had so often complained of the lack of it. This evening, if she wished.

Rössler came back, followed by Müller.

'Your wife has already left, Herr Schreber. Don't worry, you will be home soon, I'm certain of that.'

'Send someone after her!'

Müller came behind him and Schreber's Bath chair tipped back.

'There is no need,' Rössler assured him.

'I say that there is!'

The chair turned until the open door was in front and the light from the corridor came in. Schreber turned away from it and back to the doctor.

'I say that there is! I insist!'

Rössler inclined his head very slightly—a sign for Müller? Schreber was wheeled out of the room.

'I insist! Send someone!'

Rössler faced out of his window, despite the fact that the blinds were shut, and polished the lenses of his glasses as if he could hear nothing.

'Please!'

Passing through, Müller pulled the door shut with a snap.

Wheeled from Rössler's
room, Schreber is not
deterred. He tries to
leave the asylum on
foot, but Müller bars
his way. Climbing a tree,
memories of his child-
hood come to the fore.
All this is much to the
displeasure of Müller,
who is responsible for
the safety of his charge.

IX

The hallway outside Rössler's room led in two directions: left (to the entrance hall and the gardens) and right (away from them). Müller, lips pursed and white, wheeled the Bath chair off to the right.

In the window glass, Schreber caught his reflection and that of the orderly. The rattling of the wheels on the parquet floor echoed itself in Müller's arms, which were held so tight that each movement was transmitted to his shoulders, and then to his neck, and his head juddered like a man receiving an electric shock.

The corridor stretched off ahead. Schreber, all at once, stood up on the footplate of the Bath chair like a charioteer.

'Take me out of this place!'

Müller grabbed the waistband of Schreber's trousers and pulled him back down.

'That'll do, Judge, thank you!'

Schreber grunted.

How dare he? This lump! He grit his teeth and stood up again, and now his blanket slipped onto the ground and became tangled up with the chair's wheels. The whole apparatus, in the blink of an eye, was tipped forward, emptying Schreber onto the floor.

The orderly was too slow: Schreber hopped away from the mess, turned and raced off down the corridor toward the French doors that opened onto the garden. His stocking feet slipped on the polished wood and his thighs resisted the unexpected exertion, but he wasn't dead yet! He hadn't rotted away yet! He was a living man, and hadn't his father taught him to always keep himself in good fighting condition? He had, and he left that slant-browed dullard standing with his eyes wide and his chin on his chest. Doctors and orderlies! They should know their place.

'Judge! Get back here!' Müller hissed.

Schreber kept running and now the ape was after him, arms swinging, hair loose. There were the glass double doors that led out onto the lawn—no distance at all—but as Schreber made for them here was the Jewish gentleman he had seen through the window, stock still, barring his way.

Schreber came to a stop, skidding with his arms outstretched. Müller closed the distance between them.

'Be a good Judge,' he muttered, 'and stay where you are for old Müller…'

The gentleman looked on impassively, blocking the exit, and now Müller was only a few feet away. Schreber turned to face the orderly, and the only thing between them was a bust on a marble plinth. When Müller went left, Schreber went right.

'Give it up, Judge! There's a nice warm pot of coffee for you in your room, and yesterday's paper. It's kale and sausages for lunch…'

Schreber stood up straight and made out that he'd seen sense, but when Müller relaxed and came to take his arm, the judge sprinted off around the bust—Friedrich?—and ran straight at the Jewish gentleman, who thought for half a second, then smiled and stepped aside at the last moment with a generous sweep of the arm.

'After you, ball-crusher,' he said, and left the smell of his hair oil in the air.

Schreber was out into the garden.

The bright daylight made him blanch. For a second he stopped, but here was Müller, hissing.

The garden of Schreber's block was surrounded on all sides by dormitories, but there was a narrow alley leading off the southeast corner which gave onto the rest of the estate and, spying this, Schreber made for it, starting now to feel his old limbs loosening.

But Müller was too wily for him. Keeping close to the dormitory wall, he was more than halfway there before Schreber had covered any distance at all.

'Give it up, Judge!' Müller tried again.

'I want to go to Sabine!'

'We'll talk about that when you're safe in your room.' A wet smile and palms held facing out.

Schreber backed away. Back at the door from which he'd come, the Jewish gentleman was watching with interest, and now, beside him, looking away, was a second orderly, uniformed in the same long white coat that Müller wore, but because this man was so much taller, his arms protruded from the sleeves by several inches, just as his ankles did from the trousers. Müller put two fingers in the corners of his mouth and whistled. The tall orderly jerked to attention, and when Müller by gestures made him understand that Schreber was to be restrained, he too came forward, arms out and hands like a scorpion's claws, two pincers ready to grab and keep him, opening and closing.

'Let's have you back in your chair now, eh?' called Müller. 'Before there's any more trouble.' He swept around toward Schreber, always blocking off the alleyway, which Schreber could see over the orderly's shoulder and which now seemed the brightest part of the world.

The tall one was too close. Schreber moved away from each of the orderlies in turn, and if it hadn't been for the tree that

73

met his back, he would have given it up there and then. He turned, at first thinking it was another orderly, sneaking up on him from behind, but he found only a thick round trunk and before he had properly considered what it was that he had decided to do, he was up it.

Slowly at first and then quicker, he climbed until he was twenty feet or more from the ground, looking down like Pentheus spying on the Bacchae. Müller was left standing on the patio, his eyes snapping to and fro between the window of Rössler's room and the old man.

Schreber slipped off his socks, taking no notice of how the branches became thinner and more flexible as he went up. Why should he? He'd done this a thousand times as a boy, reaching for the ankles of Gustav, and never quite catching them as his brother giggled and taunted and went higher and higher.

The words of doctors and orderlies were nothing, and they blew away in the wind like the seeds of a dandelion. He wound his arms around the trunk and his bare feet pushed so his toes splayed and gripped the rough bark, staining his trousers moss green.

Hadn't he always been careless that way? Because he knew that if his mother gasped to see him so high, his father held her elbow and kept her at a distance, behind a wall, or the window of the drawing room, protected from sight by the natural reflectivity of glass. His father would have lectured her on the necessity of a boy's coming to understand and conquer little dangers, and as long as the sun shone and Gustav laughed, there was no fear that could stop Paul. Even when he realised how high he had come it was nothing, because if it was safe for Gustav then wasn't it safe for him too?

So Schreber went higher and higher, escaping somehow from the place below him. If he grazed his shin then what of it? He was no sissy. He was not soft, but instead, like all good boys, he was tough, and wasn't this what those sorts of boys did? He knew that it was.

When once he saw his father watching him, he hoped that it confirmed his father's good impression of him, that it strengthened his hopes for him, and dispelled the worries of his effeminacy that had been provoked by other things—like when he played with the undergarments of the girls' dolls. Anna had led him astray, giggling, only for the doll to be taken from both of them. When it was returned later there was a crack in her head, as if she had been wounded right through the porcelain. Then, if one was not perfectly gentle, the gap came wide and it was possible to see inside, where there was nothing.

'What did you think? That she was a real girl?' Gustav said, and he laughed.

Anna cried like she cried when she was left alone, when the boys went too high and she could not follow. For one thing, her dress was too big, all bone and frills, and she dared not get it messed up. They would insist on climbing so high, so that even the sight of it made her weep and they were egged on by her tears, laughing together.

Schreber reached up through the dense leaves and the tangles of twigs and jutting branches and when Müller came to the tree trunk, wheeling the Bath chair, the blanket shoved back onto the seat, keeping low to the earth so that Rössler mightn't see him, Schreber laughed to see it. Despite it all he laughed. He laughed harder when the idiot looked up. He was so small down below and his face was pale with amazement and dismay, because Schreber was almost at the top of the tree, which was at least two hundred years old and God knows how high.

Schreber was scratched bloody. He pulled himself up, through the canopy, and at the very top the sun was blazing.

'Get down here, you silly bastard!'

The words reached, but only barely. The wind blew in Schreber's ears and the rustling of leaves was like the waves on the shore and the movement of shingle up the beach. When Müller's words came to him, he ignored them. Instead, from

75

where he stood swaying in the wind, he searched the horizon for sign of her—for Sabine—over the roofs of the asylum, and of Dösen, and of Leipzig. They were laid out like gingerbread houses before him, their windows sugar glass in frames of icing. The scent of spice filled the air, hundreds of tiny houses all laid out in imitation of the places of the town: the bakers, the butchers, the town hall, making his mouth water, and between them roads of liquorice laid in sheets, and on one of these, surely, Sabine must be travelling. Carriages made of cake. That one? At a great distance, barely a speck, smaller than an ant—drawn there by all that sugar! Could it be her?

'Sabine!'

He waited for her reply, but there was nothing.

'Sabine!'

Nothing, and now, when he looked down, the expression on Müller's face, the tall one gone—who knows where?—was a caricature of an angry man in miniature, like a Greek theatre mask with the mouth turning down in a mirror of the line formed by the man's brow.

Schreber's skin was prickling. He looked at his forearm, rotating it first clockwise and then back again. There were tiny scratches, and they swelled up like bee stings.

Sabine was nowhere to seen.

He leaned forward, as if that small change in distance would clarify things, as if it would allow him to see her.

It did not.

He leaned further still, and still she was not there.

He leaned until only the ends of his fingers held the thin branches and shifted so one leg was free, in the air, and the tip of the tree trunk, little more than a branch itself, curved toward where he was searching, taking him closer.

But she was not there.

When he went further, he slipped from the tree and fell.

As he lies on the grass for the second time that day, Schreber's attention is taken again by the mysterious Jewish gentleman, whom Schreber is now convinced he knows from life outside the asylum.

X

From the ground he traced his fall through fizzing stars. Past branches cracked and stripped of leaves, all the way into the sky, nowhere was a limb sufficiently thick to have slowed his fall. The branches swayed—or was it his vision?—and the arrangement of the canopy slowly effaced his path, until he could no longer see the blue sky.

It was clear that he should have broken his neck.

His head vibrated even as he lay still, and if he concentrated on the sensations present at the top of his spine he could feel what must have been a substantial displacement of the vertebrae, a gap between two bones that should have been snugly together. Those nerves that ran along the length of his back felt stretched, as if they had been broken apart and stitched back. When he tried to move, the whole mechanism shook with pain.

Then, from nowhere, there was the Jewish gentleman.

He was smoking a cigarette, and when he took it from his mouth he performed a prim bow. Now Schreber thought to remember him. Suave and slim. Wasn't he always somewhere?

Keeping his distance, never seeming to move or follow him about the place, but always there when Schreber thought to check—when he felt the rising of the hairs on the back of his neck?

Hadn't he once caught sight of a shadow as he walked down a corridor, and this Jew was there? Or when he yawned or sneezed, so that his eyes blinked shut involuntarily, and, when they opened again, he felt the world as something new, and he looked around to see where he was, then wouldn't this Jew appear?

Wasn't this Jew always there, in the street, watching? Wasn't this the Jew Sabine had pointed out in the Opera, who had coughed through the overture to *Der Freischütz*? Wasn't this the Jew who had taken the carriage meant for Schreber at the station when he returned from visiting his mother? Hadn't he seen this Jew at the newspaper stand, waiting, smoking, wearing a cheap hat with a scuff on the band? Wasn't this the Jew who had been inside a carriage while its driver, a dog-faced Slav, had taken the whip to his horse, striking it across the shoulder and nose, its skin already white with foam, while it chewed and pulled against the harness, the carriage inching back and forward and welts came across the horse's face, its hair stripped? Didn't blood come from the end of the whip when the Slav brought it back over his shoulder in preparation for bringing it down again, so that a drop landed on Sabine's glove, and Schreber was outraged enough to hold the driver's wrist? There was anger in the Slav's eyes, that a man should be prevented from disciplining his own beast, whether the animal understood it or not. Skin brown, tanned by the sun and by his work. In the lines that ran beside his nose down to his mouth there was dirt, and he stank of sweat and black bread—sour and musty. Schreber held his wrist and the man turned, much more broad than Schreber was, broader even than Schreber and his wife combined were. His wrist was thicker than Schreber could easily hold, and it was clear from the look in that man's eyes that he considered using the whip on them. The Slav grit his teeth and, behind him, in the carriage, wasn't there this Jew? Sitting there, watching, eyes heavy and pensive, skin clear and pale, no expression to be seen except that of careful interest in the proceedings, and of constant mild amusement? An observer, like he was now—exactly as he was now—watching Schreber, monitoring those things that he did and those things that were done to him, listening to every word that was spoken to him and that he in his turn spoke, and finding something in it all that was faintly risible? This was the same man, surely. It was the same man, wasn't it?

Didn't the sight of this Jew strike fear into him? It did.

Even though he was just a man.

But hadn't Schreber held that Slav's arm? That man who was no more than a beast himself? Whose leather shirt was specked with horse blood, and who could have taken Schreber's neck in one hand and choked him before imagining the consequences? Wasn't this the way with men of his class, probably already drunk? Couldn't Schreber smell the alcohol on his sweat? The tang of the stuff, excreted constantly, causing the delicate skin at the corners of his eyes to smart. Didn't Sabine raise her handkerchief to her face, the blood-stained glove there for the man to see?

Didn't Schreber say to him, "The honourable man shows restraint," and let his wrist go, dropping his hand to his side?

Hadn't he done this? The Jew in the carriage, only then did he turn away. When the driver curled his lip he said something under his breath in a language that Schreber had never before heard. Its meaning was obscure, but the thick guttural mess expressed something beyond simple meaning: that the driver took Schreber for an idiot. If he had the opportunity, this Slav would have whipped them both, the stuffed shirt and his wife, until they wept on their knees. It was only the presence of passersby, and his being in a strange country and of the class

79

of man not to expect easy treatment from the authorities, that stopped him. He turned his broad back and lowered the whip, and punched the horse below the eye. He barked at it, and the Jew in the carriage knocked on the wall with the end of his stick. The driver took his place up top and cracked the reins hard. A spray of sweat from the horse's flank went up and Schreber and Sabine had to step back from the edge of the road. When the carriage jerked away, the man in the rear was looking out, and wasn't this Jew's face the same: identical to the image of the man still pictured in his mind?

When Schreber turned to face him straight on, looking to compare his thoughts with reality, he saw no one.

There was no one.

It was a while before Schreber noticed Müller at his feet. He was standing as still as the tree trunk behind him, and had he been but a shade paler, he would have been as white as the alabaster bust of King Friedrich they had recently passed in the hallway.

Schreber tried to say something, but his throat was dry and closed, and the effort made the world spin. No sense came out. The gasping noise he made in place of words had Müller inching forward, wide-eyed and open-mouthed, clearly convinced the old man was either dead or on the verge of death. The sound was so like a death rattle that Müller fell to his knees.

He crept forward like a baby.

'Judge?'

Schreber reached up his hand and Müller shut his mouth, swallowed and looked back to the asylum. Whatever it was he saw, or did not see, the orderly shuffled quickly forward, grabbed Schreber's hand and held it to his chest.

'Can you move?' he said.

Schreber tried and found that he could.

'Shall I put you in your chair?'

Schreber shook his head making it throb and causing a veil to descend over his vision, which only shutting his eyes seemed to cure. When he opened them again the veil was not passed, only lessened.

'Sabine…'

Müller licked his lips and touched his chest in that place where a man places a flask of spirits in his jacket pocket, cursing himself when his fingers, again, found nothing.

'Let's get you inside before…'

'No… Sabine…'

Müller looked at him and then back again at the asylum.

'I couldn't see her… like little ants… it was the sugar…'

Müller touched his chest and the names of the saints played silently on his lips. He whispered a prayer to Karl, his martyred brother, his father's favourite, and he promised him: 'If he lives, I'll never drink again.'

Schreber tried to sit up, but only made it a short way before falling back. The veil came down again.

Müller grabbed him by the shoulders to prevent any further sudden movement.

'I'm going to put you in your chair. Judge? Can you hear me? Judge? If it hurts, sing out, but I've got to get you inside.'

Müller placed Schreber in his chair much more delicately than he had before, but the shifting about caused pain. The world whipped around, impossible to steady, until Schreber shut his eyes.

The orderly took Schreber back to his rooms—wary as a pickpocket returning to his den.

'Let me tell you something,' Müller said, as he wheeled the chair so close to the wall that Schreber could feel the brickwork catching on his cotton shirt 'If you ever want to get out of this place you're going to have to be a good little boy. There's nothing they don't like more than trouble, and while you can cut up in front of me and I've got no choice but to take it, you let a doctor catch you and that is it. You can forget about your wife. You can forget about your home. You can forget about all of it. Do you understand?'

Schreber's eyes were shut and his jaw was set against the pain in his head, but he did hear it.

'That was too close. I've got my job to lose, and that's bad enough, but you've got your life to throw away. And there's worse places to be than up here, let me tell you. There's downstairs. Do you want to go downstairs? Is that what you want, Judge?'

The chair hit smooth stone beneath its wheels, and the pain eased a little.

Fridoline comes to visit. Schreber is initially delighted, but the girl acts strangely and becomes willful when challenged on certain details which do not accord with her father's experience of his time spent in the asylum.

XI

The rooms were not at all unpleasant, being like those one might be given in a rather genteel hotel whilst visiting Lake Garda for the summer, and the medicine—a tincture given thrice daily in a little sherry glass—blurred the edges of the place, and though Schreber strained always against the longing to run, it was, at least, not uncomfortable to take Müller's advice.

There was a heaviness in the world that came after taking his medicine, a sensation of compression, and while his anxieties did not disappear, they too were subject to this effect, so that they seemed lessened.

One day—it did not seem so long after—when the pain was gone in his head and neck, Müller came in and announced that there was to be a visitor.

The orderly was used to him, and he washed Schreber, and dressed him, and put him in his chair without any fuss, and went away. Soon there was a light rapping on the door, so light that at first Schreber assumed it must be from a room down the hallway, but it persisted, and with each tap the door shook, very lightly, in its frame. He shifted in his chair, and arranged the checked blanket so that it was straight across his knees. He put the heels of his shoes together. He smoothed his moustaches.

'Come in, please!'

The door opened.

Schreber leant forward smiling, but when it was open only a few inches the door stopped. He froze where he was, halfway out of his chair and, as he waited, the smile wavered on his lips and his arms trembled.

There was the sound of whispered reassurances, of Müller's voice. The licking of his teeth.

The door swung in again and there was Fridoline, boxed in its frame.

Almost…

She was taller than he remembered her, her face a little changed: Thinner. Longer.

'Now don't you worry, Fräulein,' Müller said from off. 'Just remember what we talked about, and I'll be waiting if…' Müller, with his hand on the doorknob, glanced past the girl and toward Schreber. 'Well, if there's anything you should need,' he said, and nodded to her. She nodded back and swallowed. She turned and, looking down at the ground, inched into the space the opening of the door had made.

'Come, come, my girl! There's no need to dawdle!'

'Yes, Papa.'

'Close the door, child.'

'Yes, Papa.'

When she was in the room her pace improved, but she looked back often, toward the closed door.

'Well, it's wonderful to see you! You look terrifically healthy. And so tall!' Schreber said.

'I am well.'

'Perhaps it is because I am seated...' Schreber thought he might stand, but his arms were weak and the world was so heavy. Was this really her? How could she have changed so much?

'And how is Dresden? Did the party go well? I'm sorry I couldn't be there...'

She stared at him blankly. There was no insolence on her face, but she said nothing. Almost a woman now!

Schreber coughed and pulled the blanket straight on his knees.

'And Mother? How is your mother? When is she coming?'

Fridoline looked back again to the shut door.

'Is she well?'

'Yes, Papa.'

Still a girl... Still little Fridoline. It was because he was seated. Perspective. All of that. A trick of the light.

'And you are being a good girl?'

She looked at her shoes and nodded.

'Excellent! It is a girl's duty to help her mother. Never has that duty been more important than now, even if only for a short while. Still, I'm sure I needn't tell you that. You've always been such a help. Haven't you, dear?'

She was very quiet. Not at all herself. Schreber sniffed and blinked. Not herself at all. So tall!

'In any case,' he went on, perhaps a little quieter than before, 'I shall be home in a few days. My doctor tells me that I am doing well. He made me sleep, for quite some time, and then there was a little accident, and now I am on the verge of complete recovery. He gives me medicine.' Schreber reached for the sherry glass, but Müller had taken it away. 'My nerves, you know.'

Fridoline nodded, but she didn't look up.

'Are you pleased to see your old Papa, then? You are very quiet. It has been quite a shock for you, all this, I suppose?'

Fridoline nodded.

'I'm sorry, girl. Truly. It is a father's place to provide order for his child, and you more than others, coming late, are in need of it. At least you do not want for anything else. Do you want for anything else?'

Fridoline shook her head.

'Good. Good. Very good. And, all in all, this whole affair, when it reaches its conclusion, as my doctor assures me it will, in two weeks, possibly a month, it won't have taken much more time than some fathers take on a business trip. Eh?'

The child was biting her lip. She nodded and smiled a tight smile, stitched at the point where her teeth pinched the skin.

She said nothing.

'Is there something wrong? Some problem with the skivvy? Or Cook? If there is, you need only tell me and I will write you a letter here and now. They listen to me. Let me get my pen.' He turned to reach for it. 'There must be paper here, in one of these drawers... Where's that blasted pen...'

'Papa...'

'It must be here. There is ink... I see the ink... But where is the pen? Ah!'

Schreber turned back smiling, with the pen in one hand and a sheet of letter paper in the other, but she was weeping. Silently, she was weeping and she was no longer biting her lip—it was turned out.

'Papa, please come home! Tell them to let you go! Mother says you must stay, but I want you to come home. She says you are too ill, that after such a long time it's all no good, but I say you should come home. She said I shouldn't come here anymore, that it makes you worse, but I say you should come home with me. Now! Won't you come home with me now? Dr. Dannenberg says it's no good keeping you here if you aren't getting any better.'

Schreber put out his arms and beckoned her forward as he always did when her lip curled over in that way, as it had on the first day he had seen her, and she had cried at the sight of him. Sabine had stood behind her, unsure how to reconcile these two:

her husband returned and the adopted child, her eyes flicking between them and, just as often, up to the heavens. She needn't have been concerned. He saw the ghosts of all the other girls and boys he had held in his arms, tiny and still, and his arms went out naturally, as they did for Klara and for all those nameless little things, and Frida came forward on that day, and on this, and buried her face in his chest.

He stroked her hair. His girl.

'Frida, my sweet girl, you mustn't upset yourself! Silly thing! It's all perfectly fine and normal. A course of treatment in a sanatorium. Like at Baden? You remember? Powders, and baths, and early nights, and all the meals served in your room? It's no different at all! The doctors and orderlies are just like the hotel staff. Nothing to cry about! The only difference is that we must do what our doctors tell us. And they charge a good deal more for their services! They aren't satisfied with a few pfennigs! But if they tell us we must stay, then we must stay. This Rössler—my doctor—he is a good man. He thinks I will be cured in no more than two weeks, perhaps a month... A little holiday, nothing more!'

'That is what you said last time... That is what you say every time... It hasn't been a month...'

'You're getting upset. This is adult business and I know it can be difficult to understand.'

'But I do understand. I understand very well. Dr. Dannenberg says I'm quite the young lady. Even Mother says I've changed since... She says I've changed. I ran the house when you and Mother went away and even since she's come back I've helped with everything, and I'm not a little girl anymore. Cook says so, and so does Sarah, and if there's someone needed to sort out a problem it's me they might come to now, because Mother... Sometimes they'd rather come to me than risk Mother, because she is much worse-tempered since she was taken ill... so it falls to me. So I'm not just a little girl!'

'I know, dear. Really. You've always been a great help and comfort to us all. I couldn't have wished for a better daughter. From the first day I came home, I said to your mother that God couldn't have blessed us with a better and brighter child. Ask her. She will confirm it. But there are some things that only your elders can properly understand. Anyway, what is a week or two, here or there? Or a month.'

'It has been more than a year, Papa! And they say terrible things about this place. There is a place below,' she whispered, 'from which people never return.'

Schreber smiled and shook his head indulgently.

'You are confused… There is no below…'

Fridoline stamped her foot and shook her head.

'It has been more than a year! You arrived last November and were very ill until the spring. Then you seemed to get well, for a little while—Mother came to see you, do you remember?—and then you went worse again. And now… won't you come home with me? For Christmas? It's almost Christmas again, and last time you promised…'

'Fridoline, I have no idea what you are talking about. My doctor assures me that I will be well and one must, where possible, follow doctor's orders. We may not like it, it may be inconvenient and tiresome, but we must follow doctor's orders! You will come to understand this. There really is no alternative. It is only a few days. A month at most. He is quite assured of it. You are so like your mother.' Schreber smiled. 'Such a fondness for the dramatic!'

Fridoline pulled away from him. Her face was the picture of concern!

'Come now. It will be fine in the end. There is no need to cry.'

'Please come home with me…'

'Here! I will call a meeting with the doctor. I will discuss with him whether I mightn't make it home by Christmas, and if he agrees, that is precisely what I will do. There, does that satisfy you? Then you and Mother and I will decorate the house and invite some of your friends to dine with us. What do you say?' Schreber expected the child to smile, but she did not.

'You will not come home with me today, then?'

'Child, I do not like your tone.'

'You will not come?'

'They will not… No, I will not.'

'Then you must stay.'

Schreber smiled.

'The older you become, Fridoline, the more you will understand the way of things. You consider yourself quite grown up, but you do not know or understand everything. Be patient. I will be home in good time, but it will be when my doctor and I are satisfied. I do not arrange my affairs by your diktat. Let that be an end to the matter. Now, when might I expect your mother? If she is better, I do not see why she shouldn't come immediately.'

Fridoline looked at her shoes.

'I will tell her you wish to see her.'

'Good girl. Now, let me see you smile before you leave.'

Schreber pushed her hair back from her face and held her by the shoulders. She fixed his gaze and did not smile, but her eyes grew large, and it seemed as if she would never blink. Then she looked away, down at the floor.

'Make sure you wear your scarf in the cab back to town. I know you! Any excuse.'

'Yes, Papa.'

Seemingly without being prompted, the door opened, and Müller stepped into the room. He and Fridoline exchanged a glance, and the girl left.

So tall!

Fridoline leaves. On closing the door, Schreber finds an object has been placed where it does not belong. He watches it, and, later, somewhere between the world of things and that of dreams, he finds a little warmth by which to sleep.

XII

Schreber stood by the door and listened to the girl's steps, and after that sound was gone it was some time before he remembered to light the lamp.

There was clicking. Müller in the hall? Müller's metal tips on the polished wood... Something forgotten? A fourth dose, ordered by Rössler?

Schreber waited for the door to open.

It did not.

The door did not open and the noise stayed at a constant volume. There was no end to it! Was the fool marching on the spot? Click, click, click, click!

'Müller!'

Nothing.

He moved his head backward and forward, like a pigeon, listening first with his left ear and then with his right, his eyes almost, but not quite, shut, and his mouth almost, but not quite, open.

The sound was coming from the other room. The bedroom. The sky outside darkened, clouds covering the sun.

The clicking... Where was it?

He walked slowly, head first, all the time listening, trying to ignore the dull slap of his leather slippers on the floorboards.

As he crossed into the bedroom he saw the clock.

It was the one he had known since he was a child, a circle of white with roman numerals and spindly hands, with wood around, shiny dark wood that curved down to meet the surface of his bedside table. Around the clock face was a thin band of metal, like gold, but flaked back to the nickel in spots because of its great age. It was the clock his father had owned, and then his mother, after his father had died, and then Anna, after Mother.

What was it doing here?

It was the one the children had watched, in silence, to ensure that it was not too early. It was the one that Gustav had wound every morning, testing the key against the spring, aware always of the tension that separated the clock from being fully wound— able to function, able to be relied on, able to be accurate—and from being over-wound, where the spring might snap, and time stop, and no one know whether it was too early or too late.

What was it doing here?

Schreber walked over to it. He peered all around it.

Someone must have brought it here. Someone must have put it here while he was asleep. Who? Not Anna? It couldn't have been Anna. She was too frightened to go near it since she dropped a glass in the larder, looking for milk, and it had smashed and gone in amongst the things on the floor and ruined the week's food, glass fragments too small for the eye to see being a grave detriment to health, and now it's not even fit for pigs. Anything glass—the little hinged door on the clock face that Gustav bravely opened to put in the key, the little dog with the pointy tail and white globs for eyes—anything made of glass, or clear, or transparent—anything like that—she was afraid to touch. But now it was here. The clock. How?

Schreber sat down on his bed next to it.

The day was becoming increasingly dark. Outside, the clouds were so thick that it seemed night was coming early. Yet the clock showed that it was only four. Five after. He opened the clock's glass door and ran his finger over the hands—two fingers: one for the minute hand, and one for the hour, and he pushed the tip of another into the square hole where the key went.

His window was open and the breeze from the garden flapped the curtains against the wall, quietly. Schreber went over to the window and pulled hard against the counterweighted sash until the frame and the window met, and then he slid across the catch. The curtains stilled, but the clock still clicked, and its hands still turned. Four and six. Schreber stood by the window and watched the clock. He watched it and gradually the room around him filled with blackness, the corners first, then the objects, and then the air, everything except the clock's white face.

The clock stopped and Schreber found that he was only inches from it: his nose was almost pressed against the glass.

He reached for the key, only understanding after his hand was already moving that he had no idea where it would be. He tried the drawer in the bedside table, but there was only an old *Leipziger Tageblatt*. In the moonlight he searched the room, squinting and bending to see onto every surface and looking into every corner, watching for the shape of the key—a little tube with a flattened end that the fingers held.

Schreber got onto his hands and knees, lifted the blankets that overhung the bed, and peered beneath. He edged forward until his head was under and the covers fell back over his shoulders, and then he lay down and swept his arm here and there across the floor. It was as if he was reaching for a toy—a white wooden train with red wheels—and he crawled until he was under the bed, up to the waist, but it didn't matter how far he went, he couldn't find anything. There was no key and no train.

He reached as far as he could, half expecting there would be an answering touch: a brother or sister's hand stretched out from the other side of the bed. First recoil and then, when the fingers approached each other again slowly, a giggle—Anna? The weight of her on the mattress above, bowing the springs.

A girl's voice.

When they touched again it was boldly, pushing each other away, fighting cheerfully for the territory within the reach of their hands. More giggles and—to a pinch—a yelp and a laugh, full blown and deep, from a boy whose voice had broken— Gustav—but who was still a boy, and Schreber, Paul, the little one, laughing and laughing without knowing why.

Anna laughed to see them both laughing and rocked with it until the springs of the bed creaked and she got up and bounced up and down. They were laughing too much to think it through, even Gustav, who should have known better in the darkness of a winter's evening, still early, so that in the summer it would have been light, but past the time when they should all have been asleep in their own beds, toys put away and the door shut, the lights snuffed out. Instead, this riotous, calamitous racket violated the silence of the house and suddenly, like a crack of thunder, any prelude unheard or unnoticed, the door opened with such force that it slammed the things off the little table. A glass half full of water was smashed, and the light of a candle shone bright in the room. Through the gap under the bed, two feet, bare and red.

'Get up!'

When Paul stood to attention he cut his foot on pieces of glass.

His father's rage—his red face and wide mouth, eyes slit, half-closed, and lines etching out over his cheeks and forehead like spider's web—was worse than the wound. Red blood and stinging, small shards of glass in his flesh. All bearable. When he dared to lift his foot from the ground, only a little, he felt the tackiness of blood under his heel and his big toe. His father ordered him forward and when he went he left a trail behind him.

When Gustav moved from his spot and came to put his arm around Paul, to ask him if he was hurt, it was the defiance that did it. It was the still unfamiliar deepness of the boy's voice that did it. It was the impudence that did it. Their father's hand sliced through the air, sleeve dragging behind it. There was a sharp report, like a rifle shot. The hand—his father's hand—the wedding ring yellow against red skin, huge and stiff, that moved his wrists, came hard against Gustav's cheek, who was passing from boy to man, but who still could not help but make a sound. Klara, seeing this, was mortified to silence and now Anna came out from under the sheets:

'You're a bad man! You're a bad man! You are a bad man!'

She was frightened of glass, this girl.

So how could she be the one who had come here, bringing the clock but not the key? How could she have put this thing in his room without the key? Why? So that it would die unwound? Its hands stilled?

Schreber is found by
Müller the follow-
ing morning in a poor
state. The orderly gives
in to the temptation to
punish a symbol of his
family's downfall, and
his patience is tested by
Schreber's endless ques-
tions.

XIII

The door hissed on its hinges.

'Judge, Judge, Judge…'

Müller. The orderly made a sound between his teeth, like a
warning chirrup from a beetle, and rattled the trolley into the
bedroom. Above the brass wheels clattering in their housings,
a higher note: the loosely stoppered bottle, and a glass placed
close by it, striking together as the trolley moved across the
boards of the floor. It went over to the window, and a little
later, there was sudden weight on the bed above.

Müller drummed his palms on the tight, undisturbed sheets,
one on the muffling blanket, and one clean on an edge where
the blanket was turned back.

'Judge, Judge, Judge…'

The orderly got up and drew the bath, dragging his feet. When
he came back he paused for a moment in the doorway and then
went to the trolley, where he poured Schreber his morning dose.
It sounded like wine in the pouring. Perhaps he stood and looked
at the half-filled glass. Perhaps there was a drip on the rim that

97

Müller wiped away with his fingertip. The finger held up. He could have wiped it on his frock-coat. He could have rubbed the drip away between his finger and thumb. Or put it to his lips.

'Sorry, Karl,' Müller said, under his breath.

He reached down and perhaps he took Schreber's glass. Did he drink the medicine—the bromides—and refill the glass? It was so quick that it might not have happened at all.

'*Judge!*'

Schreber's legs, poking out from under the bed, went stiff.

'Time to get up, Judge!'

The edge of the blanket came up so that the morning sun poured in.

'I thought I was in a strange place,' Schreber muttered. 'I was in a tiny room; the walls were all around me. My brother and sisters...'

There was wetness. Schreber reached down and under himself.

'I have had... an accident. Where am I?'

'You are in your rooms,' said Müller, 'where you always are.'

'I couldn't see anything. There were boards in front of my face, and when I tried to step back, there was nothing beneath my feet.'

'That'll come from lying under the bed. Let me get you out,' Müller said.

Müller grabbed Schreber's right leg and in one pull dragged him into the light.

Schreber turned slowly over and blinked. His face felt skewed over to the left, away from where his cheek had rested on the floorboards. There was dust in his hair. He sat up, hinging from the waist carefully, as if he might snap, and it was clear that his jacket was filthy and his shirt would need to be boiled.

'Where was I?' Schreber said.

'Under the bed, Judge. Under the bed.'

Schreber looked at the man. Was he talking Dutch?

'Why would I... I don't understand,' Schreber said, and across his face passed the various signs of a man who is piecing together the events of a day he cannot properly remember. His lips moved to the sound of unspoken words, and now and then he frowned and made cryptic gestures with his hands.

'I was standing in the dark… and then,' Schreber tried, but everything was a blur.

'You know, Judge…,' said Müller—he walked around to the other side of the bed, peered under, and when he rose he wore a pinched look—'…it is often more comfortable to sleep on top of the bed than underneath it. In my experience. And to use the lavatory when you wish to pass water.'

Schreber looked at the bed and then over at his bedside table and then, at last, over at the clock, which rested on the table in the same place it had been the night before. Müller reached over and untucked the sheets.

'Cleaner, too,' Müller said, 'although, you've saved me the job of washing the linen at least. What have I told you about too much water before bed? It'll have to be reported. Now take your medicine.'

'The clock.'

'Come on, Judge, take your medicine and let's have you in the bath. We'll get those clothes off and down to the laundry.'

'Who brought that clock?'

Müller followed Schreber's pointing finger. He rubbed his forehead and came over to loosen the old man's shirt.

'After breakfast, eh? Medicine first, then we'll pop you in the tub, the woman will bring up some eggs, and we can discuss the clock after that.'

'Was it Anna? Was it a little girl? She might have her hair in pony-tails. Blonde. She carries a doll? Was it her?'

'Yes and no.'

'I don't understand.'

'Look, Judge, I can explain it to you, but not while you're sitting on the floor in the middle of the room, drenched in your own piss, in yesterday's tweeds. Do you understand?'

'Was it her?'

'Right,' Müller said. 'We'll have that jacket off for a start.'

'Was it her?'

'Have you taken your medicine, Judge?'

'Was it her?'

Müller took the shirt from Schreber's back, upended him over his knee—sitting first on the bed—and he pulled down the old man's trousers and under-things and when he was naked, still asking after his sister, Müller carried him over his shoulder, marched him off into the bathroom, and dumped him into the hot bath water.

'It's too hot!' Schreber barked.

Müller nodded. The orderly licked his lips and looked back into the room they had come from. To the trolley?

'It's too hot!' Schreber said again.

'Sorry…' Müller muttered, 'sorry.' He left the room and there was the sound of glasses rattling. Unmistakable.

When Müller returned, Schreber was doused, lobster red, with cold water from the jug on the nightstand. Then Müller mouthed silently some few words, three or four times in succession, and left the room. When he came back, he wiped his mouth with the back of his sleeve.

Schreber tried to get out of the bath, but Müller pushed him back in. It was a gentle restraint, but Schreber slipped and his head and face went under the water and when he came up he spluttered and spat and gasped like a fish in an angler's net.

'You stay in there, Judge.'

Müller swallowed. He looked back into the bedroom, where the trolley was. It seemed for a moment as if he was going to go over to it again.

'You stay in there,' he said. 'You need a good soak to clean you up.'

He put his hand on Schreber's shoulder, sitting by the bath, holding the old man in place, but looking always into the other room.

'Anyway, the eggs aren't here yet.'

'The water is still very hot…'

'What?'

'The water is too hot.'

'Right… right.'

Müller reached for a clean, dry towel, and gestured for Schreber to stand.

'You do not intend to boil me then?' Schreber asked.

Müller frowned and looked away.

'Don't be silly.'

He dried the old man down and passed him his gown.

'I think I can hear the woman with the eggs.'

Müller left, and in the emptiness of the room, through the steam, Schreber heard her bringing his breakfast tray and smelt the eggs and ham faintly. He slipped his arm into the dressing gown, sore from the heat, and followed Müller into the living room.

'How did she carry it?'

The woman closed the door behind her.

'In her hands, how else? Sit down and eat.'

'Not the maid. Anna, I mean.'

Müller sighed and shepherded Schreber around to where the breakfast waited for him.

'In her hands,' he repeated, 'how else?'

'Did she touch the glass?'

'I wasn't paying any attention.' He pulled out the chair, and when Schreber made no attempt to sit in it, Müller gently chopped at the back of his knees with the flat of his hand. When Schreber sat by reflex, the orderly pushed the chair under the table before he could resist. 'My dad used to own this place, you know. Farmer. Not the buildings. Just the land.'

'Who did she come with?'

Müller put the knife in one hand and the fork in the other.

'She came alone. He had to sell it, the land. Legal fees. My brother, Karl. Got himself in trouble.'

'You're lying!'

'Am I? I'm not. Judge cut his head off for it. Karl.'

'How could she come alone? She is a little girl. No girl her age would be allowed out carrying a valuable clock through the streets of Leipzig without an escort. The notion is utterly ridiculous! What makes you lie? Who was with her? Was it Flechsig?'

'That anything to do with you, Judge? My Karl?' Müller picked up Schreber's fork hand and speared the egg yolk with it. 'Hard again… Don't worry, I'll give her what for.'

'Did she come with Flechsig? Answer me!'

'Who…? No, she came on her own, and she was no little girl.'

'Then she was not Anna,' Schreber nodded to himself. He took control of his own hands and carved a piece of ham.

'The woman was Anna Jung, née Schreber, and she was your sister. She came to visit you, at last, at your request, and finding you… indisposed, she left you the clock—your mother's—and she went.'

'Gibberish!'

'And you think you're going home for Christmas?'

'I am cured! I am entirely well. Of course I am well.'

'Yet I come in this morning and you've pissed your pants and are sleeping half under the bed.'

'An old man's accident.'

'And now you can't understand that your sister might be an old woman and not a girl?'

'It is you who doesn't understand,' Schreber said, chewing his eggs and ham.

Müller sighed.

'When you've had enough to eat, Judge, I'm to take you to see Rössler. He wants you down at the bottom of the garden, first thing.'

Then Müller tidied up, loading what could be loaded onto the trolley and, when he thought that Schreber could not see him, knocking back a last dose of his bromides.

'Sorry, Karl.'

Medical gymnastics, past and present, the former used as a means of ensuring moral and physical wellbeing and done well, the latter as a means of scientific diagnosis and done poorly. The mysterious Jewish gentleman demonstrates an unsettling familiarity with the intimate details of Schreber's life. A poor dog is rescued by Schreber's father.

XIV

'Let's begin with some simple stretches. Follow my lead.'

Rössler hopped from his left foot to his right, with his arms up. He was framed in the central arch of the gazebo, wreathed by spreading ivy, and he resembled nothing more than an elderly pixie. Schreber looked down at his feet—his shoe leather was dark with dew and criss-crossed with inch-long grass trimmings.

'Left, right, left, right! Come on, Herr Schreber! I'm not doing this for my own benefit!'

Schreber raised his feet in turn. There was grass on the soles, too.

'Arms up!'

Schreber put his arms up.

Over Rössler's shoulder, with one foot on the stone step and his hand on his knee, was Müller, smirking and looking back up the lawn for someone with whom to share his amusement. Finding no one, he was forced to rely on his own company, which was, apparently, sufficient, because soon he was shaking with silent laughter, clasping his fingers over his lips. Rössler pivoted from the hips and described a semi-circle with his torso. When Schreber executed the move the doctor stopped and took his pad of paper. He made a note. The degree by which he imagined Schreber deviated from correct geometry? The length of time he took to right himself after performing the movement? To aid him in his observations, Rössler held his pencil upright at arm's length and sighted down the arm.

'What does this remind you of, Herr Doktor Präsident?' said a voice from over his shoulder. Schreber span and there was the Jewish gentleman, so close that their noses almost touched. He gave off the scent of cigarettes and gentian bitters. Schreber leapt back.

'What does this remind you of, ball-crusher?'

'Herr Schreber!' shouted Rössler. 'Face front, arms up! Please! We are hardly begun. I promise you it will be worth the trouble.'

Schreber turned to him and took a wide step to the side, so that he was away from the Jew.

He took a step, too.

'He is like your father, isn't he? Do you remember? Down at the bottom of the garden.'

'To the front!'

If Müller and Rössler recognised that the Jew was beside Schreber they made no sign of it. Müller continued to laugh and Rössler to demonstrate the required gymnastics. Schreber determined to ignore the Jew, too, and put up his arms and hopped, as he was directed.

'Not bad,' said the Jewish gentleman, speaking directly into his ear, 'after all this time. Not bad at all. Though I have to say I've seen you do better.' The movement of the words through the air tickled his skin. Schreber hopped forward.

'Try to stay in one place, Herr Schreber! As if rooted to the earth. Like a tree. Although, of course, not so much that you can't jump when asked. I'm sure you get my meaning. Try again, please!'

'Who are you? Why do you watch me?'

'You don't remember me?'

He stepped to the front, smiled widely, and kept very still, so Schreber could see him properly. It was the man in the carriage, he was certain of it. And the man who tapped his cane on the railings at Angelikastrasse. But who was that man?

'I don't know you at all.'

'Really? I'm disappointed. Not surprised, I suppose. I don't make much of an impression, do I? I've never had that kind of face, voice, whatever it is that other men remember. Women, on the other hand…'

'I have seen you before, I think, but…'

'But you don't know me? It's no matter.'

'Herr Schreber! Please do not speak, just perform the exercises as I ask you to. It will go much more quickly that way.'

Schreber shut his mouth and kept his focus on Rössler. The Jewish gentleman was there at the periphery, adjusting his lapels. Schreber dipped at the knee and took in air through his nostrils, and as he came back up he let it out with a snort through the corners of his mouth.

'Excellent! Again, please!'

Schreber breathed through the nose and dipped again. On the up stroke he couldn't help but let some spittle pass his lips. The gentleman reached into his jacket for a cigarette and smiled compassionately, as if between friends—these little indiscretions are nothing, for men like us.

'Good! And now with your hands on the crown of your head.'

Schreber did it.

'Five more, please!'

By the fourth, Schreber had no choice but to breathe in through the mouth. The Jewish gentleman's cigarette smoke—*tabac noir*, thick and white and salted—came in with the cold morning breeze, making the old man cough.

'It was not like this when we were boys, all this huffing and puffing, all this coughing,' he said. 'You were quite the perfect child. Healthy and robust. Isn't that right? I, on the other hand was what your father called a "lop-sided degenerate." But now… Please, attend to your hopping. I don't mean to distract you.'

'Arms out to the side and then jump up with the right foot, and come down on the left!'

Breath was hard to catch and the Jew was right—in his childhood Schreber could have continued crouching and bending and jumping from leg to leg for ever. Rössler inclined his pencil to the horizontal. All those years ago this doctor would have had an eternity in which to observe and make notes. But Schreber was no longer a child.

'I feel faint,' he panted to the Jewish gentleman, and his left arm fell from the horizontal.

Rössler made a sharp sound under his breath, but checked himself. 'If you wish, you may return to your chair to regain yourself. We can continue in a little while.'

Müller came down from the pergola at a trot, wheeling the Bath chair, and Schreber sat in it. The Jew stood in front of him, put his cigarette in the corner of his mouth and held out his hand.

'My name is Alexander, if that helps,' he said. Schreber took his hand without thinking, and gave his own name.

'I know your name, sir,' Alexander said.

Schreber nodded, still trying to catch his breath. Rössler came over without as much as a glance at Alexander, who stood a little to the side to allow Rössler to pass.

'Herr Schreber,' the doctor said, adjusting his glasses with one hand and clutching his notebook to his chest with the other, 'it is my understanding that the human body, of which the mind is but a constituent part, acts as a single mechanism. What affects the operations of one part often has an effect in another, and by acting on organ A, we might render an effect on organ B, and by observing part C, a fault might be brought to light in part D. With me so far?'

Schreber and Alexander both nodded. The smoke from Alexander's cigarette found its way over to Müller and, to Schreber's relief, the orderly began to cough. Rössler looked over at him, and he stifled the cough with his sleeve.

'Well, with machines like the brain and, for that matter, any of the other internal organs, actual observation—in the live specimen at least—is very difficult—although not strictly impossible... I digress—it is a rule amongst physicians that we must attempt, where possible, the least invasive means of treatment before we embark on the more... fundamental ones. Do you understand?'

'Not...'

'I cannot look at your brain, sir, but I can look at the rest of you and work out from that if there might be a problem. Clear?'

'Very familiar idea,' said Alexander. 'Your father might well have agreed. In fact,'—he pulled deeply on the last of his cigarette and then flicked the dog-end in a high arc off down the lawn—'I think I might recognise the notion, the substantive part. Isn't it in the *Pangymnastikon*? Don't you recognise it?'

'Yes,' Schreber replied, to both men.

'Very good,' said Rössler. 'You see what I'm getting at with this, do you then? Very good!'

The doctor nodded to Müller, who tipped Schreber up so that the soles of his shoes hit the grass, and when the judge leaned forward, Müller pulled out the Bath chair and followed Rössler back to the gazebo with it.

'He is a good doctor, I've heard,' Alexander said. 'Not in your father's league—he does not publish—but then, might this not give him more time for his patients? Mightn't it alleviate the suspicion one always has of professionally successful men? That their attentions are not always fully on the matter in front of them? That they always have one eye looking, as it always must, toward their reputation, or some more important business, or the wider considerations of their field? I don't know. It's just an idea.'

'I don't know,' Schreber muttered. 'Is this to be my treatment?' he called out to Rössler.

Rössler took off his glasses and cleaned the lenses with his handkerchief.

'No, no! This is not treatment, Herr Schreber. My aim this morning is to make a close observation of you, and by doing so make a diagnosis of your problem. Treatment and diagnosis are not the same thing. I will attempt to diagnose any problems with your gross nervous function before moving on to understanding the psychic causes of your disease. From there we can consider further intervention. Clear?'

Rössler returned his glasses to his nose and raised his arms again. Schreber nodded.

'You see, he wants to make a good stab at a cure. Just like your father. He wants to get a good look at the problem so that he can bring his science to bear on it. Like Moritz did.'

Schreber's arms fell abruptly to his sides as if the strings had been cut.

'You knew my father?'

Alexander smiled. 'I did know him. And this Rössler reminds me of him. A poor imitation, but an imitation nonetheless.'

Indeed, the way Rössler was standing—stiffly and perfectly upright, with his head back and his chest out—was very like Schreber's father, and the cool breeze that made goose-pimples rise on the old judge's arms was just like the air on the cold mornings of his boyhood, standing in the garden of the Institute.

'Didn't your father stand in front of you in the same way?' Alexander said. 'And weren't you expected to watch and listen just as this doctor expects you to watch and listen now?'

Schreber nodded.

'It's almost like being there again, isn't it? On that day. Do you know the day I mean?'

Yes.

It was like that day. 'I don't know you. Please leave me to my exercises.'

Alexander did not leave him.

'Didn't your father come down, as he always did for the inspection of the children, precisely half an hour after your mother fed and watered you, and washed the dirt from behind your ears and under your nails, and straightened your collars and cuffs? Didn't she pick specks of invisible dust and stray hair from your velvet jackets?'

She did, and afterward his father checked that they had not soiled themselves in some perceptible manner in the period between their mother leaving and his arrival. Then he marched them out, arms stiff by their sides like those of clockwork soldiers, down to the part of the lawn that was under the big tree.

'Didn't he stand there in front of you, occasionally in shadow and occasionally in light, depending on how the branches of the tree waved, with his jacket off, laid carefully on the grass beside him? There in his white shirt he puffed out his chest, and gestured that you should do the same, all of you, brothers and sisters alike, though, if truth were told, he always took more care that you boys did as was asked, and the girls had a little more leeway. Isn't that right?'

It was, Gustav always said as much, and their father made one posture after another, a serious look on his face, and the children repeated them, smiling sometimes.

'When the easy business was finished he rolled up his sleeves, didn't he? First he'd take off the cuffs and put them on his jacket, and then he rolled the sleeves back up past the elbow and he started on the combinations—a jump and a stretch, a bow and a sweep. A hop and a twist and a sweep and a jump. Jump, bow, stretch, turn, hop, hop, twist, jump, bend. It got very complicated! As much a test of memory as of the muscles and sinews. Like a dance, though I don't think any of you would have made the comparison. Too effeminate! By God if there was something old Moritz didn't like it was that a boy should be effeminate! Isn't that right?' The Jew frowned and Schreber knew that it was true. To be effeminate was the worst thing a boy could be: To wear his mother's things, that was certainly not done. Or to pamper the little ones.

'Old Moritz—Papa—he jumped higher and stretched lower and went faster and faster until by the end you children were flushed. Once, his collar came loose and flapped at the side. Do you remember that? Perhaps you don't, but I can tell you that it did! Your straight and respectable old father, even he wasn't completely immune! But then, you know that already. You know that already. No one's immune. Are they? His collar coming unbuttoned…'

Then Papa walked off, back to the house. Gustav followed behind with the jacket and cuffs, returning a few seconds later to take them on laps of the trees until they were called in.

'Rössler wants you.' Alexander flicked a wrist in the doctor's direction, pursed his lips, and took another cigarette.

'Copy me,' Rössler said, and bent down to touch his toes. He barely made it halfway.

Alexander frowned.

'Dear, dear! Very bad…'

He walked over so that he stood beside Rössler. When the doctor moved, Alexander, cigarette placed firmly between his teeth, mimicked the movements the doctor made, except that this was not mimicry, it was something better: the perfect representation of the movements the doctor only hinted at. The Jew touched his toes and, it was clear to see, could have gone further and put the palms of his hands down flat on the grass if he had chosen to do so. Schreber followed suit, though he could not do much better than the doctor.

'How old do you think I am?' Alexander said with a smile. Schreber shook his head.

'Guess. Please. I won't be offended.'

'I have no idea.' Not young, but then not old either. There was no telling from his dress.

Alexander reached down and touched his toes and then, as if to give a clue, he leapt up in a star jump.

'I am your age, more or less. It is something, wouldn't you say, for a man of our age to make these movements? To touch his toes and leap? Not every man can do it. Your father could, or should I say, would have been able to, if he had not been taken so young.'

'You seem to know a great deal about my father.'

'A great deal. We had much in common. We were both sickly children and we both made men of ourselves—or had men made of us, which is a little different. But I suppose in the end we all succumb to our original poverty. Don't you think? He in his way, and we in ours?'

Rössler was demonstrating a squatting posture in which his arms were raised first up and then out to the sides. Schreber was too concerned with Alexander's words to notice.

'What business is any of this of yours?'

'Please attend to me, Herr Schreber,' Rössler snapped.

'Do as he says. He might know what he is doing. Anything is possible.'

Alexander crouched and beckoned to Schreber to do the same.

Schreber stopped.

'If I can do it, you can,' Alexander chided.

Schreber did his best, but Alexander was disappointed.

'Let me tell you a story,' he said. 'It might make this pass a little quicker.'

'You may do what you wish. I have no interest.'

'You might. The story is about you. Shall I begin?'

Schreber went down on his haunches and said nothing.

'There once was a house in which things ran like clockwork. You could predict everything. There was never any doubt as to who should be where, and what might happen when. The people in this house—a family—they knew that they had only to follow the pattern of the day, and to do the things that were supposed to be done, and that everything would be fine. They were well off, this family: not ostentatiously so, but comfortable. The owner of the place was a doctor of sorts—I see you are starting to recognise yourselves—and this doctor had two sons and three daughters, and the doctor and his wife arranged matters so that order prevailed in their house. All to the good, no doubt. Well, one day everything changed, and not for the better.'

'Herr Schreber, a little higher in the arms if you can.'

'On that day the doctor was struck by an iron ladder, on the head, while performing advanced exercises in the gymnasium. An accident. No fault of his own. He followed his regimen the day before, and there had been no hint of anything unusual, nor anything the day before that, nor the one before that, nor off, back into time, for days and weeks and years. No one ever suspected that there would come a day when the order of things would be interrupted by this strange turn of fate. Isn't that right? It was a surprise, wasn't it?'

Schreber tried to appear as if he wasn't listening, but Alexander didn't stop. Rössler bobbed up and down in front of the gazebo and Schreber focussed on him. But the words kept coming...

'Surprise or not, the fall of that ladder is inexplicable. You would know. I'm right, aren't I? There was nothing to see? It was a mystery. For everyone? Perhaps. Though, if one were to have looked closely—very closely—at every square inch of that gymnasium, it must have been possible to see the signs—fatigue in the jointing that attached the ladder to the wall, perhaps. Or crumbling in the plaster. A little give which, through repetition, when the doctor removed and replaced the ladder every day, became a looseness, although never enough for the doctor to notice. A tiny increment each day, below the threshold of human sensitivity. Perhaps this could have been detected if an interested party had taken it upon themselves to go around with a magnifying glass, inspecting the gymnasium. It is irrelevant, because no one did examine the place in that degree of detail. What would have been the point? So, the strange day came and the ladder was removed from its fitting, as usual, and placed against the wall. He used it to exercise the muscles of his calves and thighs, ten steps up, ten steps down, ten steps up, ten steps down, and then, those parts of his body properly exercised, the ladder was returned to its fitting, apparently safely. The next set of exercises was begun. Your father was diligent and his diligence was reinforced by routine and repetition. All very laudable. All very reliable. Exemplary behaviour. Right?'

He was right. It was all right.

'The only problem with this perfect predictability was, of course, that there was never any chance that he would *not be* where he always was, predictably, reliably, laudably, directly below the ladder as it hung from its fitting—put out of the way to maintain an efficient tidiness in the room, reflecting what he believed was an efficient tidiness in all areas of his life. A less conscientious man might have escaped your father's fate by not adhering quite so strictly to the routine. He might have stopped for his coffee early, or been distracted by the paper. But not your father. Not Moritz. He was bound to be beneath that ladder when it fell. Where else would he have been at that time of day?

'I suppose a suspicious man might wonder whether the other people about the place—I should have mentioned that this doctor's home was also his place of work, a sanatorium for orthopaedic cases, and that it was frequented by the boarders of that institute, as well as by the staff and their families—we might wonder whether if, amongst the other occupants of the house, there was someone with a grievance against the good doctor. Someone who might lack the courage and manliness to confront him directly, and who might—let us speculate—have whittled away at the fitting with a purloined dinner knife, hanging one-armed from the climbing rope beside the ladder. But we are not suspicious. There is no need to posit the existence of such a criminal and, even if we did, there could be no proof, not this long after the event. Besides, the law of Occam's razor argues against unnecessarily complicated explanations of events when simple ones are available, as any man of science will tell you. As your father would have told you. No, it is enough to say that the ladder fell, and that your father was beneath it, and that the ladder struck him on the head. It did not kill him, although it might well have done for a less vital man; an iron ladder is, after all, nothing to be lightly shrugged off, and when falling from a height it might easily crush a man's skull. A reasonable man might, indeed, expect it to. He might rely on it doing so—in other circumstances—but, rather, on this day it merely caused the man's nerves to become disturbed in his skull, and made vibrations where there should have been none.'

Schreber whirled on the Jew, and jabbed at him with his finger.

'I ask again, what business is this of yours?'

Alexander stepped back and smoothed down his waistcoat.

'It is merely a story,' he smiled, 'something to pass the time. Rössler wants you back on one leg. It is easier to obey him. It keeps him quiet. There, he returns to his notes and there is a smile on his face—good news? A solution to the Schreber mystery? We will see. To return to the story—the previous afternoon, your father exercised and was struck by a ladder. He retired to bed. This was in the early morning: he retired to bed before even taking his lunch. Absolutely unprecedented. Wasn't it? And this was not to be an isolated deviation. The next morning, neither your father nor your mother came down to greet you children, and the maid was forced to seek your parents out, wondering whether there would be a change to the breakfast routine, though quite unable to imagine why. She found them in the bedroom, the doctor, your father, fully dressed down to his boots, lying on the neatly made bed with your mother standing by, chewing her hair. The girl was sent out to fetch your own doctor. This is all by-the-by. What is important is that there were no adults available to take you children in hand. You were left in a vacuum, one which would have been nothing in a normal house, where, let us be honest, chaos is more the natural state in the presence of five young children. But, in this haven of order, where each day was precisely like the next from the moment of birth to this one day, the contrast was jarring for you all, to say the least.

'The eldest child, your brother Gustav, was faced with a silent room. You and your sisters swayed and pulled your lips and looked at the door. Gustav was bright and, in the absence of authority, knew enough to understand that he was next in the proper succession of power in the house. He said:

'"I'll be Father."

'A reasonable suggestion. He went on:

'"Anna, you be Mother."

'Now, Anna was equally bright and equally sensitive to the structures of their lives but, as two bright young things might, came to an utterly different conclusion to that of her brother. She looked at him like their mother had looked at him once, when he swore—purely by accident—having heard the word spoken in anger by the maid and deciding to use it himself in a similar circumstance.

'"Don't be naughty," Anna said. "We will wait here until someone comes down."

'Gustav straightened his back and pushed his chin down to his chest so that when he spoke his voice was deeper than usual and he looked out over heavy brows underlining a wrinkled forehead.

'"Now children, get in a line," he said, and though he didn't look a bit like their father, the little ones obeyed, recognising if not an agent of authority, then the tone that one might properly use.

'"Stop it!" Anna said, and she rushed over and tried to wipe the silly look from her brother's face, to prise his chin up from his chest and smooth out his forehead. Gustav pushed her away.

'"Paul, you be Mother if Anna won't do it."

'And here we have it. You are a second son, a third child, and you were given a difficult choice: naturally you would wish to defer to both your older brother and older sister, and here were conflicting requirements. You were also, no less than the others, at a loss in this strange world where neither father nor mother were present. Breakfast was already ten minutes late, and none of you had been so much as a wiped with a flannel. Your nightshirt was still on, and your legs were cold. Isn't that right? Now here was Gustav, making your father's face—more convincingly than might be imagined—and you were confused as to the level of Gustav's actual authority. And Anna was clearly disconcerted, where Gustav seemed calm. So you followed your instincts and did as you were told. We might make assumptions here about a boy's natural inclinations. We might wonder whether you were predisposed to adopt the motherly role. Indeed, to the lay observer, you did appear to be less of a boisterous boy than your brother was. Couldn't you be seen, occasionally, touching the dresses of your sister's dolls? Or stroking their hair? But I see you do not consider this the proper place for such conjecture. Back to the facts! You arched your eyebrows and pursed your lips and waved your left hand around from side to side, not so much in imitation of your mother—though it was a passable try—as in a pastiche of the generic feminine. You looked more like Anna than anyone else. This enraged Anna even further, but when she came over to you, you pushed her aside, despite being her junior, and when she recovered, the little ones were dancing around you and laughing and pulling at your nightshirt. The noise made Anna look toward the door and up at the ceiling, but no one came to impose order, so you went and took your place at your brother's side, reaching down to hold his hand, and together you stood by the doorway. Anna dived back under her bedclothes, but the little ones jumped around shouting "Mama, Papa, Mama, Papa," and laughing. It was quite a scene!

"'Quiet!" shouted Gustav, and the little ones were shocked, at first, but soon saw the game, and they went quiet and stood watching, the corners of their nightshirts in their mouths so their pudgy legs were bare up past their knees. Stop me if I get anything wrong, or out of place, but this is accurate so far, isn't it? It fits with your memory? Don't feel you have to speak, if the exercise makes you breathless, a nod will suffice… I'll continue anyway.

"'Mother," Gustav went on, not looking at you, or seeing fit to elaborate on his one-word declarations.

"'Yes now, children," you said, after a sideways glance, "do as your father says and get washed and dressed and make yourself ready to do our exercises."

'The children did not move. Gustav turned his head aside, disdainfully, and you, understanding your brother's performance of fatherly frustration, went to the children and stripped them of their nightwear. Then you led them over to the nightstand, where you doused them with the cold water that was always left out for them by the maid, today being no exception, as different though it was from all other days. When they were wet and cold you went to dry them but Gustav said:

"'No, they will become soft that way. They must dry in the natural way, in the fresh air," and, smiling to himself, he went over to the window and pushed it up so the cold wind blew in. When the heavy, musty, night-warmth of the bedroom was blown out into the garden, the children began to shiver. You came forward with the clothes the maid had laid out for them. Again, Gustav stopped you.

'"Make them dance themselves dry!" He had a little smile, one that you had never noticed on your father. Pleasure? Something your father never showed and yet… deep inside, was this the first prompt to much future examination of your father's motives? I go too far? Perhaps. Anyway, Gustav went on.

'"Mother," he said, "I don't want to see one speck of water on those children."

'"But," you said, "their teeth are chattering."

'"Ah!" said Gustav, indicating that he did not share your concern.

'You put the children's clothes back on the bed and whispered to the little ones, something about a game and, after a little uncertainty, they jigged here and there on the spot, quite naked, and you hovered nearby watching Gustav for signs that they were dry enough.

'"This is ridiculous," said Anna. "They'll catch a chill and then you will be for it. I'll tell Mama everything, and she'll tell Papa and have both of you whipped."

'Gustav thought about this, but by the look on his face it was clear that he considered the argument defective. He turned to you.

'"But I am Papa," he said, "aren't I, Mama?"

'"Yes, dear," you said, but you weren't as convinced anymore, and when Anna came over and grabbed the clothes and started dressing the little ones, you were more than prepared to let the game drop, weren't you? Didn't you even go off to find your train, the red wooden one, very fine, very expensive—from that shop on the Felixstrasse—you remember the one? With the guard painted in at the window and brass studs on the wheels. You had left it under the bed, but when Gustav saw you were going to drop the performance he ran over to where Anna was, grabbed the clothes and pulled them away from her. Anna was strong, and when Gustav could not take the clothes from her, he shouted for you and here you were on familiar ground, this sort of tug-o-war being run-of-the-mill nursery play and something you could innocently enjoy, without the strange prickling sensations, down there, that you had only just started to notice. You started to tickle Anna under the arms, a game she always liked, and she laughed and squeaked, but at the same time she grunted in anger and annoyance, when the tickling waned a little, until after a few seconds she let go of the clothes and started to cry. Gustav turned away, unconcerned, but you went to put your hand on her shoulder. She pulled away.

'"Now, Mother," Gustav intoned, "are these children dry, or will they need to run the water off in the garden?"

'You looked between brother and sister. She was crying and he seemed so sure of himself. You took up the maternal role again and checked the shivering children for water. They were dry, the breeze had seen to that, so at last Gustav gave permission for them to be dressed, by which time Anna was back under the covers of her bed and now Klara was crying from the room next door. Gustav looked at you as if he couldn't understand what it was you were waiting for, and you understood the look. You were very sensitive, even then: a perceptive little boy, bright, sucking in the world. It was a look you'd seen pass between your mother and father so many times, seemingly for as long as you could remember, and so often that you almost didn't need to think about it, it was just understood. You trotted to the door, your hands at your side, as your mother's would have been, although you had no dress to keep straight, no weight of fabric to stop from swinging, no line to preserve.'

Rössler came over and put his hand on Schreber's shoulder.

'We'll take a break here for iced water. Please, take a seat. Müller, bring the chair over and then go to the kitchens. Might

I ask how you are feeling, Herr Schreber? You seem pale and distracted. You look off over your shoulder.'

'Do you see that Jew?'

'Focus on me, please, Herr Schreber. Look at my fingertip if you will, as I describe a circle spinning clockwise.'

'He is right beside you. He knows everything.'

'The fingertip, please.'

Schreber reached out his hand, intending to grab Rössler and force him to look at the Jew. Rössler was not inclined to be grabbed and stepped back. From his new vantage he looked Schreber up and down.

'I suppose it was silly of me to expect more co-operation from you than you are used to giving, Herr Schreber.'

'Please look behind you, it is a simple matter.'

'Are we to return to this? Please examine me; please listen to me; and this new one, please look behind me? I thought you wanted to make progress. Was I wrong?'

'He is behind you. He tells tales from my life to me, and there is no way he can know what he knows.'

Rössler nodded.

'Here is Müller with the water. Take some from the tray, please.'

'Müller, do you see him? The man over Rössler's shoulder?'

'Which one? the garden is full of them,' Müller said.

By the time Schreber pointed weakly at the Jew, Müller had looked away. Alexander smiled, perfectly relaxed, smoking a newly lit cigarette. Rössler shot Müller a look, and he returned to his place behind Schreber's chair.

'Drink up,' Rössler said, rubbing his creaking back, 'and we'll get this thankless business over with.'

Alexander came over.

'They don't see me. They have no interest in me. I have been here for years—since the place opened. There is nothing that could happen now, nothing that I could do that would make them pay me a single moment of attention. Except, perhaps, if I were to slit my throat. Then they would notice me, although, I fear, only as much as was necessary to clear me away and write up the report. I am hopeless, they say. Hopelessly insane.'

Rössler turned his back on both of them and returned his jacket to the grass.

'Soon they will think the same of you—that you are lost, I mean. This is just the final effort: an act, if you will, to placate their consciences. They are generous in giving you that. See that one there, bald, with the long scar like a frowning mouth that runs across his forehead?'

Schreber could see him. He sat in a chair very like Schreber's and his head lolled on his shoulders.

'That one got sliced into on the day he arrived. A miner. He took his pick to the pit props as he and his colleagues were extending the seam in a new direction. He couldn't be stopped. Brought the roof down on top of six men. No one knows how he got out. They found him doing it again, and it took another six men to hold him down. He said he'd seen the devil. They brought him here strapped to a board of wood. The doctors couldn't get any sense out of him, so Rössler cut out a part of his brain. If you ask nicely, next time you're in his office, I dare say he'll show it to you. He has it in a jar. The poor fool hasn't said a word since. So we should be grateful it's only the gymnastics for you... He's at it again.'

Alexander stepped to one side. Rössler had started the new set of postures. Schreber got up from his chair and followed suit.

'Anyway,' Alexander said, 'let's not dwell on morbid matters, eh? So, where were we? Yes, your mother and father. They were busy and Gustav has you acting the role of mother. That's right. And Klara was crying. So what does a mother do, when her child cries? She rushes to it. This is what you did, because you are a clever boy, keen to do things right, even when you aren't sure you should be doing them at all. You got so caught up in the game that you forgot that there were real parents somewhere in the house, didn't you? Out of sight, out of mind.'

'It didn't occur to me to listen out for Mother or Father.'

'Just as I thought. You do remember, then? I am not altogether deluded? That is good! I have remembered it like this for many years. It has seemed to me that—and you must forgive me for taking liberties here—the very playing of the game established, somewhere deep, their absence, simply by the fact that you would not dare mimic them in their presence. Here a reversion occurred in your mind—if you were mimicking them, then they could not be there, rather than it being the other way around: that you were able to mimic them because they were not there. Would you agree?'

Schreber nodded, but then Rössler had him lie on his back and raise his legs in the air, and talking became difficult. Alexander, thoughtfully, went on.

'You didn't listen out for them, and nor did you look for a turning of the door handle, as you generally would have done, but instead you went for Klara, hands first, certain only that Gustav—Father—was behind you in the doorway, watching on, making sure that you—Mother—fulfilled your maternal duty. And you did. Gustav was there and watching and when you picked up the baby and she didn't stop crying, Gustav said:

'"The child is hungry, woman," and he sniffed and turned away until he could be mistaken for a person looking in the other direction, except that when he opened his left eye he could see you clearly. At first you did nothing. You held Klara and rocked her, like you normally did, on those early mornings—or perhaps one should say those late nights—when the child woke and cried, and your fraternal instincts got the better of you. Am I right? Don't trouble to answer, I know that I am. But now, when you saw that Gustav's half-stare was still on you, you thought for a little while and then—and this is what sticks in the mind—you pulled your nightshirt up so that your chest was bared, and you put Klara onto it, as you had seen your mother do, or sometimes the nurse.'

Alexander took two or three steps forward until he was looking down at Schreber, lying on his back on the grass. He leaned right over, the polished tips of his shoes only an inch of two from Schreber's ear.

'She rooted here and there, out of instinct, on the flat skin of your chest, squirming like a maggot. Gustav shrieked in delight and disgust, and his pretence was dropped and he became himself again. Who knows why? Perhaps in the face of such a breach in the order of the world it is impossible to dissemble, no matter how innocently, just as Klara herself could do nothing other than follow her true nature. She sucked and her little hands gripped the air, looking for something and her wet lips were over your chest, on the flat, bony ground of it, where she would usually find her milk.

'Of course, there was nothing, and, as must be expected, she became upset. Her face went red and she cried harder, and you, not knowing what to do, pressed her harder against your chest, as your mother did and sometimes, too, the nurse. She was crying so loud that you didn't hear a thing. Nothing. Not the door opening. You were so closely attending to your sister that you saw nothing either, not even Gustav stiffening, and putting his hands behind his back. If you had listened closely, you would have heard the sound of your father, gritting his teeth. You'd have seen the laughter wiped from your brother's face. If you hadn't been wrapped up in the game you'd have been aware of the whiteness of your own thin legs poking out from where your nightshirt was suddenly lifted. You would have felt it lift, even, and you would have turned to see the progress of your father's huge red hand through the air, it coming fast as a swooping falcon, so that when that slap landed on you, you would not have been so utterly surprised. As it was, it was only by miracle that you didn't drop Klara head first onto the white wooden boards.

'Your mother was by your father's side, with her hands up to her face, and when the slap hit you jumped. She gasped and stepped forward, reaching down, ready to grab you and Klara both and lift you away to somewhere, away from that place, but your father, upright again now, took her by the arm and pulled her to his side and turned his anger on her. With a glance he said more clearly than words that he considered this aberration to be some fault of hers, her coddling influence once again undercutting his good work, and now this, the worst. From the way her face fell she agreed with him.

'I have to say that I was surprised, because she always seemed a mother first and foremost, but, at her husband's side, despite her reservations and obvious love for you, she found the strength to ignore the looks on your face, the surprise fading and your lips pursing, eyes narrowing, red coming everywhere, up from your chest to your neck and your cheeks blazing. Klara was quiet now. I don't know how much she could have known—nothing probably—but she felt something, and was silenced by it. Perhaps infants, even before speech, have some understanding of the hierarchy of human emotions. Rössler might be able to tell you. Or it might have been a coincidence, but she let her petty hunger go and was watchful. She watched your mouth widen until your teeth were showing, and then you wailed and wailed, and if anyone seemed to be the baby, forgive me, it was you. Your father was immune to the noise, but your mother... she saw her baby who had once been, who was now separated from her by years, your wide mouth and shut eyes, crying, and though you could not have seen it, she tested the grip of her husband on her forearm, and it was only his years of domination that prevented her from pulling away. That, and, perhaps, his prickling anger: it filled the room like steam from an untended kettle. No one moved, even though your tears moved them all, and your mother would have given anything to fall onto her knees and pull both of you little dears toward her and hold you against her breast.

'But your father was the stronger. You cried and they watched and there was a stalemate. Heaven knows how much time passed. It felt like an hour. It was Anna who ended it. She ran past Gustav and stood in the middle of the room and she spoke a torrent of words, none of them you'd remember, I suppose. I doubt you would have heard them above your wailing. Anna stood straight with her hands behind her back, except when she needed to point to one or other of the boys, and she explained everything. She was fast and intense, a firecracker, just as she has always been and all eyes were on her.

'Her words were charming, somehow, in their earnest intensity. When you sensed that the attention was taken from you, your eyes opened a slit and it was then that you saw your father, and what had been anger in his eyes and the clenching of his jaw had transformed itself to something else, something you had never seen. Like you, he had tears in his eyes, and on his cheeks, and his face was red and white, like the knuckles of his hands. I think you were the only other one who noticed it, whatever it was. Shame? Love and guilt? It was a complicated emotion and something in you couldn't bear to see it. You edged forward, safe in the distraction that Anna provided, and then Gustav joined in the speaking and the focus of the room shifted to him. He was high-pitched, wavering and nervous, croaking with tears, and you stepped from board to board, feeling the cracks between them with your toes, and all the while watching the tears well in the corner of your father's eyes. You edged forward, unseen, and took your father's hand and stood there like a statue, listening to them speak. You held your father's hand tight, the hand that had only recently slapped your bare arse, and your father held your mother's arm, his fingers pinching into her, and the speaking just went on and on, and the grip of your father's fingers on your mother's arm was so tight that she couldn't bear it anymore and she called out:

'"Moritz!"

'Everything went silent. Your father dropped to one knee. The hand that had been at his wife's arm now covered his face, gripped the skin of his face, his other hand clutching hard at you. There came a strange whining noise into the room, like a wounded dog's keening, and it was a long time before anyone realised it came from your father.

'No one knew what was going on, least of all your parents. In the end your mother took the baby, and she led the others out of the room and closed the door behind her. She knelt down and made them all gather around her, and in the quietest possible voice she told them that their father was very unwell, that he had been hit by a ladder, and that they were to be very good little boys and girls and never again to do what they did that morning. When they all nodded and nodded with sad little faces, she kissed each one of them on the top of their heads and took them away and dressed them with warm clothes from the laundry. When that was done she opened the door a crack, and when she saw that your father was still there, on his knees in the middle of the room, whining, with your hand held tight in his, she came and prised off his fingers and led you through the house and out into the garden. There you did your exercises, and all of you tried to pretend there was nothing wrong or different in the way your mother did them, even though she did not know the routine. Now, faced with our Rössler here, similarly failing to provide the correct example, bending wrongly, not reaching to the proper extent, lapsing from symmetry for God's sake, even as he thinks to claim that authority that your father had, doesn't it bring it all right back? Like a slap in the face? Or on the arse? Look at him—his movements are hardly better than those that you did as a child. Worse.'

Even though this Jew was vile, it could not be argued that he was mistaken, though how he knew what he knew Schreber could not begin to understand. Schreber felt a longing for the straight body of his father and the certainty of his beliefs.

When Rössler's own collar came loose it was the end of it.

A button failed, and Schreber wished that his father had never died. There was a wattle of loose skin at the doctor's neck, which prickled with white hair inexpertly shaved back. It bulged through the gap in the starched collar, a fraction more with each partial bend until there was a thumb's width protruding, and the sight brought his father back so strongly that Schreber could almost not bear it. His father would have run thirty miles at the sight of an ounce of fat building on his frame. He would have scrubbed himself raw with pumice, and scraped his flesh down to the bone with a thrice sharpened razor to prevent just that bulge of flesh, that prickle of hair. The sensation of his father's disgust at this doctor was so strong that Schreber ignored the man's instructions and, much to the delight of the Jew, he went into the routine he remembered from his childhood, remembered down in his bones and in the muscles of his thighs and in the breath of his body. The Jew clapped his hands together twice, as Schreber's father often did before beginning, and he performed the routine too, learned from those long mornings in the garden where they had all worked hard and true at the exercises, his father too, his legs straight, knees back, never hiding behind his role as educator, as this Rössler did. Now, when Rössler indicated a certain twist or lean to the left or right, Schreber defied him, bending in a way that should not be possible for a man of his age and condition, and, though his face whitened with the effort and sweat began to pool in the small of his back and slicked down from under his arms, he went on, sure in the truth of his father's teaching. The Jew followed him perfectly, egging him on.

After a while, Schreber shut his eyes, the better to concentrate on the perfection of the angles of his limbs, but he was certain the Jew was beside him, matching him turn for turn. The fluidity with which he went from one posture to the next was absolute, and if his chest heaved, what of it? The body would be subservient to the mind, the flesh to the will, the son to the father. A tickling at the back of the throat as each new breath was dragged down against his lungs' attempts to force the old one out was nothing to Schreber, had been nothing to him as a boy. The proper end of the exercises was dictated not by his puny body, but by the world itself, by the scripture of gymnastics, by numbers and the science they represented, by certainties more carved in stone than the flesh was carved. If lights danced behind his eyelids and his ears buzzed like bees, then that was nothing compared to the necessity to stop not at ten, but at twenty-five. Schreber bent and jumped, to show that fat-necked doctor what it meant to move the body, to have control over the gross physical machine, and Rössler, despite his arrogance, was a fool, a man who allowed the hair of his body to grow where it would, a man who allowed his skin to loosen with age and let his collar come loose, a man with no understanding of discipline, or of health. He wanted to make his father proud, kneeling like a soldier defeated—by what, he couldn't understand—and even though the welt on the back of his legs was still ever so sore, he looked up to the upstairs windows of the house, and he hoped to see some movement that might mean his father was rustling the curtains. He might see how badly his wife was drilling the children, and, despite his defeat, he might come down and take that intricate care over them that he had always taken before, every morning. If he was stern then it was through love, hadn't he said so a hundred times? Like a general is stern with his men, in their best interests, to make strength in them that might one day save their lives. He was no less loving of his children, so that whatever he did, however they imagined they suffered, this was a loving kindness. When they were older they would understand, as they watched the flabby, ill-disciplined boys and girls of their schools wither and fail in the face of life. They would fall to their knees at the first obstacle, whimpering, while the Schreber children would march on to great things! They would never shy from pain when it needed to be felt, or exhaustion in a good cause, their bodies and minds would never let them down. So much was the effort their father put into their health and happiness that he himself was brought low. His fingers clutching so hard at him, so that he had to bite his lip, Papa on his knees, clutching his face, the fingers on his other hand pushing into his eye sockets, that strange sound like the wounded dog, speared through its side, that they had once come across in the park, pathetic and wide-eyed, keening, the victim of some childish viciousness, kicked and beaten and laughed at.

'Father, we must take him home!'

His father said nothing but shook his head slowly. There was a pool of blood that coloured the ground at the dog's side. Paul reached down to touch his little head. The dog shuffled toward him, but the stick dragged, and there was a shriek. Paul's hand hovered, too frightened of hurting the little thing to comfort it, and tears came without restraint.

When Paul looked up at his father there were tears there, too, like there would be in Klara's room, when his father was defeated, kneeling. In the park he had been strong, and he knelt down and twisted the dog's neck, cracked his little neck, made his eyes go glassy and his head loose. His father picked Paul up, as he never did, and they marched away.

It was only when Schreber found that he was not moving, lying again on the grass with the vicious snap of smelling salts in his nose, that he opened his eyes.

There was the ape, no longer laughing. There was the doctor—his collar now miraculously rebuttoned, the sweat from his brow dried and the wattle gone—leaning over him.

The Jew was nowhere to be seen, and Müller picked Schreber up under the knees and across the back, as if his legs were useless, and placed him gently back into the Bath chair.

'I think we have enough to be going on with,' said Rössler.

A memory of a time
before his father's ill-
ness, in which a family
of Jewish boarders are
trapped. One of them
is called Alexander.
Isn't that the name of
the mysterious Jewish
gentleman who tor-
ments Schreber?

XV

The five of them stood in order of height: Gustav first, then
Paul, Anna, Sidonie, and, last, Klara, moving from foot to
foot, the tiles so cold and no time to find their slippers. In the
candlelight, the walls around them came closer and moved back
with each flicker of the flame. Their mother ran from room to
room, gathering things: a shawl, a shoe, a packet of bread and
butter, all of which she put into a big doctor's bag. Outside
there was shouting.

Their father stood by the door.

Down on the street: the sound of breaking glass and men
calling to each other.

Boots clattering on cobbles.

Their father buttoned his long blue coat, pushing the brass
through the slits in the fabric and polishing them with his sleeve
when they came through. His tall knee boots were pulled up
and his hat pulled down so that the peak hid his eyes. The gold
chin strap sparkled.

Someone screamed outside.

Father stood straight and turned to face the children. He was neat and stiff.

'There is nothing to fear, children!' he said. 'No matter what you see or what you hear tonight, fear is of no use to you!'

He went over to a window and pulled aside the curtain.

'No amount of noise from the street, no Catholic, no Jesuit can ever threaten you if your will is strong. Do you understand?'

Paul, like the others, nodded once, but none of them understood what he said.

'You are strong, brave children. Fine girls and boys!'

In the street there was a terrible crashing.

Wood splintering.

Rifle fire.

Their father licked his teeth and marched to the window. He opened it and leaned out. Their mother was back now, kneeling before them so that she could look them all in the eye. She whispered that they must be obedient and not worry because their father and the other men of the militia would make sure they were safe. They would all go to their grandmother's for a few days. Wasn't that wonderful?

The children said nothing, even though it was a great thing to be allowed to go to their grandmother's house, where even Father smiled as he sat and smoked in the best chair.

When Father called them to attention he stood in front of them, heels together and now he looked like a God: not the God of the vicious Catholics who would burn a house down and turn a child by torture to their papish ways, but like a God of the olden days, such as those in the books that Gustav got down from their father's shelf. He was like Woden or Thunor: he stood strong and straight. His boots shone in the candlelight, and the bright, brass buttons were like stars.

Their father clicked his heels and left the room, the steel tips of his boots ringing on the stone flags, quicker and quicker as he went down the stairs.

When the door opened onto the street, the noise of shouting grew very loud and angry. Mother took Gustav by the hand and then each one took the hand of the next in line and they followed her into the hallway. Though the lamp had not been lit and there was nothing but darkness and the light from outside, they didn't complain; they went quickly, paying no attention to the door through which Father had just left, and lined up against the wall.

'When the carriage comes to take us to Grandmother's we must all go to it without a moment's fussing. Do you understand, children? There will be no time for silliness!'

'What is the noise, Frau Schreber?'

Their mother looked up.

There, in their doorway, was the boarder and his family, still in their nightgowns. He leaned at a peculiar angle on account of his deformity, and so did his son, but the women of the family also made a poor show, and the mother had not even taken the time to run a brush through her hair before coming down.

'Nothing, Herr Zilberschlag,' Frau Schreber said. 'Please go back to sleep.'

'It doesn't sound like nothing,' said Frau Zilberschlag.

The daughter squirmed and whined. Frau Zilberschlag cooed at her and shifted her higher on the hip.

The boy spoke.

'Papa,' he said, 'why are they all dressed up to go out? I thought it was bedtime?'

'It is bedtime, Alex dear.'

'So why aren't we in bed?'

'That, little one, is exactly what we are out of bed to find out, isn't it?'

Herr Zilberschlag smiled at Frau Schreber, but she said nothing and after a while he stopped smiling.

They were weak, these Zilberschlags. Their eldest boy was about Paul's age and it wasn't really his fault, but he had a twist in his spine, and it made him feeble. And they had no money, because of the fees, so that their mother couldn't buy the material she needed to mend their clothes, let alone make new ones.

'Are you going somewhere nice, children?' Frau Zilberschlag said, and before Frau Schreber could stop her, Sidonie replied that, yes thank you, they were going to their grandmother's.

'The country? Very nice. And why wait until morning? Strike while the iron is hot! Very sensible.'

Outside there was a bang that shook the glass in the windows and then, almost straight after, one of the windows came in. All at once, a curtain billowed, glass shattered, and a rock the size of a man's fist landed in the middle of the room. It skidded across the boards and came to rest at Herr Zilberschlag's feet.

They all looked at it in silence.

After a long time Paul said, 'You can't come with us.'

His mother shushed him and gathered the children together, fussing over their coats, but he went on.

'You can't come with us!'

'Paul!'

'No, Mama! There is no room in the carriage. And look at them!'

'Young man, we have not asked to come with you,' said Herr Zilberschlag.

'You couldn't go anyway. Your nightclothes are grubby. You're all crooked. Your backs go off to one side. You have to live in a medical institute! You can't come anyway!'

'Paul! You will be silent this instant!'

'It is nothing, Frau Schreber, really.' Herr Zilberschlag came over and knelt in front of Paul. He meant to be nice. He reached forward and tried to touch Paul's hand, but Paul stepped back.

'Papa says you get what you deserve! There are people like us—like me and my brothers and sisters, like Mother and Father—we make sure we are good and strong and good things happen to us. And there are people like you.' Paul hesitated, suddenly aware everyone was watching him.

'Go on,' said Herr Zilberschlag, 'there are people like us…'

'Paul! Get here now!'

'There are people like you, Catholics and Jews, who wake up late, and stay half-asleep all day, and if you were set fire to in your beds then that would be no one's fault but your own.'

Herr Zilberschlag nodded and looked back at his wife, but neither of them had anything to say.

'Why don't you get yourself a uniform?' said Paul. 'Why don't you go out with the militia and fight, like Papa?'

Herr Zilberschlag stood, with difficulty. The twist in his spine—it made it tricky to stand up all in a moment.

'There are many reasons, Paul.'

'All excuses. Papa says that some people are only any good at wheedling their way out of things. If you were straighter, not so twisted, you might be able to wear a nice uniform like Papa's, with a hat and brass buttons.'

There was a knock at the door.

'That will be the carriage…'

Frau Schreber opened the door and beckoned for the children to come forward, but it was not the carriage driver. It was a tall man in the same uniform their father wore, except it was torn at the arm, and this man had no hat. His brass buttons were dull, and his moustaches were uneven.

'Might I help you?' Frau Schreber asked.

The man said nothing. He looked off over her shoulder and when he saw the Zilberschlags he smiled. In the front row of his teeth only two remained whole—the others were ragged black stubs.

Outside there was laughing and Paul caught sight of a man running in his nightshirt. His white legs were bare up to the knee and his feet jarred against the cobblestones as he ran. There was a man in blue running behind him, with a stick, beating him like a man beats a horse. The man in his nightgown fell and the stick was raised high.

The man with black teeth beckoned to the Zilberschlags.

He stepped up, as if to come in.

He smiled.

The door slammed in the man's face—red painted wood—and Paul's mother pulled across the bolts.

Gustav ran to the door.

'But Father!'

She took the boy by the elbow and walked him away, struggling.

At no time did she look away from her boarders.

'Upstairs, children.'

'But what about the carriage?'

'What about grandmother's?'

Frau Schreber pushed them up the stairs, and nodded politely to Herr Zilberschlag as she followed them up.

Schreber visits Rössler with a request. The doctor is distracted. When Schreber forcefully attempts to secure his full attention, he makes a mistake.

XVI

The corridor was empty. Through the windows the late afternoon sun made blocks of cold white light on the floor, jointed where they met the opposite wall. Schreber looked behind him, to where the stairs from the orderlies' quarters emerged from below. No one. He made his way without hesitating to Rössler's office. He knocked twice and flinched to hear the sound echo in every direction.

The door swung open.

'What is it?' Rössler snapped without looking up from the starched white shirt he was attempting, without much success, to put on. His bulb-knuckled fingers kept slipping on the smooth mother-of-pearl studs.

'Well?' he said, still not looking up.

Schreber clicked his heels and sniffed, at which point Rössler at last deigned his visitor a glance.

'Oh… I thought… Müller!' He shouted, 'Müller!'

Rössler bent down and, audibly creaking, pulled at the strap of his left dress boot, which made no progress over his heel.

'My nephew… formal dinner. Müller!'

'He isn't available, Herr Doktor.'

'No, so it seems. Do you wish to see me, Herr Schreber? It is just that I am rather…'

'For a minute, if you are able. I would very much appreciate it.'

Rössler hopped on one leg but, despite becoming red in the face, was unable to coax his boot on.

'Bloody gout now is it?' Rössler cursed, 'Can't a man get dressed without his body making things difficult for him?' he sighed, and let the polished boot slip down so that it lay like a pool of black oil beside his thick woollen stocking.

'Herr Schreber, please come in.' He went over to his desk, sliding slowly on his stocking foot and letting the booted one edge him along. 'Age,' he said, and didn't see the need to elaborate.

Rössler nodded to the patient's chair, only noticing his dress jacket as Schreber went to sit on it. Suddenly a man twenty years younger, Rössler was across the room in a flash and holding his jacket straight. He brushed it with the back of his hand twice and hung it on the coat rack. He looked at the clock on his desk.

'I'm afraid you catch me at a bad time. My nephew will be here imminently, and he is not the kind of man who enjoys being kept waiting—quite the opposite. So…?'

'One question. I wish to return home by Christmas. Is this something you expect to be possible, now you have your diagnosis?'

Rössler raised his eyebrows and examined Schreber closely, apparently to see if he was joking.

'My expectation is that a cure should not be difficult, and that I should be well enough to take some time away from the asylum to attend to my duties at home. Is this your understanding?'

Schreber waited, but Rössler said nothing, and now, his state of undress forgotten, he was instead turning over piles of paper on his desk, looking for something.

'My daughter, Fridoline, was here…'

'Your daughter?'

'Yes. Frida was very keen that I should be home for Christmas.'

'You admit, then, that you have a daughter?'

Rössler found the papers he was searching for. He rifled through them until he found one in particular which he pulled out and held up, letting it twist between his fingers until Schreber could see the writing on one side.

'You no longer believe that she is,' Rössler turned the paper back over and, putting his glasses up onto the bridge of his nose, read it: '"a cruel fiction, a parody stitched together from the corpses of innumerable tiny birds, whose aim it is to mock and crow and speak of the corruption of the Schreber family line"?'

Rössler lowered the paper and stared over the top of it, like a hawk.

'I don't recall saying those things. But I'm sure I promised Frida that I would be home by Christmas. I am a man of my word and I would not like to be proved otherwise.'

'Do you recall that you said that "she has been taken over by the soul of a palsied whore who stares out from her eyes and takes lascivious pleasure in deriding your masculine pride"?'

'Do you think I might be home for Christmas?'

'That "her wrists and ankles are moved by the agency of the lower God?" Your own words, Herr Schreber, not mine.'

'I do not recall saying anything of that sort.'

'No?'

'Will I be home for Christmas?'

'No.'

'But I promised.'

'It would be wise to make no further promises. Without, at least, consulting with me first. Your condition is too severe. You don't believe me? Let me read from your notes… This is for last month: "In the main part there is no change… very rarely speaks with doctor… says that he is being tortured with food he cannot eat… constantly tormented by hallucinations… sleep poor… stands in bed, stands in front of window listening intently… unreachable…" Does this sound like a man who will be returning to his family for Christmas? Now I really must get ready. We can talk further in the morning, if, of course, we find you still disposed to do so.'

Schreber shook his head vigorously, but Rössler returned to the matter of his boots and whether there was any chance he might get them onto his feet. Schreber stood over the doctor, who was now sitting on his rug, grimacing and holding the top edges of the boot with his hands and forcing his leg to straighten into the boot.

'Sir, I do not know what kind of man you are,' Schreber said, 'though I have my suspicions, but in my family a man's word is his bond. It may be a trivial matter to you—to break a promise to a young girl—but to me it is something I would not do unless there was absolutely no alternative.'

'This damn boot! Müller! Where is the man?'

'Is there absolutely no alternative?'

Schreber knelt beside the doctor, the better that the man should see that he was in earnest.

'I implore you!'

'Müller! The carriage will be here any minute…'

'You aren't listening to me. This is a matter of great importance.'

'Müller! All I need is a horn. I felt sure there was one here…'

'Perhaps an *exeat*? A supervised visit? Anything.'

'I was given a silver shoehorn as a gift. Lord alone knows where it has got to.'

'Please?'

Rössler went quiet and let the boot drop. He looked off over Schreber's shoulder, and a thoughtful expression played across his face. He rubbed his cheek, and pushed his glasses up his nose. He ran a hand through his hair. Schreber waited, his knees aching from kneeling.

'Please?' Schreber repeated, and he held his hands together, as if in a prayer.

'Please what?' Rössler asked with a frown, 'Müller! If I'm late I'm going to have that man fired!'

'You aren't listening to me!' Schreber barked.

He leaned over and grabbed the doctor by the lapels and when he tugged him forward so that their faces were no more than a few inches apart and the doctor at last seemed to pay him some attention, he was breathing fast and heavily, so that Rössler blinked with Schreber's every exhalation. The doctor said nothing. Schreber opened his mouth to speak, but somehow the words did not come.

'Did you call for me, sir?'

'Yes, Müller.'

'Would you like me to…?'

'Of course…'

Müller was over, bringing with him the sour odour of liquor. It stung Schreber's eyes and Rössler sniffed twice, pointedly. Müller seemed not to notice, picked Schreber up under the arms, and pulled him away. At first Schreber did not let go of the lapels, but Müller tugged and he came loose.

'Shall I…?'

'Take him back to his rooms.'

'Yes, sir. Your carriage…'

'Outside already? Yes, I thought it might be.'

'I told him to wait.'

Rössler turned away from both of them.

Müller whispered in Schreber's ear, 'Now you've done it, you silly old sod.'

In his rooms, Schreber writes a letter of apology to Fridoline. His thoughts turn to the importance of a child's having brothers and sisters on whom she can rely. He remembers a day in the garden of the Institute which, though difficult, was ultimately one of his happiest moments. Later, he cannot find the letter he was writing.

XVII

Schreber smoothed the paper with his sleeve before taking up the pen. The breakfast things lay on their tray at his feet, untouched. He pushed them out of sight with the toe of his slipper and ignored the chime his glass made as it fell and hit the side of his plate. He lifted the lid of the inkwell and charged the pen's bladder with the lever. A thick drop of black hung precariously from the end of the gold nib. When he moved the lever backward it shrank, but when he returned the lever to its proper place the drop swelled. There was no blotting paper, so he wiped it on the sleeve of his dressing gown. He picked off a snagged thread and coughed.

My dearest Fridoline,
Silly little thing!

So like her aunt—so like Anna—though neither of them would admit it. A firecracker! He hated to see them upset. The turning over of the bottom lip—it was the same with both of them—the shadow that came into the sockets of their eyes, like bruises, deepening as their eyes reddened. To be told there would be no excursion, for this reason or that—to the zoo, or to the lido—he hated to see the disappointment and the sadness.

My dearest Fridoline,

Despite my promise, I am very sad to say that my doctor does not hold out much hope for me making it home for our usual Christmas celebrations...

That he was the source of the disappointment, that was the problem, when he broke his promises, or caused a fuss. It didn't matter if nothing was said, it was the unmistakable atmosphere, an understanding which passes between people without the need for words, transmitted in a more basic language than speech, heard not by the ear, but felt by the skin on the space between the shoulder blades. Or, on the back of the neck and then the prickling of the hairs of the arm—not words, but sensible nonetheless. Disappointment. A quivering lip and, perhaps, a little sniff. A handkerchief taken to the corner of the eye. They were very similar, Anna and Fridoline. And Sabine.

'Why is it that I must be the one to tell her?'

Schreber watched the end of his pen, motionless on the paper. Beneath it the full stop was growing. The ink leached into the fibres of the paper, and the nib shook with the vibrations of his nerves. His hand twitched for no reason—for absolutely no reason—and spoiled the page with a long thick upward-leading mark. Schreber grunted and put down the pen. He slid the paper off the desk and onto the ground. It curved down, cutting the air quite slowly, before coming to rest on his breakfast tray.

Voluptuousness has become God-fearing.

He took another piece of paper from his drawer.

Dear Fridoline,

The raincoats returned to their pegs.

'Your father does not feel well.'

'But he promised!'

'Next week?'

But he promised. Poor old Fridoline, taking off her fur-trimmed suede, the one with the big black buttons, and when the last button was undone she hung it herself, taking her scarf next and drawing together the two ends, putting the middle of it in one of the coat pockets so that it would be there when she next needed it—her own innovation—placing the paper packet of walnuts in their shells on the table by the door, the top neatly crimped. Such a good child, never complaining, except that lip, curling over, just like her Aunt Anna's—exactly the same—a strange coincidence but unmistakable despite Sabine's blank stare whenever he pointed it out.

'The child is only a Schreber in name—she will not resemble any of you.'

But it was there nonetheless. He was not imagining it—the disappointed curl of the lip.

Dearest Fridoline,

Easier to read, this time. The ink had flowed more easily. The nib had not caught on the right angle between the letter 'r' and the letter 'i' and there was no consequent overshooting of the dim, half-obscured line from the guide sheet below. The lip. Hadn't Anna done just the same thing as a child?

Please know that there is nothing that saddens me more than breaking a promise to you, but this is just what I must do.

Would there be tears? Or would that be too mild a reaction? A girl cries over many things. When she cracks the porcelain on the head of her doll, or when her hair is pulled—that little scoundrel! He should have clipped his ear, whatever the boy's father said. A girl might cry for a thousand other things. Wasn't this worse?

I remain well and my doctor is confident I will make a full recovery in only a few days or weeks, but not by Christmas.

To be abandoned by one's father? A terrible thing. It could make a child turn in on herself. Without a father's author-ity what was a child to do? Go to her mother? Sabine? Seek comradeship and support in others? Anna had her brothers and sisters. Whom did Fridoline have? The skivvy? Cook? With Father gone, Anna had relied on the others. Up to the point at which the household passed into anarchy and beyond it, when the law seemed to have collapsed. Wasn't that true of all of them?

My greatest regret is that you have no brothers and sisters on whom to rely.

Because, in the absence of discipline, they took to each other the roles and requirements of the system and acted it out, after a fashion, in the manner that it had been acted out upon them. A most valuable thing, to know one's place. When they played in the garden, the law of nature was the proper ruler and their activities found natural limits in the extent to which things could be done, and at what speed, and by what measure. The other children, whose fathers and mothers had not changed or gone, were markers for them.

There is much to say for communal living, particularly for children, as they require others to play with, their own internal resources not yet sufficient to occupy them. The same can be said for the outdoors, where the world contains enough variety to fill a day. It was when they were obliged to be in—when the sun went down, or before and after meals—that the weight of their father's removal from the place became most apparent. It was on Gustav that the change was most visible. He stood straighter than he had and his chest was puffed out, and in his actions a sternness of mood became apparent. Would this happen with Fridoline? She had never been a boisterous girl; more inclined to needlework and her paints than wholesome play in the garden.

'What do you expect her to do out there all day?' Sabine said.

They stood at the window, and she stood lost by the damson tree, a perfect red circle at her feet: a hoop, untouched. Sabine huffed and went down, and, after a delay, Schreber saw her take the girl's hand and she brought her in. This was where she stayed, and when the hoop was next picked up, beneath it there was a ring of flat, washed-out, yellow grass.

In the garden one day Gustav hit Paul. There had been some trifling incident—Paul had allowed the seat of his trousers to become grass-stained by sliding down the steep approach to the lake's edge. Seeing what he had done, and knowing that this would cause trouble for his mother, he had allowed himself a tear or two. Gustav became enraged, and the look of fear in his brother's eyes made it worse—little sissy!—and he swung down a slap from on high, moving his hand in a snap from the position of a Roman salute down and across Paul's cheek, too hard—much harder than he had intended—so that the slap sounded through the garden like a dry branch snapping from a tree.

The boarders' children stopped in their play and one of them, Alexander—a boy who always appeared to be craning over to his left, as if he carried a heavy weight on one shoulder only—came over and said:

'That was a beauty! Right across the cheek! Do it again!'

'Shut up!' said Anna, who had come running at the sound, and now knelt by Paul. He was trying to swallow the lump that had come into his throat. He was blinking and blinking as if it would stop tears.

Gustav's mouth was suddenly dry, and he looked back toward the house.

Nothing.

He licked his lips and told Paul to get up and stop behaving like a girl.

Alexander laughed.

'You tell him, Gus,' he said, 'that prissy little girl. Get up, girl!'

'Shut up!' Anna said. 'Tell him, Gustav!'

'No cripple tells me what to do, and no girl either.' He dragged Paul up roughly by the arm and span him round so that the stain on his bottom was visible to all of them.

'He's made a right mess, hasn't he, Gus?' Alexander said.

The other children gathered around now and they pointed at the grass stain and smirked at each other. Gustav took two steps forward and pushed Alexander in the chest.

'What did you do that for?'

Alexander was as tall as Gustav. Thin black down covered his top lip, but the twist in his spine meant that Gustav stood taller, and he was lean and strong where this boy was underfed. Alexander glanced over his shoulder, toward his friends, and they stepped forward, so that he smiled and stepped forward himself. He looked Gustav in the eye and beckoned to him. Gustav clenched his fists and stepped up, and then Alexander, the coward, stamped his boot down Gustav's shin, dragging the skin down in a curl, like chilled butter scraped off the block, down to where Gustav's sock gathered above his ankle. Gustav couldn't help but kneel down, because it burned terribly.

Alexander sniffed and smiled and turned back to look at his associates.

'You little brute!' Anna said, and she rushed him, paddling with open hands at his face and chest.

Alexander giggled as he pushed her away.

The wound on Gustav's shin, clear at first, was now prickling with spots of blood. Gustav knelt and put his fingers either side of the wound, and he turned to Paul. He didn't have to say a thing.

Paul went forward. Those spots of blood. The curl of flesh that touched his brother's sock—white flesh that no longer felt anything and over which blood had started to run. Dead skin rubbing against the small, grey sock fibres onto which blood dripped, hanging in perfect little spheres. His father's hand passing through the air. The landing of a blow. The direction of his wrists. He grit his teeth. That ugly child! That filthy twisted cripple that had dared hurt his brother—his father—both of them. Stronger than anything. Clear in their hearts. His father's hand. Gustav's hand. Coming down to strike him. To shame him. That dirty little bastard! This hideous creature—like a gnome or a troll—who dared to assault his brother. Coward! Not even in a manly way, but like a coward, like a girl. With the feet! A man uses his hands.

Paul grabbed for Alexander, who was smiling and looking back for approval. Paul was smaller, younger, and though he was righteous in his anger he had no understanding of how to fight. He grabbed out, finding the boy's balls with one hand, through his loose shorts, and his ear with the other. He crushed and pulled with all his might, gritting his teeth until they cracked, shutting his eyes, his face still stinging from Gustav's slap. Alexander dropped to his knees but Paul did not let go. He pulled and he crushed and screamed in the child's face like a demon or a dervish. The boy shrieked, but Paul shrieked louder, and it was only when Gustav pulled him away that he stopped shrieking.

Alexander slumped over onto his bent side and his chest heaved. He was sick onto the grass, his friends frozen behind him, open-mouthed.

'You dirty ball-crusher!' one of them cried.

Gustav grabbed Paul's arm again, but now his face was open and he was smiling. Anna took his other hand and squeezed it gently, and though Paul's breath would not slow, and he felt something in his throat, they were happy with him, and he found himself happy too.

The three of them walked toward Sidonie, who was already halfway up the garden, talking to herself as she always did, and the boy didn't move. His friends—Sylvie and Klaus and Johan—kneeled around him and asked him questions to which he could not reply.

Gustav slapped Paul on the back, between his shoulder blades, quieting the tingling that turning his back on the cripple had started up.

'Come on, ball-crusher!'

Paul felt in himself pride, suddenly, that he had been the instrument of this boy's punishment, and, in that feeling, the shame that Gustav's slap had brought on him disappeared, and he knew that he had reason to be proud, that his father would be proud of him, for his strength and bravery, like a knight from a story, the monster righteously defeated, and when he looked at his hands he knew them to be strong.

Schreber picked up the pen from where it had fallen at his feet. The breakfast tray was gone. His slippers were no longer on his feet, and instead he had on his all-weather boots, laced high above the ankle. They were wet, as were the hems of his trousers. He sat up. On the table there was a cup, half-filled with tea. Steam rose up from it, gently. A piece of buttered bread was on a plate beside it, untouched.

Dearest Fridoline, he began again, but now he wrote directly onto the tabletop.

Where was the paper?

Where was the letter?

Schreber moved all the things about on the table.

Nothing. Only the buttered bread and a half-finished cup of tea that he did not remember starting.

Schreber takes his
meal in the commu-
nal dining area. The
mysterious Jewish
gentleman, Alexan-
der, warns Schreber
of a change for the
worse in his circum-
stances. Schreber rails
against Alexander and
the other inmates of
the asylum. Müller
takes him away.

XVIII

That evening, Müller informed Schreber that he would be
taking his meal in the communal dining room and, despite his
protestations that a man of his standing should not have to eat
with the ordinary inmates, Schreber eventually allowed himself
to be taken and given a seat by the door.

At his table were men from other buildings in the asylum
complex. He recognised none of them, but bowed to each. Not
one returned his kindness, engaged as they were in thumping
the handles of their knives down against the table and sweeping their elbows randomly into wine glasses and salt cellars.
Schreber took great pains to sit upright in front of his plate,
and arranged his cutlery neatly before the meal was served to
him. He never slumped in his chair, or allowed his elbows to
come near to touching the table.

When eventually the soup was splashed into his bowl, he
used the appropriate spoon to transfer it past his moustaches—
its lack of seasoning and sour flavour unremarked—while the
men around him spat on the ground and wailed in disgust,

or thrashed their heads from side to side while their orderlies forced the spoons into their mouths, almost empty of any of the food they were supposed to be delivering, the largest part finding its way onto the fronts of their shirts, and into the creases of their necks. Everywhere there was a great shouting and fuss, while Schreber made not one breach of etiquette: not so much as a single impatient glance toward the kitchen when his soup was done and, his appetite unusually piqued, he considered taking something more substantial. He sat and waited like a good boy, no need for the strut to be attached to the rim of the table, the iron bar that arrested the progress of the chest forward and kept the spine aligned properly to the requirements of natural science. His hands were crossed on his lap and he looked at the man across the table from him.

Of course, it was the Jew.

The man was staring hard at him.

Something came from the far end of the table—was thrown spiralling across—a glass, the water spraying out and wetting the cloth, sent by a man who could not control the movements of his limbs.

'Strange,' said Alexander, 'that men like him are allowed their own rooms? Don't you think?'

Schreber took a piece of bread from the basket.

'It is no concern of mine.'

Alexander smiled and nodded and lit a cigarette.

'You seem well, Judge.'

'Herr Doktor Präsident Schreber, please.'

'Very well. I came by your room but you were not there. Müller told me I would find you here.'

'And here you find me.'

Alexander nodded, and across a sea of elbows and shouting, meat and potatoes were served to them. Schreber picked up his knife and fork, but the Jew began to speak, so he returned them to the table. The Jew did not, and, without cutting off the fat, placed a wedge of beef into his mouth and spoke around it.

'He was very busy, your orderly,'—with each word a little stream of gravy progressed further down the Jew's chin until gravity carried it down, back onto his plate with a little splash. The Jew smiled and, with his silk handkerchief, wiped his face. Then he took his cigarette from the edge of the table where he had laid it, and pushed his plate away.

'Enough for me, I think.'

Schreber took up his knife and fork and carefully removed a piece of gristle from the edge of his meat. It was tough, and his knife—as with all the knives—was blunt. He managed to pull the white mass from the darker meat, but some ligament remained. The moment he loosened the tension between meat and gristle, the ligament brought them back together. He turned the meat around and tried again.

'He was packing things in crates. Müller.'

Schreber shook his head and returned to his plate. The man next to him—he was a Slav—lurched suddenly over into Schreber, sending his fork skittering across the tabletop. Schreber sniffed and got up from the table.

'I think I'll return to my rooms. I'm not terribly hungry.'

'Yes, yes,' Alexander said, 'except…'

'Except what?'

'Please.' Alexander indicated for Schreber to sit back down. 'I saw your clothes being taken from your room as I came to dinner.'

'Nonsense.'

'And your desk.'

'Why would anyone remove my desk?'

'To give it to a man who needs it?'

'Ridiculous! I need it. I must write letters.'

Schreber walked away from the table.

'I think you might prefer it if you stayed here. While you can.'

'I don't understand you.'

'No. I see that. Please, do sit down! They will bring us winter bread.'

Schreber sighed and sat down. Alexander leaned over the table, first clearing a space in the debris.

'I have been here for a number of years, Herr Doktor Präsident Schreber, as you know. I am familiar with the signs and with the routines of this place. A man's effects are never moved from his room without reason. It is a waste of energy.'

'What are you trying to say?'

'I heard you screaming today. I stood by your door, and I heard you screaming.'

'Nonsense! And I don't see what business it is of yours whether I scream or I do not scream.'

'It is no business of mine whatsoever, except that, as a friend, I feel I must offer you a word of warning. It is my opinion, from what I know of this place, that you are to be taken below...' Alexander put his used cigarette out in the gravy on his plate and lit a fresh one. 'And this is not a good place to be taken. They say it is the home of the lost. Men rarely return. If you wish, when you are below, I can arrange for your family to know. Perhaps they will come to find you. You have a wife... I know.'

'Sabine will come for me shortly in any case. I'm sure of it.'

'Should I write to your daughter, then?'

'I wrote to her only yesterday.'

Alexander raised his eyebrow.

'That is not my understanding. A young girl came here before last Christmas. A dark-haired and serious child. No letter was sent to her.'

'How would you know?'

Alexander smiled.

'I make it my business to know everything. What else is a man to do in here? It is not a difficult task, to call on the mail room occasionally. If I have a telegram to send, for example. I can certainly make it appear that I have such a need, if I wish. It is not difficult.'

Schreber got up again and this time was determined to leave the table, but the Jew reached across and grabbed him by the elbow.

'Do not be so keen to leave this table. It will be your last meal as a free man. Now, show some sense and sit down. You still have some vestige of your rationality, that much is obvious to me, even if Rössler doesn't see it. Use it.'

Alexander let go of him and Schreber did not leave.

'I don't believe you.'

A small weasel of a man, Giron—a Westphalian—lifted the table at the far end, sending a cascade of half-eaten food and cutlery down toward where Schreber and the Jew were sitting. The Jew had the presence of mind to stand up before the wave reached him, but Schreber was too slow. Potatoes and the cruet set rolled past and the gravy boat came to rest upside down on the table immediately in front of him, splashing his trousers. The Jew took Schreber by the arm and dragged him up, first gently, and then, when there was no answering response, as roughly as he needed to. He took him into the hallway.

'Do you see?'

There was Müller, wiping sweat from the back of his neck with a grubby white handkerchief, a bundle of clothes tied with string at his feet and Schreber's books and clock piled beside them.

'Do you see? I wasn't lying was I?'

'You are nothing. A plaything.'

Schreber walked back to the dining hall. He pushed past men who were little better than dogs, scrabbling around on the ground with their orderlies tugging on their leashes. He pushed one of them from his chair and the fool barely noticed, curling up into a ball, still chewing. Schreber got onto the chair and bellowed out:

'You are all nothing! Dirt! Look at you! You are disgusting! You are like animals! I do not belong here!'

One of the orderlies came over and tried to take him down from the chair.

'You are no better! Take your hands off me!'

Schreber aimed a kick at the man's head.

'I demand to be taken home! I do not belong here! I cannot live among these cursed play-with-human-beings! I am a respectable man. I am a judge! I could have the lot of you put away! I could have you executed!'

Alexander was in the doorway and Schreber turned on him.

'This Jew, he follows me everywhere! He knows everything. Get off me! It is him you should be grabbing. He must be punished. Call for the police!'

'What's all this?'

'Müller! Take me back to my room. I intend to leave tonight. And tell this Jew to keep away from me.'

'What Jew?'

'Him!'

Schreber pointed directly at Alexander, who nodded and lit a cigarette.

'Who?'

Schreber jumped down and grabbed the Jew by the collar, and dragged him forward.

'This man! Are you blind? Keep him away from me!'

Müller looked at the other orderlies.

'When did all this start?'

One of them shrugged, the others looked away.

'Right. Come with me, Judge; let's see if we can't get you settled into your new place.'

Müller put one arm around Schreber and lifted him over his shoulder. Schreber kicked and struggled but the orderly was too strong for him.

'I am not a prisoner!'

'Stop wriggling!'

'I cannot be kept against my will!'

'That's right…' Müller said.

As he was taken out, Alexander walked behind him.

'It's not finished yet. Don't despair!'

'Get away from me! Call for the police! If I wish to leave I must be allowed to do so!'

'That's right…' Müller said.

'Sabine! I want Sabine!'

'That's right…'

'Find her! Get away from me! I don't want to go!'

'That's right…'

Schreber is introduced to his cell. Despite his efforts, he is not able to secure his return to the world above ground. Müller's attitude is less respectful here than it was above.

XIX

The cell had a single barred window like a letter slot. It was set high in the wall of the cell, low to the ground outside. The wall was thick and there was no view, except an oblique slice of a small yard where black-skinned coalmen delivered, and where their horses pissed onto the ground. At the correct angle Schreber could see as much as he liked of the side of a drayman's boot, or of the evacuations of that same man's horse, but nothing of the sky or of the sun.

No trees.

He turned away from the window.

The room itself scarcely deserved the name. A room, at the least, exists to encapsulate bare space so that it might be accorded a function. At the least, it offers a man something that its absence could not offer him. That it shelters is one condition, but it is not sufficient—a tree might give shelter, a cave, a box, any enclosed object of sufficient size, all these things might give shelter. A room must also do something else. A bathroom contains a bath, a bedroom a bed, a kitchen an oven, and the rooms so furnished are given a purpose: a bathroom becomes a room that allows a man to wash, a bedroom to sleep, a kitchen to cook. This room was nothing like that. It did not even provide shelter. Not adequately. It was cold and damp and the wind rattled the pane of glass in its frame. It was utterly empty of objects, except as much as dead insects—a spider and a fly—might be classed as objects. There was no bed, no bath, no oven. It was only once a man was in the room that it took on a function: it became a cell, a place that enclosed the space between its walls and within which a man was contained. Should he be taken out of it, that place would cease to be a room and become what it was—walls, a floor, and a ceiling.

Schreber ran his hand over the brick onto which no plaster had been placed and from which the paint curled and blistered. He scratched with his shoe on the floor, which was not wood, but seemed to have been shaped from the clay on which the asylum rested. It was neither properly hard nor even. There was a smell of mould, or mildew—strong and peaty—as if he was buried already in soil. He took two steps back and only stopped when he met Müller's chest with his back. Schreber turned and poked at the orderly. 'I cannot be left here. It is not sanitary.'

Müller snorted and took the finger in his fist. He didn't squeeze it, or twist it, but when he spoke it was as if he might.

'Don't you like it?'

'It is like the grave. I will not be buried.'

Müller moved Schreber's finger down, and the arm with it. When he let it go, it stayed where it had been put, but Müller's hand went to his chest and from a pocket he took a flask and drank from it. Whatever was in it made Müller blink and swallow hard.

'The doctor believes,' he said, after a cough, 'that with a different regime, one without all the fanciness, you might be able to sort yourself out—that is exactly what he said to me, *verbatim*—and when I've bedded you in he will come down and check on how you're getting along. He said,' and here Müller did a little impression of the doctor, crouching down, 'after no time, perhaps as little as a week or a month, you will find yourself better.' Müller smirked and stood back up straight. 'In any case, you'll be down here nice and quiet, not up there making a nuisance of yourself and acting like Lord Muck and grabbing your betters by the collar. Right?'

'I will return to my rooms in a week? He said this?'

'That's what he said.' Müller took the flask out again and shook it by his ear, listening to the sound of a little liquid, sloshing backward and forward.

'In a week, then?' Schreber said.

'If there's a room, and all being well.'

'And what of my medicine?'

Müller looked back at the door. There was the trolley and on it were bottles and glasses. Müller pursed his lips and swallowed.

'That's my concern.'

The orderly was different down here. Larger in the dark than he was upstairs in the light, the breadth of the doorway and almost as high.

'Is there a lamp?'

Müller shook his head slowly.

'Light comes into the room through the grill above the door. When I want you to have light, you'll have light, and when I don't want you to, you won't.'

'There is no wardrobe, no wash stand, and no desk.'

'You won't need them, because you'll be wearing a gown, and I'll bring in a bath and a bucket if you need one. You need to rest your nerves.'

'I don't like it.'

'You aren't supposed to.'

'He promised me I'd be going home!'

'I don't think he sees it like that.'

'Send message to my wife that I must be taken home immediately, whatever the consequences.'

'Well, you'd need to talk to Rössler about that. And he isn't here. And he doesn't come here, either.'

'This is not acceptable! I want my wife!'

Müller backed out of the door, keeping Schreber at arm's length with no more effort than would be required to stop a child from crossing in front of a tram. He turned the key in the lock and left, whistling. He didn't miss a note, no matter how hard Schreber banged on the door with his fists. No matter how loudly he shouted after him, or what names he called him, he whistled and as he took the first step up the stairs, setting the wood creaking, he sang:

> 'Oh, why did Mother Nature make
> Me only a lady's chambermaid?'

Schreber ran to the wall into which the window was set. He reached as high as he could manage, but his fingers were still inches short of the glass. He looked around for something to stand on, knowing before he did it that there was nothing. He stepped back, and through the glass he could see the sockless ankles and calves of a boy in shorts with stiff leather dress shoes two sizes too big. Schreber shouted up to him.

'Hey! Boy!'

The boy's shoes rubbed the skin at his heels as he trotted backward and forward, blistering them. He was carrying something from the cart to his master. Back and forward. Time and again.

'Boy!'

No sign of recognition, just bare legs and the occasional glimpse of his shorts when he stooped or bent at the knee.

The glass was too thick.

Schreber took off his shoe and hurled it as hard as he could at the window. The glass did not break but the sound did at least attract the boy. He stopped still and the shoes edged from side to side, turning slowly to face the source of the sound. One shoe tapped the glass with its toe. Schreber picked up his own shoe and threw it back again. The boy stepped back.

'Help me!'

Suddenly, at the window, a face appeared—a boy's face—smudged black as a negro's. He looked around, searching, puzzled. Schreber waved his arms and the boy saw him. There was a moment when their eyes met and then the boy's face split in a smile, his teeth and the whites of his eyes bright like the white keys of a piano next to the black. Schreber smiled back at him and gestured to the window that the child should open it. The boy began to laugh and Schreber, too, felt like laughing. He tried to make his intentions known, miming the opening of a window and the more he mimed the harder the child laughed. He nodded and laughed and pointed and Schreber mimed all the harder, acting out how he would climb up and out of the window, or allow himself to be pulled up by a rope. The boy nodded and shook with laughter, sitting down cross-legged in front of the window, and if Schreber let up his act, the boy tapped on the window and waved him on. When Schreber got out of breath and had to take a rest, the child gestured to someone off stage and then there were two black faces at the window, the second one much older—his grandfather?—and when this man smiled his teeth were not white but were tobacco brown—those that had not been lost.

Schreber mimed the opening of the window again, and the two faces laughed together. Then the boy stuck out his tongue. It was pink and wet and he waggled it up and down.

Schreber stopped his miming.

The boy put fingers in either side of his mouth and pulled so that it became wide and he rolled his eyes. The grandfather knocked on the window, and when Schreber turned a little to look at him he pulled his top lip up and his bottom lip down, and swayed from side to side. When he tired of this he made a pained face and banged on the sides of his head with his fists. The boy and his grandfather laughed and laughed, and Schreber watched them with only one shoe on and his toes becoming stiff with the cold. They wanted to see more, and they banged on the window, but then they were moved away. By an orderly? By Müller? Schreber could not see.

An hour later, a workman came to board over the window.

As the day went on and Müller did not return, Schreber waited.

This could not go on! Sabine would be told, and when she realised what was happening she would come for him. It was simply a matter of waiting.

What light came through the cracks in the window boards gradually blurred into darkness. He made a clicking sound with his tongue, by accident. Nothing. In the general course of a day that click would not have been noticed. It would have been masked by other sounds of more interest and import. It was a body sound: like the creaking of bones, or the rustle of flesh on flesh when dry fingertips are rubbed together, but in the absence of anything else this clicking of his tongue boomed. The meaningless clicking of his tongue—a vacuum accidentally caused between that organ and the palate as he swallowed with a dry mouth—echoed. Schreber made the clicking sound again. And again.

What is to become of the whole cursed affair?

If there had been anyone there to hear him, they would have been struck by the impression that Schreber was imitating a beetle—a cricket or a scarab—and when night fell Schreber was still clicking to himself.

The body will rot and the head (will go on living).

In the night there was a crowd, it must have been six, seven, at least, all hooting and shouting. Women too, singing. Lasciviousness. Ribaldry. Knowing cackles and lewdness, and the women standing for it. Enjoying it.

Someone banged on the door with the metal tip of a cane, and Schreber pulled back so that his shoulders curved and fitted into the right angle two walls made.

There was silence. He moved further, so that he was pressed into the corner.

More silence.

They moved on to the next door.

Now banging.

Müller, drunk.

Shouting.

Singing.

The next door opened.

'Where is he, the old fool?'

'Get him up!'

'I can't see him! Where are you? Oh, my lord!'

There was laughing. Apoplectic laughing. It went on for an age, and each time it seemed to stop it began again. Women and men. Dirty laughing and banging.

Then the door shut and it was muffled.

Schreber sprang up.

Enough of this!

He stood below the window and rubbed his hands together.

Whooping and clapping.

He inhaled sharply and jumped, stretching up. His fingers met the sill of the window before he came down—it was no more than an inch deep, nothing to hold onto.

He brushed off his shirt and tried again, this time succeeding in gripping one of the bars. Was there give in it? There was give in it! Only a little, like a tooth one suspects of being loose, but enough. He dangled by one arm from the bar. A little give!

'Judge! Your breakfast is here.'

A tray slid through into the cell, and while the hatch was still open Schreber could almost see the world outside the door— polished flagstones, another door across the corridor—and then the hatch closed, and it was gone. Müller's eye appeared at the peephole.

'Come and get it, Judge.'

Dry toast, porridge, and a glass of water.

Schreber stayed where he was.

'Well, you play it like that.'

The eye retreated and silence returned to the room.

Schreber scrambled over to the window and was up again, swinging from the bar. And now a little dust! Falling into his eyes as he looked up.

Müller's eye was back at the hole.

'What are you up to?'

Schreber dropped to the ground. He wiped the dust from his eyes and put his fingers to his lips.

'Nothing to say, Judge? Sulking? I suppose you think you've got good reason to sulk, left alone with no mattress, and your own company. Don't blame me. Rössler said you ought to go for a little while without your little comforts, on account of how luxury and rich food, such as what you've been getting upstairs, can contribute to confusion and bad temper brought on by indigestion. Poisonous influences. Making you misbehave. That's what he said. Giving you a false impression of yourself. Making you think you're better than you are. Walking around the place with your nose back like you've got shit on your lip.' Müller chuckled to himself and Schreber could tell he had been drinking by the edges of his words, which were dull and heavy. 'I don't want to be here either, do I? By rights I should own this place. Karl should. We'd work the land together. But no. Expensive lot, you lawyers. And bloody useless. So now I'm Rössler's man. I just do what he says, and if he says that Herr Schreber should be on dry toast and porridge and that I shouldn't rush to get him his mattress, then I just do what he says. You understand that, right? Just following the law? Right, Judge? Nothing personal. Blind justice…'

The eye blinked and retreated, returning almost immediately, pressed up as tight as it would go.

'What's the point of me coming down this end of the corridor anyway, if I'm not supposed to aggravate you? Leave him to his own devices, he said. Let him get settled, he said. Stop aggravating him, he said. So that's what I'm doing.'

Müller stopped talking, but the eye remained, turning circles. When it left, the talk returned.

'Don't think I've forgotten about you, just because you've been stuck down here. I remember you, don't worry about that. I'm always thinking about you. About what you've done. What you are…'

Beneath the door Schreber could make out Müller's boots shuffling back and forward.

'You want a blanket? Have a blanket.'

The hatch opened and a neatly folded blanket was shoved through.

'Don't say I don't do anything for you. That's a good blanket. It's got holes in it, but so what? You think you deserve better? That's the best you're going to get. Anyway, doesn't seem right to put the good ones down here when they could be better used upstairs where the boys are more likely to notice the difference. Not like your lot, who can't tell the difference between a blanket and a nice fur rug. And even if you can, then so what? So what?'

The blanket lay there by the tray, and Schreber made no move toward either of them.

'Boy down the corridor passed on last night, God bless him! You hear all that? Some problem with his chest. Banging on it like a drum he was! His mouth was open, and his eyes were popping out. Quite a sight, I can tell you! We all thought so… Nothing I could do for him. The doctors won't be woken. They're very determined about that. So I didn't even ring for them. He's still in there. The men from the city are coming for him. Sent a boy round to his family house and it turns out they moved on a couple years back and no one knows where they went. Shame. Isn't that a shame? Right?'

Müller went quiet and the eye disappeared, but Schreber wasn't fooled. He could see his shadow beneath the door.

'Come on now, Judge, it's time for your porridge. You can't tell me you're not hungry. You haven't eaten for days and even you must be feeling it. No? Suit yourself, I've got work to do.'

Schreber didn't move. He heard the orderly's breath catch on the back of his throat and whistle through the gaps in his teeth. His mouth would be half open, as it always was, waiting for a reply that would never come.

Dust!

After a long silence there was the sound of an argument—half of it: Müller's side—loud and hard, and punctuated with derisive laughter. Perhaps, very faint, the protestations of another man, which came at last to nothing.

There had been a time, not so long ago—two years? Three? Certainly not more than three—when Sabine had said to him: "Is that where an eagle makes its home?" She indicated the top of a tall tree at some remove, and Schreber gave her a little lecture on the birds of the region, Bohemia, and on the constancy evidenced in the mating habits of certain species of those birds. Though he was not a man given to excessive shows of public affection, he took her by the waist and drew her to him and kissed her, thinking to draw a comparison between their love and that noble fidelity displayed by the eagles. Though she pulled away and made a fuss of her dress and the arrangement of her skirts, she smiled at the corners of her eyes and Schreber felt in himself a perfect and wonderful contentment for the span of several moments, long enough to watch a bird swoop between two distantly spaced treetops, and for Sabine to correct the disarray he had unwittingly brought about.

He reached up with his other hand and, holding two bars now, he planted his feet against the wall and pushed until it felt as if his arms would come out of their sockets.

'Well, Judge, what you were expecting? Where Rössler'll tell you with a harsh word, down here I use a tug on your ear, or a little slap, just so you know where you are. It's nothing personal, it's just easier that way. I've got to keep you in line. Otherwise it's all talk, talk, talk. Half of it doesn't make sense, and the other half goes round in circles, and there's not much you can say to a jab in the ribs with a night stick is there? When you are doing things you know you shouldn't. Like hanging from the window. And you might get a bit of a shove when it's needed, friendly like, to get you to do something your peculiar way of looking at the world says you oughtn't to do, but what we all know you have to do anyway. Like eat.

'Upstairs I'd talk you round. Give you a choice bit of ham, or a nice boiled egg, because if you're up there that's the kind of thing that might work on you. Because you wouldn't be one of the dyed-in-the-wool lunatics. Down here, though? If you don't eat your porridge by yourself, Judge, then one way or the other you'll find someone will make you. If that means I have to force the spoon past your teeth and hold your nose until you choke, then that is what I will do. Nothing personal. Doctor's orders. I do what I'm told. A man's got to eat his porridge, whether he thinks he's got a stomach or not.

'Take the new boy next to you. William, his name is. Ironmonger. Now, he reckons all his food is painted on his plate. You give him his dinner and he looks at you like you're the one who's mad, not him. He won't be told. So what is there to do? Should I stand there and talk him out of it? I haven't got the time, Judge, even if I thought he'd listen. Which he wouldn't. So I pinch his snout until he has to open his mouth to breathe and when he does, I shove something in there and clamp it shut. He doesn't like it! Why would he? But he has to swallow in the end or I won't let him breathe. Simple. I'm in and out in a couple of shakes and on to the next. A clever sort like yourself can see the sense of that I'm sure, Judge.

'What else can I do? I can't let you all starve to death. The doctors don't take kindly to it. They won't come down here—that's more than their lives are worth—but they do expect those that they send down here to come back up when they're called for. They want them alive and paying their bills, not dead and returned to the loving breast and all that. I suppose you think I'm a bit cynical? Well, we'll see how you feel in a couple of months.

'I've got boys who've been down here since the place opened. The doctors don't see them anymore, haven't done for as long as I've been here. I give them their medicine, and they don't get better. They never get called for, no one comes to see them. What's the point of that? Except that someone's paying the bills? Keeping the buggers out of the way, so that they don't cause a fuss at home. I'm sure you can sympathise. Didn't go down too well back at yours, I suppose, all that bellowing and touching yourself up when you think no one's looking. Dressing up in the missus's knickers and giving yourself one in the manner of Onan from the Bible when you think she's calling on a lady friend. And then she comes back early? They don't like it, these prim and proper types. Frightening the guests with your talk of devils, and phantoms, and ghosts, and all that other scary stuff. Not the done thing at all, is it?

'Not that I'm saying she's got you out of the way down here on purpose, but being as she's had a stroke and mightn't be expected to look after a normal husband, let alone a barker, well, where's her choice? You lot—you loonies—all you think about is yourselves and your mad ideas. Well, I have to tell you, it's harder looking after you buggers than it is being mad yourself. Do you know that? Who do you think clears up after you? Who do you think has to listen to the gibberish you come out with? It's hard enough for me—who doesn't care what happens to you as long as I get my money—but those wives and children? What about those poor sods, watching you lot go to rack and ruin? It breaks my heart to think of it.

'So you'll understand if I don't feel too sorry for you, won't you, Judge? Not to mention I don't like judges. Not after what they did to Karl. You didn't know him, I suppose, my Karl. Did you? No? Guillotined. Fitted up. Tried and chopped.

'So, there you go. I'm not one for judges. In general. That's not to say I blame you, Judge. I don't. I know you had nothing to do with it. You didn't did you? No? Just you have that manner. High and mighty. Holier than thou. Even down here. Even when you're waist deep in your own shite you try it on. Reminds me sometimes.

'Anyway, are you going to eat that porridge, or am I going to have to help you? It's good. Same as the stuff they get upstairs. Bit less milk and a bit more water but the same oats. Plenty of salt, so there's no need to turn your nose up at it. I have it myself, when I have the time. When I'm not wiping old boys' arses and listening to their rubbish. There's another one like you down the hall. He thinks God has a thing for him too. It's quite common. You ask the other orderlies about it. There's always some silly sod who reckons God has a plan for him down here. You're not the worst. Christ, no! You're bad, don't get me wrong, otherwise you wouldn't be down here, but you're nothing compared to some of them. We had one a few years back, just after we opened, *he thought he was God!* Convinced of it. Didn't last long. Got cholera. Since then we've had the drains redone.

'Right—I've got to run along so we'll have that porridge started and finished right now, or I'll have to take measures. No use pretending you're asleep either. I can tell from the way you're breathing that you're pretending. It's not as easy as it looks! Everyone gets it wrong. You, for example, breathe too slow and regular. And you're too still. You'd know, if you'd ever worked the night shift down here, and if you'd ever done the night checks, that no one sleeps that still. Least of all you lot! It's all legs twitching, and twisted blankets, and gob wide open, and choking sounds, and farts, and all of that. No one sleeps nice and quietly on their side. So sit up, before I sit you up, and get your teeth round this porridge, because that's the easiest way for both of us, and I wouldn't want my natural good-heartedness to be temporarily overcome by my hatred of wig-wearers, even retired ones.'

Schreber has a visitor.
There is a disagreement
between them.

XX

Schreber's shirt itched at the collar—too much starch. His jacket
was heavy and damp. It smelt of hand-rolled cigarettes and beef
dripping. Cheap beer. He put his hand in the chest pocket and
pulled out a tram ticket.

'What is today's date?'

Müller put the brakes on the chair and came round to the
front. He set his feet apart, put his hands on his knees, and took
a long look. Schreber waited for a reply. Müller made none.
Instead, he licked the corner of his handkerchief and with it he
wiped a smudge from Schreber's cheek.

'That'll do… not perfect, but…'

'The date?'

'Fifteenth.'

The date on the ticket was the fourteenth.

'Was it raining yesterday evening?'

Müller put one foot on the front wheel of the Bath
chair, to stop it moving, and pulled Schreber toward him
by his lapels.

'For a man who won't eat his porridge, you really do weigh a lot.'

'When you took my jacket, was it raining?'

When Schreber was standing Müller dusted him down, patted him flat and, as a last touch, took his comb and ran it through the old man's hair.

'Not bad at all…'

'Herr Müller, you cannot fool me.'

'Amazing what a bit of spit and a hankie can achieve.'

'I know that you have been wearing my clothes.'

'Now, Herr Schreber, are you ready for your visitor?'

Once in Rössler's office, Schreber could not sit still. He peered over his shoulder, back at the door. He jerked towards the window. He looked down at the floor underneath the desk. He felt in his bones a sensation like that pain one has while moving from boyhood to adolescence—an ache—and with it, not quite completely distinct from it, was the idea that he was about to do something wrong. Guilt in advance for something he had not yet decided to do.

He shuffled, setting off a crackle of static between the fibres of his clothes and the red velvet seat cushion. Through the window the garden was vivid green. He licked his lips and when he coughed it was like he'd let off a firecracker. He turned to look at the door. Nothing.

He bit his lip and stood up. Half a dozen steps and he could unlatch and open the window. Very easy. He paused, and in that time he saw every object in that room: Rössler's eye glasses upside down on a pile of papers; his pen beside them; the grit left by wine in the bottom of a wide-bowled glass; the trace of an outline snaking up that same glass almost to the rim where the wine had dried away; the smudge of Rössler's lips; his neck-tie, curled like a snail shell and put on the table; the scuff in the rug where the doctor rested his feet and the weft aligned in the opposite direction to the rest of the fabric; a segment of orange on a saucer; a ball of paper marked by the shadow of the ink on its inner surface, words written in reverse and transformed by crumpling into nonsense and already discarded anyway. On top of it all was the insistent sound of Schreber's breathing.

Then the door handle turned and he sat down quickly.

All the things before him faded into the background except one: the door knob. It was dull pewter and secured by screws to the turning mechanism. The knob was marked, perhaps by the workmen who had attached it, scratched and dulled by their tools. Schreber sniffed. The door only opened a little, but he could hear Rössler, his tone strangely subdued. If he leaned forward he could see the knuckles of the doctor's right hand—his ring, with the eagle crest, that sometimes he rotated one way and then the other when he was talking, or when he was thinking and was not to be interrupted.

He stood in the doorway and said:

'We are doing our best for him, Frau Jung, but the progress, if there is any, is very gradual.'

Schreber didn't hear the response, but the door swung toward him by six inches so that Rössler's arm was visible, his wrist appearing out of his sleeve, thin and then bulbous like a burr on a branch. Then, without warning, the door almost closed, the catch resting on the door jamb, where it knocked on the wood in response to every breath of wind. Schreber sniffed.

Frau Jung?

He turned to the window again. Half a dozen steps… but now, rather than see the room and its every detail, he saw nothing clearly. Everything around him lost colour and detail and became a whirl, such as is seen when observing a zoetrope before the proper rate of turning is achieved. Objects were a smear of something on the retina, nothing that could be made sense of. He shut his eyes and massaged them, and in the blackness he saw women and girls, and then one girl in particular, a girl he had seen when coming upon her unannounced—he too young to be the source of concern, only a boy—with her foot on a stool, her petticoat raised up to her thigh, and between her legs only darkness. She chided him, 'Get out, little boy,' but with a smile, and her legs opened wider if anything, her hand running down to it, pulling across her drawers. He turned and ran.

Schreber sniffed and the door opened again. This time it came wide, and Rössler was standing in the doorway. Without his glasses he looked very old indeed, the eyes like black marbles, lost in their orbits. When he brought his hand up to his face he found nothing to push up, and he had to let it fall back down by his side, loose and unfulfilled.

'We need another chair...' he said.

Rössler went to that part of the room where he sometimes ate meals and took the chair from the round folding table temporarily draped with white lace, and moved it beside Schreber's, at a distance of perhaps six feet.

Into the room came a woman.

She was familiar, something in the sweep of the skin that led from the bridge of the nose to the cheekbones, and also in the deep set of her eyes, and the bulge above her eyebrows, and the hairline that took the beginning of the hair so far back that it started to become masculine. She was familiar. Like someone he knew: not that person, whoever it was, but like her. She looked at him as if she knew him. It was not how Rössler looked at him: not like a doctor, who examines a man every time he sees him as if it is the first time, to make certain that there is not something important in the appearance that he might otherwise miss. Even while a person speaks, the doctor watches everything, down to the colour of the lips and the clearness of the eye. This woman's attention had nothing of that quality, but instead she made contact directly with him, only breaking it to give the most cursory glance around, as if assuring herself that she was safe to ignore everything else. Her expression gave Schreber to believe that she was pleased to see him, as a woman might be pleased to see someone she loves and who has worried her by his absence.

Who was she?

Rössler stepped between them, briefly, and then stood at a point equidistant, like the priest does at a wedding, or the referee at a boxing match. While they looked at each other, he mediated, outlining the rules of engagement, and then he left with his words still ringing in the air: that she might get his attention by use of the bell on the desk, and that an assistant would come at the shortest of notice, she need only call out.

Neither of them moved for several moments, and the connection between them was not broken until the woman broke it, and for all that time Schreber could not understand who she was, although she looked just like someone. His mother? His father? His sister? But she was an old woman.

'Is there anything you want to say, Paul?'

Schreber shifted his attention to her mouth. Her lips were smooth and pink, like Anna's, only the skin that connected them to her face was lined. She was like Anna, only drained somehow. The flesh of her face was dried like a flower that is pressed between the pages of a book, the water drawn out so that, if there is ink on the pages—if it is a book that has been used in extremis, a book of psalms used where no proper pressing book was present—that ink is blurred, and the words are only just comprehensible: *so my redeemer liveth*, or some such nonsense. She was the same, like Anna, but pressed and dried. Like the flower book, the room around her seemed incomprehensible now she was here, as if the missing vitality had leaked out, had been drawn out by the room, smudging everything.

'Are you Anna?'

Anna sat in the seat opposite Schreber and crossed her hands on her lap. She smiled, but said nothing. She watched him and he watched her, his words hanging in the air unanswered. She wore black, though to mourn whom he could not tell. When she moved her hands her dress rustled, and when she breathed there was a rustling too—dry and sharp and quiet—coming from somewhere deep inside her.

'What do you want from me, Paul?'

The words fell dead in the room and Schreber could not think of a reply.

'What do you mean?'

She squirmed in her chair. Rustling. Camphor.

'You called me here,' she sighed. 'You begged me to come, if I'm to believe the doctor. He tells me a lot of things. Things I do not understand.'

'I don't want you for anything,' whoever you are…

'Then why ask for me to come? Do you think I've nothing better to do?'

'I am sorry.' Schreber smiled at the woman. Would this be an end to it? If he rose now and walked to the door would she simply take her leave of him?

If he went to the window?

He got to his feet, but the woman did not join him.

Instead, she was picking over every detail of him. Schreber saw himself in the mirror above the fireplace: a sallow-faced fool with wide eyes who twitched like a bird, and fidgeted. His clothes were inches to big for him, the shirt not even touching the skin of his neck, his arms poking through the sleeves, and the lapels of his jacket meeting and crossing where they should have been a finger's width apart. And beside him was this woman and it was obvious, immediately, who she was. His sister.

Schreber nodded.

Anna.

His elder sister.

She turned to see where he was looking and met his gaze in the mirror.

How must he look to her? Standing beside her in the mirror…
a believer of tragic nonsense? Could she see her brother in
this man in front of her? Was he like the boy he had been? It
was clear that he was not. He would never regain that lively
attention that had so characterised him, even as a boy, and that
questioning mind, and now here was only a parody. She might
easily walk out of this place and never return.

'Do you remember that day, Anna?' Schreber said, 'When he
came to get us? He was in his uniform. He took you first from
the schoolhouse and then both of you came for me? Mother
took the little girls to town for new dresses and Gustav was in
the woods with the *turnverein*? Do you remember? I don't know
what fancy took him, or whether he had no choice, but he took
us by carriage to his club. Do you remember that day? They all
thought we were marvellous, the militia-men, and I sat on his
one knee, and you were on the other. That big wooden table,
picking sweetmeats off a metal dish, while they sang songs. Do
you remember?'

She smiled and nodded.

She must remember it: her father and her brother and the
sound of song, a marching song—"Fridericus Rex"—the men
puffing out their chests, and her mouth full of candied figs. She
would have seen the smile on her brother's face, as if he had
been born a prince. Perhaps she felt it too, in the company of
these strong men whose buttons shone and whose faces were
red, caught up in the manliness of their song, its martial theme
undercut by the winks that met her whenever she caught their
eyes. Their father's attention was turned around the room,
and not on them, so content was he for them to be part of his
world. They were contained by his aura and within arm's reach
so that he felt no need to watch for transgressions, and they felt
no need to commit them. Paul tried to sing, picking up the
lines that were repeated, joining in with the chorus, his mouth
open so that she could see the chewed mess inside. It escaped

the attention of his father, and the other men did not care, so why should she? So she sang too, a few lines, and this made the men clap, and they egged her on, and when they stopped she volunteered a little recital of her own—*The Little Dog that Swims in the Rhine*—and they all clapped along, and from there the memory faded, and Schreber was singing under his breath that very song, and in his eyes there were tears.

'"The Little Dog that Swims in the Rhine,"' she said.

'I am kept in a cell, dearest Anna. Can that be right?'

She sighed and crossed her hands once more over her lap.

'You are very ill, brother.'

'Am I?'

'Your illness has returned, and you must be treated as the doctor sees fit. It is only by virtue of my knowing the Gerhardt widow that you are not in jail. The first year we had hope… But now your doctor…'

'He is a fraud.'

'He is not.'

Schreber nodded and there was silence again.

'What were you thinking of? To abuse the Gerhardt girl in that way! I still do not understand.'

'It was nothing.'

'Hardly! They were intent on having you prosecuted. I had to *beg*—do you understand?—*beg*. When will you realise…'

'She was nothing. A plaything.'

Anna pursed her lips and stared at the back of her hands.

'Do you intend to write?' she asked, and the question was so carefully spoken, so stripped of inflection or weight, so studiously neutral, that Schreber understood even without hearing her thoughts that it was the question she had come here to ask.

He answered plainly.

'I cannot. When I try, I find the paper suddenly gone. Or the pen. Or I awake somewhere else, on a different day, and my thoughts are elsewhere.'

'Very good. I will not hide the fact that I am relieved.'

'Let's not discuss this matter again, Anna. It is as nothing.'

'To you perhaps.'

Schreber returned to his seat and took his sister's hand. She pulled away, at first, but then thought better of it, putting her other hand atop his.

'I am sorry to have caused you trouble,' Schreber said. 'My intention was honourable. I hoped to help you understand… I am a little surprised it has caused you such worry. Isn't it just the thing we used to sit and talk of? Astronomy, theology, politics? And it is only one book! Think of the many, many books of our father's that are published. I have the publisher's contracts if you wish to see them. They are at home in the bureau. I have taken great care that Father's work be given its best advantage, and they sell wonderfully well. There is a good income to be had from them still, to this day. Do not concern yourself over the words of one nerve case. Mere supposition… nothing when compared to his great words.'

Anna brought a handkerchief up to her nose and blew it.

'You underestimate the interest in scandal. Still, if you are content to write nothing else, then the matter is closed.'

'Can you take me home, Anna? I feel I will die here.'

'Dr. Rössler tells me you believe yourself to be pregnant. He tells me that you believe God has given you children.'

'I have said no such thing! I want to be taken home.'

'He says you believe yourself to be in a colony of the Monist Confederacy. That you are rotting away.'

'I have only been here a matter of weeks. I have told him nothing. Please take me home.'

Anna frowned and began to say something, to correct some false opinion of Schreber's, but she seemed to think better of it, and the moment passed.

'And what would you do at home, if I took you there?'

'What do you mean?'

'What good would it do?'

Schreber stood up abruptly, and while he did not intend to push the chair over it fell anyway, clattering against the table and knocking off a glass that was too close to one edge.

'Why do you question me? Is it not enough for a man to wish to be in his own home, amongst those things he recognises, in charge of his own household? If I wish to return home, then why shouldn't I?'

He would have shouted—he intended to shout this all out—but there was something in his chest—pain—that made it impossible to muster the force and instead it came out like an insistent hiss. Schreber coughed and banged his fist on his chest but it made no difference.

Now Anna stood up.

'I will not be harangued!'

'Don't go, please! I am not well. I want to be among the people I love. These men... I am surrounded by dogs. I despise them! They treat me as if I were a fool... worse! A criminal or a child. I see you and now I realise that I *must* leave here. Is that too much to ask?'

Anna turned her back on him but she did not leave.

Schreber came over to her and gently turned her by the shoulders. Anna took a deep breath.

'Your wife... if there is an obstacle...'

'Sabine? How is she? If she is unwell, then we will hire more help.'

'She is well. She is almost entirely recovered. That is not the issue.'

'Send her here.'

'I cannot dictate to your wife, Paul, nor even her daughter. No one can, as surely you must know.'

'She must come! *I* demand it.'

'Let go of me!'

'No! Did you bring Mother's clock here?'

Anna lurched for the bell on the desk, but Schreber held her. 'Did you bring her clock here? It is a very simple question.'

She twisted free and stood straight.

'You already know that I did, brother.'

'I know nothing of the sort.'

'I told you the first time I came here. You told me that I had forgotten the key. You became angry. I told you that all clock keys are the same. They are all the same!'

She rubbed her shoulder and took slow steps back until she could open the door. When she turned away, finally, she looked just like she did as a girl—in her profile, at least.

'But you hate glass!' he hissed.

'Goodbye, brother.'

'I carry the glass things! Because you are frightened of them. It is for me to carry the clock! What if the glass were to break? Don't you need me to carry the clock anymore?'

She stood with her back to him in the open doorway. She did not look back.

'Goodbye, brother. Take care,' she said, and she left.

Schreber stood in the empty room, with his hands reaching out, and it was only after Müller came in for him, and strapped him into the Bath chair, that he remembered the window.

In the darkness of his cell, where a hand is not visible even when placed directly before the eyes, and Müller has still not arrived with the mattress, Schreber considers the accident that changed his father from a man of energy to a migrainous wreck. He is shown a series of disturbing anatomical diagrams, and recalls the degeneracy of some common boys.

XXI

He was so suddenly changed, Father, from the man who took two stairs for every one an ordinary man took—or even three—and who cartwheeled down the garden in his vest. Once, Paul had watched him break the ice on the lake with his fists before diving in.

When he came up again he bellowed like an ox.

But after the accident? His head was bowed and when he climbed the stairs back to bed in the afternoon he gripped the rail until his nails shone out white against his red skin and the veins popped and snaked on the backs of his hands. They moved beneath the skin, slipping under pressure from the movement of his blood, and from the strain of his muscles and ligaments. The internal excess of heat boiled over at the indentation on his temple. He would take one hand from the rail—stopping altogether, halfway up—and bring his leading foot down a step. The scar on his head, where hair no longer grew, was like a crescent moon.

He could stop at any time, wherever he was, and he would hold perfectly still except for his lips, which trembled beneath his moustache. Those strong hands became tremorous, like dying birds, and hovered, fluttering, before landing where they fell.

To believe the muttering statue they saw before them was the same man who had flipped and turned and sprinted from one part of the garden to the other, a man whose children ran behind, laughing to see the exuberance in their father, a man who was also so proper that he did not think twice of beating them for their own benefit—for those two things to be the same? The idea was ridiculous!

If the children had stood around this statue and blasphemed Christ and God himself then it would not have been able to raise a hand to any of them, not even the youngest. The beating hand was clamped to its brow, and the other was required for support: holding a banister, or flat and splayed on a polished tabletop. Indeed, it was a matter of debate whether, during these spells, the statue could hear a thing, because it would not react—not to the whisperings of Mother or to the shouts of the children—and it was only after minutes, sometimes ten minutes at a time, that it would continue its progress to its room.

Even then it was slow: slower than anyone in that house. Slower even than the twisted children whom he had treated, to whom he had lowered himself to attend. Each one of them was quicker, even young Hans, whose legs were bowed from the knee to the ankle, so that if he stood in the right way, the way Gustav told him, his bones made the segments of a circle the remainder of which could easily be drawn in the mind's eye. Even that child could make the journey from top to bottom, creaking and complaining, crying, but it could be done in a fraction of the time it took that statue.

Its eyes were tight shut, protecting against everything: light, sound, the movement of the air in a room, the smell of coffee boiling, strawberries—anything at all—they were intolerable. There were times when it put its hand across its mouth, barring the progress of even the air in and out. But it was never enough.

The waft of the afternoon breeze was enough to set the nerves of its mind vibrating like a piano string, strung to such a high pitch that it was heard as pain throughout his body—in the bones and in the liver, scorching the bladder, evoking sympathetic responses in every organ. It did not stop there: the pain continued into the functions of the organs. There was pain in the purification of the liquors of the body, in the imagination that was generated in the mind, in the flow of blood around the body, in the receiving of visual perception. In all things where the representation of pain was possible, it came.

As if by miracle, this man was transformed from the exemplar of health—as the embodiment of his own words—and made into this bent and bowed statue. He was made into disease.

What of the man who wore the uniform, with brass buttons and a peaked cap? How could that man be made into this? By a fallen ladder? Impossible! By a bang to the head? By a cut the length of a finger? A slight—so slight!—depression in the skull, not even a fracture: a swelling, that was gone in a week or less, stitched and cleaned and under gauze so quickly that it was barely noticed? Incredible!

What could his father—who was so good, who knew the ways to be good and made them clear to all those people he met: to the crooked children in the Institute, to his own family, to everyone, through his words—what could he have done to deserve this punishment? The man who was the punisher, who decided on the best and most useful punishment, how could that man become the subject of punishment? There was no sense to it! No justice!

On those times when he stopped halfway up the stairs, it amounted to nothing when Paul begged his father to come back down. He did not come.

They all stood in the hall and wept for him.

His wife, their mother—she wanted so much for her husband. She was once so delighted to see the plans for this house, the

Institute, in which her husband was now imprisoned. She felt the excitement in her gut when the keystones were laid in place. She wept for joy on the first night they had slept here, the empty space around them ripe with becoming. Everything they had accounted for in their plans—so much space—room for a facility of world renown, a fit home for the man she believed her husband should be. The years that passed and the petty successes and failures of their ambition did nothing to dull her excitement, knowing as she did the essential worthiness of their cause, and that of the place itself. Now she wept, and when she passed the stairs, hoping to find her husband at his work but instead seeing him motionless halfway between flights, the tautness of his back stretching the fabric of his jacket and the air bristling with his pain, she wept, as did they all. As would anyone who had seen the head of their house reduced to that state. It was all made so much worse by remembering him as he was before: a man, strong and strict.

Made weak by nothing.

By an accident.

By God.

They were made angry too, despite their faith. If they would not admit it to themselves, the focus of this anger was God nonetheless.

When his father died and was laid in the coffin, Paul returned from university. The object laid out in the chapel was nothing like the father he had known. It was not only because the absence of life had taken the bloom from the face—that aura, unappreciated during life, but which is so clearly gone on the event of death—that might have been expected. It was not simply that this ineffable aspect of his father was missing; it was more than that. The man was shrunken. His father had been drained. His weight, his muscularity, his colour—everything that had been him—was taken away.

He was framed in wood and soft silk. His collar was buttoned high and tight. His lips were painted red and his eyes were lined with kohl, with the cheeks sunk in. It was very easy to imagine the skull. The jaw beneath the skin. The teeth. The hands were now nothing but raw bones, incapable of gripping anything, incapable of directing anything. If one were to pinch a wrist between forefinger and thumb there would be no effort required to move that wrist where one wished it to go, to make it do what one wished, regardless of its owner's desires and intentions.

Paul looked at him unblinking, as a man now—almost—but not a boy. He looked at him with a dispassionate eye. He took him for an object.

The cadaver was poor in appearance. If it had been said of his father that he was a small man and very slight, of unimpressive physique and inadequate health, then there was nothing in the box that might have been used to refute that statement. If claims were made to his father's brilliance and efficacy, and expectations given to a viewer of the contents of this box, his corpse would have raised an eyebrow, at least, and comments would have been made.

His mother laid her hand on his shoulder and smoothed his jacket. She put her hand on his hip and guided him away quietly, but he did not come. He stood and would not be moved.

He reached into the box, and his mother gasped. He took his father by the wrists, and lifted his arms.

'Paul!'

'He might sit up. If we tell him.'

'Paul!' Gustav stood between his brother and father, and the arms fell crooked against the chest.

'Why don't you tell him?'

His mother leant over the coffin, and Paul thought for a moment that she would do the work, attend to her husband as a wife ought to.

'Open his eyes!' he said, but she refused. She pushed Paul away when he came forward again, and it took Gustav to return him to his seat.

The box was lowered into the earth in the presence of hundreds. Those who had been unable to find space in the church were not dissuaded from attending the burial. They paid their respects. Men and women Paul had never seen: the parents of children who had been eased of their suffering. Readers of his father's works who imagined themselves close, though they had never met. Some of them dared to touch Paul, thinking to offer him solace, but it had the opposite effect, setting off spasms in his muscles.

His mother, after the funeral, with the ringing of the bells still in her ears, calmly took everything of his father's—his shirts, his pictures, his books, his papers, his shoes, his favourite foods—took it all and piled it in the middle of the garden and set light to it. She rid herself of the connection, of the burden of her attachment to a man who was now dead. If Anna couldn't understand, if Gustav dragged her back to the house, the taper in her hand still burning, and the girls wept to see it, Paul understood. The pile of things over which was draped the long blue coat with the brass buttons, the pile from which the eyes of his father watched from broken framed portraits, it might still have remained untouched. Gustav exceeded himself in his authority, wondering how he should take the place his father had guarded jealously, unprepared and over hard in the execution of the role, holding their mother's arms behind her—even though she was not struggling—and on her face was serenity of the most plain kind, no hint of hysteria. Anna wore the emotion for all of them, shrieking at a pitch that would have shamed a banshee. If it had not been for Paul, who took the flame from his mother's hand and laid it at the base of the pile, those objects—those bonds of which his mother wished to free herself—would have been saved. Instead the smoke crawled along the grass, keeping low and dense.

Then the weeping of the girls, and the cracking of glass from the centre of the pyre, the leaking of water and sap from treated wood popping in the heat that built, his mother silent, her arms wrapped around herself, rocking a little from side to side. Here and there an orange flicker, like the lamps of boats out on the lake at night, seen from the far shore, obscured and revealed by the movement of waves. Slowly, from the top, darting jets of flame and then, after a while, fire everywhere, and then only fire and blackness, ever shrinking, until there was nothing but the coals that lie in the fireplace when the fire is exhausted.

Like his mother, when the fire was over, he felt unburdened, knowing there was nothing remaining to keep him in this place, and that he could do nothing but prepare himself for the trial that was to come. He must make clear his case, set forth, by action, his plea for clemency in the eyes of God, to atone for the sins of his father and for his own failures as a man. Because hadn't he failed? Even years later, wasn't he a failure? Didn't he adorn himself with robes and take the seat of a man who is given godly powers on earth? The power to decide, to know, to pass judgement on other men? Even on those other men who would judge too, abstracting himself from the world to apply the letter and word of the law. Blinding himself to the little facts of things: the coincidences and movements of objects through the world, the tides of men's wishes and desires—their intentions. He set himself the task of separating the chaff until only the truth remained. Then, scientifically, objectively, perfectly, measured this truth against the word of the Law. When that was done he turned his back on the matter, letting the others deal with the mess. The flood of matter that would need to be staunched, he left to others. The necks sliced, or the bodies caged. Just as the Inquisitors, the hated Catholics, had handed over the products of their courts to the secular wing so that they would not have to sully their office, their robes, with the blood of women and men, so his robes were unsullied, his office. Yet now, crouching in that cell, he knew that he was stained, as a man is always stained, and no office or garment could stand between him and his own judgement. It was not those small things of which he was accused, the deaths he had personally ordered, or the weeping, or the misery, but a much greater crime: a crime of the soul, to have lived when his father had died, when his brother had died, to have exceeded his proper authority.

Flesh. A man, his needs and desires and thoughts and memories: nothing. A machine of skin and bone and blood. Clockwork, like the Mechanical Turk. A device of exceptional cleverness, of immense complexity, but a machine nonetheless. An empty shell, that worked through its routines like a metal bird, singing though it is nothing but cogs and wheels and bellows. Without animus, its only motivation the twisting of the key in its back. Once that was withdrawn? Once the breath of life was removed? There would be nothing, like those beautiful children he had seen born, but who could not be compelled to live. As those that could not have the desire for life shaken into them, no more could this crouching figure be compelled to go on. Indeed, why should he?

He sat in the corner of his dark cell, in the darkest part of the night, without so much as a place to lie. The dust from the window frame gathered at the corners of his eyes, and he imagined himself in his father's box. He lay there in that box, to all appearances dead, appearing to be dead, but not dead. Boxed and buried, but the nerves so enlivened by God's presence that his consciousness survived in the corpse. He sat in the darkness deprived of all those things necessary to sustain existence, and he felt the closeness of the walnut and the silk, and felt the rotting of his own body, his devouring by insects, his putrefaction, and he longed to be dead, like his father was. Like his brother was. Like his children were.

In his dream, the room was full of them: less-than-men, hundreds crowding the hall. It was not just the similarity of their dress that was obvious—all of them in the same shirt and jacket, the same collar and cuffs, the same dark trousers tightly pressed—they had faces that repeated, expressions that repeated, selves, it seemed to him, that repeated. As he stood on the platform and looked down at them, elevated by his position, they cheered for him as the assistant to the *Landrat* came with the votes. The Socialist by his side, the only man who was different at all, reached to shake his hand, mouthing "Good luck!" He couldn't take his eyes from the men below in the crowd. He could see the same face—a waxy-faced man, with red cheeks and a curling moustache, dotted amongst the others—first a handful of times, but the more he looked, the more he saw him. That man was restricted to a very limited set of movements and expressions: a wave, a cheer, a nod of the head, a turning toward a companion, a whispered exchange, and then returning to the wave to begin the sequence again. When he looked closer, fully half of the men there were identical to this man and ran, out of sequence, the same set of gestures. In the pit of his stomach the nervousness he had felt, that he had been assured was excitement by the party men, the nervousness that had kept him awake for days and that had become as much a part of him as hunger, or the need to evacuate his bowels, that feeling changed into something else. It was something more intense, something felt in his bladder, and on the backs of his knees, and in the eagerness of the muscles of his thighs to be moving. Fear—there was no other word for it. Though the lighting in the room remained unchanged, the objects around him brightened while the air dimmed, giving everything an afterimage, like the negative of a photograph. It was not as clear or as obvious as that alteration, but there nonetheless and with an oppressive atmosphere that tickled the backs of his eyes.

He looked toward the exit through the throng of men who were all now identical and beginning to move in sequence. It was as if they were clocks all running at a different tempo, a fraction of a second out of time with each other, but whose dials were coming, by accident, to read the same time, down to the second. The coming together of their movements coincided with the progress of the *Landrat* up the steps to the stage, and when the Liberal leant over to shake his hand it was only with the greatest effort that Schreber was able to take it. Sweat pooled beneath the collar at the back of his shirt, and his mouth was utterly dry. It was clear that at the exact moment the returning officer would speak, so would the men of the crowd come to synchronicity.

So it proved, the moment of congruence resulting in their becoming still, in a gesture of listening, and the room was silent. Schreber could hear, loud as a bass drum, his heart beating, and the breath like a hurricane coming faster and faster from between his lips. Though he was sure he must have been seen and heard by everyone, no one paid him the slightest attention, and instead they watched the man in the centre of the platform.

He spoke.

Schreber lost the ability to understand words, and though he recognised they were German, the language of his father, he could not extract the meaning of them. It was as if they were in a confusing dialect, or spoken too quickly by a man with a heavy accent. Everything was partial and fragmented, of enormous significance, but with no meaning. The feeling in his stomach was intense to the point of hysteria, literal hysteria, as if a fearful woman's organ had been placed inside him and was flooding his body with the humours that brought so many of that sex to irrationality and emotional incontinence. He could feel it in himself, he who had been chosen by these clockwork men as an exemplar of something else: of masculinity, of continence, of fortitude and strength, of knowledge. Wasn't he a man who took after his father? They held him to be a great thinker—a great man—an opinion Schreber would never have disavowed. But he knew, as his family knew—even his mother—that the same man had been weak, bowed down by pain, despite his stoicism. Now if they could only see inside Schreber, their new ideal, who stood before them as a symbol of power and authority, inside him was the febrile machine of a woman's weakness. He could feel it, that terrible alien device that separated one sex from the other, making difference in them. That thing sent out its nerves throughout his body, experienced as pain and weakness and fear, exciting his own manly nerves, overtaking them, so that he felt all those things that a woman felt in place of those things that were right and proper to a man—calmness and inviolate courage. If they could have seen inside him, these men with their identical moustaches, they would have stopped listening to the *Landrat* and would have ridiculed him instead. They would have punished him, as he had been punished by his father on that day when he was found with Klara clutched to his chest. Her gentle sucking at his flat breast had filled him with an unaccountable joy, a joy that must be punished, a joy that was despised. The great hand coming down across the backs of his legs, and the flaming redness on his father's cheeks was like the redness in the cheeks of these clockwork men.

More words were being spoken, calculations made on the lips of the men in the crowd, men reacting, the turning of backs. If it hadn't been for the potency of that organ within him that now shook his knees with fear, he would have understood what was being said: that the Socialist had won, by an enormous margin. He would have found despite it all, despite what he should have desired, that he was relieved. He would have been happy to have the burden of these replicas' expectations removed from him. As it was he heard nothing, felt nothing, except womb-fear running in his blood, and the presence inside him of something that was not present before. Something that must be removed.

He lost his balance when he tried to run from that place, to escape from these clockwork men and return home. He fell heavily to one side, knocking his head against a chair. Despite that, when he was taken home and poulticed, and left alone in bed, he could not sleep. Inside him the womb leaked into his nerves the knowledge of his loss, the disappointment on the face of the men who came home with him in the carriage, possessed again of their own faces and vowing to try again.

This disappointment felt like pleasure: to be left alone, to do what he preferred to do without the pain of being something for someone. The pressure of this woman's organ within him was good now, and something else—something like the feeling he had felt with Klara—a sensual delight, spread where the pain had spread. This was the other side of womanliness, once the requirement to be rational was over. To give himself up to something external: the world, the body. He lay in the darkness between the starched sheets, beneath the blanket, and he ran his hand over his skin, thinking first of nothing. Then, pricked with guilt and remembering the requirement to sleep, the necessity to sleep on doctor's orders, the obligation to relax his body and mind, and knowing that, like hunger, the other requirements of the body could be satisfied, their tensions released, by giving in to them, he gave in to the womb in him. He let his hands travel where they wished without restraint, the building up of pressure like water behind a dam, which, when there has been rain, can become too great for the dam-wall. It must be vented. The memory of the day—of the election, of his failure, of his fall, of the clockwork men—all these things were dispersed by the simple act of running his hand across his body. If that was to strengthen the organ within him then what was his option? He must sleep! The doctor had told him to sleep no more than an hour ago, and who could sleep with this sensation playing through his body?

It was an impossibility.

In the morning, when the sun rose and the light was too much, he shut his eyes.

His attention turned inwards, and he saw images of his organs like the plates in a book of anatomy; except where those were paradigms, these illustrations were the opposite: instances of corruption and the degradation of form—diseased, putrefying matter, only barely recognisable—engravings such as those a doctor might show his students or those of his patients that he wished to frighten into the observance of some otherwise onerous course of treatment.

The plates were laid out before his mind's eye in sequence: first the bones of the feet and their conjunctive tissues, with the phalanges buckled and the ligaments and cartilage softened like cheese, so that he knew that if he moved his foot there must be pain. The mesh of nerves remained intact, entangled with God's immortal nerve. The lesser matter—the unholy flesh that God did not concern himself with—was putrefying by turns. The plates of the bones of his ankle revealed that they were rendered brittle: bubbles in the calcium, caused by gases released from the rotting of his marrow, undermined everything. This continued into the shin, which was represented as bowed, like those possessed by children Schreber had seen in the Institute, and in the slums of Dresden—in the place that was cleared to build their home. Muddy little boys and girls with drooping eyelids and heavy lips and legs that were so bent that it was easy, when they stood insolently in front of him and asked him what business he thought he had there, in their neighbourhood, it was easy to draw with the imagination a circle of which these two limbs were quadrants, the rest of the line inked in the mind.

When he shooed them away and took Sabine's hand, and, with an expansive wave, indicated where the house was to be built, the children moved only a small distance back and watched them both. One boy indicated by gesture that his friend should come near, subtly, in a manner that was designed to escape Schreber's attention, but which did not. The friend was older, and, though they shared the same bow legs, where the younger was mischievous this boy was vicious, having, it seemed then, more understanding of the gulf that existed between his own low standing and that of the couple who stood before him.

It seemed that the older boy was prompted to anger by his jealousy, and this was written on his face—in the grit of his teeth and the scab above his eye. Schreber took Sabine's hand and led her back to the carriage. He walked straight-legged and calmly, as if on a stroll through the park, as if the set of their backs and the confidence of their slow progress were proof against any violent ambition on the part of the older boy. When his wife was safely inside, Schreber turned, and a clod of wet mud landed on his chest. It had been thrown at his back, but this was much better, and the rascals whooped to see that a simple act of defiance had become so much more, spiced by the old fool's frowning dismay. The mud splattered up onto his face, into his beard, and Schreber took one step forward to the sounds of his father's outrage. Sabine grabbed him by the arm and whispered:

'They are animals, these people.'

'Then we have the advantage of them,' Schreber replied.

Other boys had come, like a pack of dogs, and one was stooping to pick up more mud. Schreber stood his ground, but Sabine urged him back to the carriage, pulling his arm when he would not come and pleading with him under her breath in words that Schreber could not hear for the rushing of the blood in his ears.

Dogs. Not worthy of his time.

He returned with Sabine to the carriage, and as the driver cracked the reins and the wheels dragged and slipped in the mud, eventually pulling away, the boys ran after them, shrieking and singing their victory. It was only the bowing of their bones—the imperfection of their development, the variation from the proper manifestation of the body brought on by their inadequate nutrition—that slowed the children and allowed the carriage to draw off, and for their laughter to fade.

Sabine congratulated him on his choice of site for the house. The carriage was back in the street, and she made a modest request regarding the design of the new place. She would like a carved lintel over the front door—musical notes from her favourite opera—a show of delicacy of feeling and of respect for her theatrical career, written in stone, an answer to any of her critics, though no one had ever thought to criticise her in Schreber's company. As she spoke, Schreber saw the curve of those boys' shin bones and their skin ingrained with filth and putrefaction, forced as they were to live like beasts. He saw how these boys would develop into adulthood, having seen so many of their type before him in the courts, and, above the sound of his wife's opinions on the disposition of the laundry room and the maid's quarters, he wondered whether there wasn't something bodily to which he could attribute their poverty. Was the bowing of the legs a sign in itself of a lack of something which was reflected later in their moral insufficiencies and their tendency to crime? He looked down at his own limbs, and he saw they were straight, so utterly at odds with those boys. Hadn't his father had always taken pains to ensure straightness? Of posture and of thought? The straight-keeper, that little device which would have benefitted those boys and taught them the error inherent in despising one's superiors. It blinkered them to the requirement that they better themselves, or allow themselves to be bettered. Stern discipline. As Schreber used upon himself, every minute of every day. Straight posture. Straight thought. Straight action.

Now, in his cell in the silent early morning, here were his bones, despite all his efforts, bowed into semicircles, and it was brought home to him how he had, in his pride, ignored his own brute animal nature in considering himself above those boys, those pups, dog-bred in the gutter. He had brought down punitive judgement on them and their fathers. On that day and on every other day that he sat in judgement. Bolt upright in his chair. Now what? Was he to be judged by a higher authority? Was his flesh to be found weak and guilty? It was.

The evidence was presented to his mind's eye, etched on a copper plate, inked and pressed onto the finest paper. Illustrations of his bones and organs, one after the other, in sequence and degraded. They were held up, compared in their detail to his understanding of the body's proper form, understanding taken from his father's extensive library, from his own amateur interest in the particulars of all the sciences—medicine no less than law—as was right for a man of intellect. The evidence, as it was presented to him, was incontrovertible. His body was sick, every aspect of it, from his thigh bone, fractured and rebuilt a thousand times, shortened and thickened, to his hip joint, widened to make room for the thicker thigh and opened out to be like that of a woman.

Then there came the most important plate. There was an octopus, laid upon his bowel. Its tentacles stretched everywhere, up into his chest and down toward the base of his spine, joining with the nerves. Within it there grew something, and if there was a source of his degeneracy, here it was. Its tentacles reached everywhere: thin fingers intertwining with his flesh and nerves and there was not an inch of him that was not compromised, like those children who played in the muck.

Out of the blue, Rössler
comes below to take
Schreber above. They
discover pertinent facts,
but neither of them are
in a position to recog-
nise them.

XXII

The door opened and there was Rössler.

Although the doctor had never seemed to take any particular care over his appearance in the past, he seemed excessively worried about soiling his clothes, and as he stepped into the room he fiddled with his white shirt cuffs and kept as much distance between himself and the walls as he could. He watched where he placed his feet.

'Herr Schreber, could you come with me please?'

Schreber looked warily around the cell, but did not move.

Rössler sniffed. 'Right away, please.'

Where was Müller? Schreber looked past the doctor. No sign of the man.

'Herr Müller is… indisposed,' Rössler said. 'Please…'

He held out his hand, but when Schreber came forward the doctor saw better what state the man was in and retracted it. He muttered something about Müller under his breath.

'I will have one of the other orderlies bathe and dress you.'
Rössler turned and left, leaving the door wide.

'This place has the atmosphere of a Turkish brothel...' Schreber
said. He rubbed his fingertips together. His nails and skin were
clean and he had a fresh pair of pyjamas and a dressing gown.

Rössler smiled. 'Would you like me to open the blind?'

'What do you want of me? Am I to go home?'

'Perhaps, Herr Schreber. Perhaps.'

Schreber leaned forward in his chair.

'When?'

Rössler smiled and made a noncommittal shrug of the
shoulders.

Schreber sat back. 'In a week? Perhaps a month? I have been
left to rot...'

'Not at all. This is how we proceed here, Herr Schreber.
Sometimes it is necessary to strip a man back to his foundations
before we can begin to treat him.'

Rössler smiled as if this was perfectly reasonable. Schreber
watched that smile, but said nothing.

'To be sure of what it is that we are working with. Like a
surgeon cuts away the dead tissue before he sutures a wound.
Do you understand?'

Schreber made no movement of any kind.

Rössler coughed and flicked through his papers.

'One must undress for an examination...' he muttered.

'Do you wish me to undress?'

'No, Herr Schreber. It is an analogy.'

'Underneath my skin there is an organ. It looks like an octopus. In it are children. They are God's.'

'Is this an analogy?'

'No. Do you wish me to undress? It can be seen under the
skin.'

'That won't be necessary. You have no natural heir, Herr Schreber. Is that right?'

'This place has the atmosphere of a Turkish brothel…'

'Yes. I'll open the blinds.'

The doctor pushed himself back in his chair. The back legs caught on the carpet, tipping the chair back slightly. Rössler tutted and lifted the chair, standing so that his thighs did not leave the cushion, his body bent forward, taking tiny steps back until there was space for him. Then he allowed the chair to return to the ground.

'Did your wife never wish to provide you with an heir?'

Rössler crossed the distance to the window without turning away from Schreber.

'There are things I do not allow myself to think of.'

Rössler stopped with his hand on the blind.

'What things?'

Schreber turned away. He looked down at the floor between his knees—at a bare heel, the remainder of the foot enclosed in the slipper. He lifted the heel and watched, as if it belonged to someone else, as he put it down again. Then he did the same with the other foot.

'I don't know.'

Rössler nodded, but he did not open the blind.

'Did your wife never wish to be pregnant? It is something that most women desire, at some point? Or was there some difficulty?'

The slippers were cheap. They were of the type Schreber preferred—soft leather uppers and a firm flat sole—but the stitching was loose.

'Some incompetency on your part? Impotency?'

'No,' Schreber snapped. 'I am very tired.'

'Then why?'

'I find it hard to breathe.'

'If there was no obstruction…'

'I cannot sleep.'

Now Rössler was in front of him. He knelt at his feet and with his thin, hard hands he gripped Schreber's wrists.

'Why didn't you have children?'

His hold was tight.

'We had Fridoline.'

'Did you?'

'Of course. She was there when I came home. Sabine arranged it all, while I was away. The adoption.'

'Indeed? Why did she not adopt a boy child? To continue your father's line? To maintain the family name?'

Schreber pulled away, but Rössler held tight. Tighter. He did not intend to let go.

'I…'

'Surely this was something necessary?'

Rössler directed Schreber's movements.

'Please, do not speak of my wife.'

'What of her?'

Sabine lay on the bed. The room was terribly quiet. The midwife was so thin. He had expected someone fatter. Someone matronly. But she was like a stick. She moved about the room without making a sound. She went here and there, tidying things away. Piling things and wrapping things: red sheets, red linens, red cotton—everything red, wrapping them in a quilt—quite ruined. Quite, quite ruined.

She dipped her hands in a porcelain bowl of water.

'Didn't she want you to have an heir?'

Sabine lay on the bed with her nightshirt riding up over her waist and a fresh towel laid over her legs. She was pale and her mouth was open so that he could see her teeth. Sleeping? Her hair was slick against her forehead.

'Didn't you want one?'

On the towel beside her was Schreber's daughter.

She was a good size—that is what the woman had said.

A good size.

With these things one generally expects them to be runts. This is what she said. She kept saying it. When the missus comes round you'd better go. A man's no good in this. She kept saying all of it.

Schreber touched the girl's head. She had dark hair. Soft and dark.

'It is my responsibility.'

'What is?'

'That is what my mother said. It is your responsibility.'

'What is your responsibility, Herr Schreber?'

His daughter lay out on the towel beside Sabine. She lay on her back, her arms out to either side of her head, hands balled up in fists. She was very beautiful.

'If Sabine cannot do it…'

'Cannot do what?'

'One must be strict with children.' It is the loving thing. To let children do what they will, to lie in bed past their time, to give in to their desires—this is the road that leads to indolence, to softness. That beautiful little thing.

The woman left the room, the bundle of linens so large that it pushed up her chin. Schreber watched her go. Then he took the girl by the wrists, the little thing, so beautiful, and he made her move where she would not. He held up her arms, straight, and her head stayed up with them, so that Schreber thought for a second that perhaps there had been a mistake—that she might open her eyes after all. It was not a mistake.

He held her there, letting her feet—they were still turned in from being inside—he let her feet touch the bed, and he said to her:

'You must move.'

'Who must?'

He held her there and he said it again. Then he moved her arms apart, slowly.

'You must move.'

'Who must move, Herr Schreber?'

As he moved her arms, her head went back and her mouth fell open. He thought for a moment that she was trying to speak, that it had all been a mistake, that her eyes would open and she would speak, but the further he moved her arms apart the more her head went back on her shoulders.

'I order you!'

He shook her a little.

'I order you! I demand it!'

'What do you demand? Of whom?'

He moved her arms like his father had moved his, to demonstrate the correct mode of movement, the postures and positions of his gymnastics.

'You must! You must!'

She did not.

When the woman returned she snatched the child from him, saying nothing, clutching the beautiful little thing to her chest and backing away from him, as if he was an animal from whom the child had to be protected.

'It is your responsibility.'

'What is, Herr Schreber?'

The doctor reached for the blind. 'If Sabine cannot do it… If she cannot do what?'

'Do not speak of my wife!'

Please help me, Paul.

I cannot.

Please!

I am not a doctor, Sabine. You must try again.

Even when his son was the same. He had felt the boy kicking—one hand on Sabine's belly, the other on the back of the chair. But he was just the same, in the end. He would not move. Could not move. Could not be induced to move no matter what Schreber said or did. Dead. No matter how much he pleaded and shouted. Like a creation of a lower god. An incompetent god. A god who could not understand living things. A god who knew only corpses, and made of these his playthings, animating them by pulling their puppet strings, but refusing even that.

'You must move!'

I cannot do it again, Sabine said.

'But you must, my sweet.'

Help me!

'I am not a doctor.'

I cannot do it again, he had said to his mother. But you must! If not for yourself then for him. His name. His legacy. Your father. Are you so weak?

Might we adopt a son? It is not the same. If Sabine cannot provide an heir…

'Do not speak of my wife!'

'I was not speaking of your wife, Herr Schreber.'

Rössler opened the blinds and in came the sun, blinding white, so that he could not see. He held that boy's wrists, moved him like a puppet, gave him motion and life but the moment he stopped the child would not obey, no matter how Schreber screamed.

The responsibility is yours! For your father!

Now Rössler was in front of him, blocking out the sun. He put a glass to his lips.

'Close the blinds!'

Rössler did it and came back with the glass refilled.

'It is too bright. God will see me. In my belly is an octopus and in it are God's children. Living children. There are things I must not think of.'

'I can't make any sense of what you are saying.'

One day Paul came upon his father. He was in a terrible rage at his wife. There was no telling what she had done, but he slapped her hard across the face. The way she took it, it was as if it was no surprise to her, just as it had come not to surprise

Paul. Nevertheless, he ran over and grabbed his father's wrist, in case he intended to strike her again.

His father looked at him as if he had never seen him before that day—he was fifteen or sixteen. He allowed Paul to hold his wrist: perhaps the son had become old enough to prevent these acts of violence, so that the father saw in him strength. Paul turned to his mother and opened his mouth to speak—what he intended to say is forgotten. Without a pause, and with no particular animosity, she slapped him.

The mother took the father's side in domestic matters.

Schreber closed his eyes and gripped his temples. 'Do not speak of my wife!'

'Herr Schreber, I was not speaking of your wife.'

Do not speak!

Schreber is visited by
Alexander. He comes
with a message of hope.

XXIII

There was a sound.

It came from the walls, and at first it seemed to Schreber that it was nothing: the wind, or the movement of water in pipes that ran behind the cell, across the ceiling. But it persisted, regular and even in tone. There was the hiss of a letter cut off before it could be properly spoken, or falling into silence too early, muffled by something. The bricks of the wall?

Schreber sat up in the dark and angled his head first one way and then another, like a small bird—a blue tit, perhaps—in the way those little creatures tilt their heads when they listen out for the songs of other birds, or are made wary by the appearance of a cat in the garden. He made sharp, sudden, seemingly random movements, trying to locate the source of the sound. Schreber was made to think of a man impersonating a snake, or the escape of steam from a valve.

There was silence for as long as a minute, and then the knocking came. It was hard and insistent, coming from the window. Schreber backed away on his hands and knees, not daring to look up, but listening. The hairs pricked up on the back of his neck with the effort to hear something recognisable in the sound. When the soles of his feet met the far wall he stopped. The knocking did not stop. Schreber wrapped his head with his arms, as if by doing so he could deafen himself, but when he became still he could hear it almost as well as if he had chosen not to block it out. He put his fingers in his ears and hummed a tune; it was one his father had hummed. What its name was he could not recall, but it was bold and fearless and he hummed so loud that it echoed in his mind. Where there had been speculation on what devil might be knocking on his window, instead there was his father dressed in his uniform, offering his hand to his poor son. Such was Schreber's confusion that he reached to take it, and with his finger out of his ear the knocking became appallingly loud. Then there was silence for a short while, and then a sharp crack. Glass breaking.

A voice.

'Herr Schreber,' it whispered. 'Paul!'

For a missed beat of his heart Schreber thought it was his father's voice. But it was not. It was the Jew. His flat sardonic tone.

'I heard you humming; I know you are in there! Pom-pom-pom-ti-pom, pom-ti-pom, pom-pom-pom. "Prussia's Glory"? Am I right? I've come to help you.'

'What do you want from me?'

There was a pause in which the sound of a man clapping his hands together may have reached Schreber, or it may have been the cracking of a bone from somewhere deep in his chest, but it was something. The darkness lessened for a moment, like ink diluted with water. The dead black cell became black-grey, and when he put his hand in front of his eyes there was the faintest outline: barely more than a trick of the imagination. When he moved his fingers he could see something corresponding to them move in the darkness, as if at a great distance, as if he was on the shore watching moonless waves in a black storm.

'Come over here!'

Schreber turned to the sound and there, seemingly miles away—a distant lighthouse—was a tiny irregular square of light, orange and flickering. He was drawn toward it, as an insect is drawn to a lamp: not considering anything other than that he must go there. He got to his feet and moved. There was a hole in the boards on the window.

'Are you well?'

The glass was broken off in a single piece the shape of a dog's tooth. He jumped up and held the bars with one hand and there was just enough room for the other to pass up to the wrist. Behind that was wood—a smaller gap here, and rough. Schreber stuffed his fingers into the hole and pushed them until his knuckles stopped any further progress. After all his work, was this all it took? To be outside?

'I can feel the wind…'

And rain.

And the warm touch of a hand, shocking like a rat bite. Schreber pulled away, cutting the back of his hand in his hurry.

'If you have come here to torment me…'

There was a long silence. And then a face appeared in the gap, lamp-lit and dripping wet. The eyes were wide, excited, but also somehow soft. Reassuring. Rain gathered at the tip of the nose until there was too much of it and then it ran down to the lips.

'Don't you remember me?'

'You are the Jew.'

Alexander wiped the rainwater from his face and smoothed back his hair.

'My name is Alexander Zilberschlag. I want to help you.'

Schreber said nothing, and Zilberschlag sighed. From somewhere he took a cigarette and lit it on the flame of the lamp. It hissed as a rain drop put it out, but he pinched off the end, lit it again, and held it downward so his hand shielded it and the lower part of his face. When Zilberschlag spoke, smoke came with his words.

'I think the hole will become conspicuous if I make it any larger. Will it do?' When he leaned forward, Zilberschlag's eye filled the hole, filled the world. 'You have not been forgotten! Is there anything I can get for you? Food? Paper?'

The eye circled and moved, searching.

'Are you getting enough to eat?'

Schreber turned away from the eye, dropped to the ground and crawled until he reached the far corner.

'I eat nothing,' he whispered. 'My organs are destroyed and remade daily. If I attempt to satisfy my hunger pieces of my throat are swallowed with the meal and my stomach is made to vanish. There is an octopus. In it are parasitical children. They consume me from within. I am damned.'

There was quiet for a long while and Schreber kept his back to the window.

'With your permission, I will write to your wife. Perhaps I can persuade her to visit. Is that something you would like?'

Schreber said nothing, but hunched over and covered his head with his arms, as if the rain was within the cell and not outside of it.

'I'm not a lawyer,' Zilberschlag continued, 'but I seem to recall that a lack of protest can be taken for assent. I must go. If the staff find me out here they'll put me in the cell next to you, but I am determined to make amends. Keep your spirits up, Paul! Remember what your father used to say—there is nothing a good German boy cannot endure! Let us hope that he was right.'

Rössler takes Schreber
on a trip. They visit the
house in which Schre-
ber was raised. Rössler's
hope is that Schreber
should see that the
place is very ordinary,
and to allay any anxi-
eties Schreber might
have. His anxieties are
not allayed, but there is
good news.

XXIV

In the morning, Rössler came, and this time he was followed
by Müller. The orderly glowered in silence. He dropped the
pair of slippers on the ground, held out the dressing gown, and
gestured for Schreber to get into the Bath chair.

'We are going on a journey, Herr Schreber,' the doctor said.

Schreber began to say something, but Rössler had already
gone up the stairs.

'Come on!'

Müller leaned over Schreber and hissed in his ear: 'You've
dropped me right in it, haven't you?'

'I…' Müller dragged the chair backwards after the doctor.
Each step jolted Schreber so that he almost fell out, and it was
only the orderly's hand clamping hard on the back of his neck
that kept him in his seat.

When they were out, Rössler was nowhere to be seen. Müller
wheeled the chair between the buildings, cutting close to the
walls, going so quickly that Schreber had to grip the sides.

'What did you tell him?'

'I said nothing.'

Müller gripped him so that his nails bit into the flesh.

'No? Nothing about the bromides? Nothing about the bath? Nothing about the food? You're for it. Do you understand?' Müller barked, and he pinched Schreber's arm.

After that he said nothing, and Schreber was happy for it.

They rushed through unfamiliar gardens, past a patch of turf that had been taken up: a perfect brown rectangle the size of a man—a little bigger—surrounded by green grass. The chair skirted its edge, the wheels so close that when Schreber leaned over he felt he could almost take a handful of the fresh dug soil. Worms lay in and out of the dirt, glistening, amongst the dirty pebbles and pale white grass roots. Schreber reached out, and the chair was swung hard to the other side, almost emptying him onto the ground. Schreber sat straight and gripped the arms of the chair.

Müller took him onto the path, new flags with barely a crack in them, smooth except for where one ended and the other began—a little jolt—nothing much. Schreber watched his feet as they cut through the grounds of the asylum. These slippers were different, stiff fabric, and when he moved them the whole toe articulated along a single line, like a fold in a piece of paper.

They came out into a courtyard and there was Rössler at one corner. He raised his hand.

'It must be nice for you to get some fresh air.'

'Are you taking me home?'

'In a way, Herr Schreber.'

Schreber got up, almost as far as to stand straight upright, but Müller grabbed him by both shoulders and slammed him back into the chair, so hard that it made his spine shudder and, unbidden, tears came to his eyes. Rössler stepped forward, staring at Müller.

Schreber tried to get up again, warier this time, with a backward glance over his shoulder, and this time Müller grabbed an elbow and tugged Schreber until he fell heavily.

Rössler came closer, so that Schreber could smell his cologne.

'Please remain seated, Herr Schreber,' the doctor said, but he was looking over his shoulder at Müller, and he spoke in a monotone so flat that his mind was clearly elsewhere.

Müller coughed and spat and stepped away from the chair.

'Müller.'

'Sir?'

'That will be all.'

'Sir.'

The orderly walked away, and as he went he pulled off his white coat. Schreber heard the cotton snap on the buttons, and as he rounded a corner passing out of sight, the orderly, now only in his vest, let the coat fall to the ground. He did not stop to retrieve it. He left it where it was.

Rössler coughed and frowned, but when he turned back to Schreber he wore a smile. 'May I take you on a little journey, Herr Schreber? There is a carriage waiting.'

'I will walk home. It is no distance.'

'Let me help you in. You will not need the chair. If we walk at all it will be only a short way.'

'Sabine will be waiting for me. Cook will have lunch ready.'

'Let me help you.'

Rössler called to the driver and he hopped down from his platform and, one either side, the two men lifted Schreber up into the carriage.

'He ain't going to do anything peculiar in there, is he, sir? Only I got a private client this afternoon, and I won't have time to do any cleanup after him. That won't be required will it, sir? Only if it is…'

'There will be nothing unusual about the trip. We are going for a little ride, nothing more.'

Rössler gently pushed the carriage door shut and rattled it in its frame with his gloved hands. When he was certain it was secure, he trotted off out of view.

Schreber turned and waited for the doctor to appear at the other door. When he did, he was smiling. He knocked twice on the carriage roof and they moved away.

'Are you comfortable? Warm enough?'

'I suppose this will be quicker…'

Rössler smiled, but said nothing.

'Here! We are almost out of Dösen. Take a deep breath, Herr Schreber! Let the good air deep into your lungs.'

'Is this the way home?'

'Deep down, Herr Schreber!'

'Is it?'

Rössler filled his own lungs, and held his chest puffed out. He smiled and gestured, flapping one flat hand in front of his belly as if it were the wing of a bird. When Schreber tried to speak again, the other hand went up and the index finger came out and wagged from side to side. Schreber took a deep breath, but it had the opposite effect to that imagined by Rössler, and Schreber began an uncontrolled bout of coughing.

When Schreber eventually opened his eyes, they were wet with exertion.

'My apologies,' he spluttered. 'A little cold, nothing more.'

'Of course. The ride will be very short—only a mile or two.'

Rössler knocked on the roof of the carriage and it came to a stop: the Zeitzer Gate, where his father had bought land, then on the frontier of the city, but now huddled between a hundred other plots. There were people, and coaches and horses, but Schreber paid them almost no heed. He fixed his sights on the house where he had lived with his family.

'The Institute, Herr Schreber. Quite a building! Only fitting for a place of world renown.'

All the rooms empty—then at least—so that a boy might hide anywhere, and Sardines became a rather tedious affair.

'Shall we take a walk around it?'

Rössler went up to the gap in the railings—such a short old man—barely half the height of the fence around the Institute's front garden. He gestured for Schreber to come, like an eager child. Schreber took a step, slowly, but his eye was directed up to a window on the third floor. The drawing of a curtain? Rössler made to come over and take Schreber by the hand, but he came of his own accord, looking up.

'Good man! Shall we announce ourselves?'

'No!' Schreber grabbed the doctor's arm. 'You mustn't ring the bell…'

Rössler withdrew from Schreber's grip, slowly, and took a step back.

'It is very loud…' Schreber explained.

Rössler nodded and indicated that, in that case, they might instead prefer to take a look in through a window. When he walked away he took a quick glance over his shoulder. Anxiety?

Schreber found his mouth was unaccountably dry, and swallowing did not seem to correct it. The old doctor was far too short to see in through the raised windows, and so he stooped and looked into the narrow slits at ground level.

'There is nothing down there to see.'

'Well, Herr Schreber, if our journey is not to be wasted then we must ask to be admitted, if only briefly.'

Schreber marched quickly up the steps to the door, arriving there before the doctor could ring the bell. On a plaque to one side of the door was written *Orthopaedic Clinic, Schildbach*. Schreber touched the letters with his fingertip.

'It is quite tarnished,' Rössler said. 'I wonder the maid hasn't been dismissed.'

The same could be said of the door handle and the knocker, and, when he looked around, Schreber saw that the flags on the ground were cracked and the glass above the door was almost opaque with dust.

Rössler indicated the bell and raised his eyebrows as if to say 'may I?'

Schreber took the knocker and rapped twice, very quietly, barely making any contact at all.

'Come now, man!' Rössler said, and rapped hard and loud.

Schreber flinched and waited, biting his lip and holding his breath.

Nothing.

Rössler tried again, tapping out a staccato rhythm.

'It is too loud!' Schreber cried.

Rössler raised his finger to his lips and listened with his eyes narrowed.

Nothing.

'Not loud enough, it seems, Herr Schreber.'

'He will not wish to be disturbed.'

'Who, sir? Your father?' Rössler asked, although he seemed to know the answer already.

Schreber sniffed, but said nothing.

Rössler rang the bell... several times.

'Very odd... Wait here, I'll fetch the driver.'

The old doctor went off at a gallop. Schreber pressed his ear against the door.

By the time the doctor came back with the driver, he had still heard nothing.

'It really would be a shame to have come out here and have to go back with the day wasted,' Rössler was saying.

'Well, sir, the place looks empty to me.'

'Mightn't we, then...?'

'Mightn't we what, sir?'

'You know...'

'I ain't a burglar, sir, if that's what you are suggesting.'

'No, no, not at all! How ridiculous! No... but a man such as yourself—a working man—a tradesman... you might... you know?'

'I'm sure I *don't* know, sir. What I do know is I ain't breaking into a place on your say so.'

'No? Very well…'

The driver stalked off back to the carriage, sparing only an appalled and derisive glance back.

Rössler pushed his glasses up his nose and sighed.

'Well, I'm afraid I've brought you out here on a rather pointless trip, Herr Schreber. Please forgive me.'

Schreber stepped up to the door and lifted it by the handle, half an inch or so, and then shoved with his shoulder. There was a click and then a soft thud and the door swung in. The doctor was saying something excitedly, and laughing, but Schreber paid him no attention at all.

The door opened up onto the hall and it was clear to see that the place was empty. He stepped inside, wiping his feet on the mat that was no longer there, unbuttoning his coat, nicely, neatly, and it was only when he realised how cold it was in that empty place, and that there was no rack to hang it from, that he returned it to his shoulders.

'Marvellous building! Terribly grand! *Terribly* grand!'

Schreber blanched at the doctor's noise at first, and then he straightened up, sniffed, and walked up to the foot of the stairs.

'Hello?' he said. The sound echoed and somewhere there was the flapping of wings and the scratch of clawed feet on wood.

'Pigeons, they get everywhere!'

Schreber coughed on the dust that seemed to swirl round in clouds, and he was taken again until his eyes watered. The rooms rang with the sound, and he clutched his arms around his chest. It was no good. Rössler rapped him twice, hard, between the shoulder blades and perhaps it was the shock, but it seemed to help.

Schreber nodded his thanks and swallowed as well as he could. He found this was not well enough, so he walked down through the hall and into the gymnasium, where a tap and basin were set into the wall. The white porcelain was cracked around the drain and yellowing, and when he turned the fixture only air and dust and a great deal of noise came out.

Rössler offered Schreber his flask.

'A little brandy?'

Schreber tried to refuse, but the coughing started again, and now the doctor was there with the flask at his lips, urging him to drink. With much spluttering, he managed to take a sip and the shock of the burning on the back of his throat forced him to take a deep breath, down from the stomach, and he found he could breathe a little easier.

'If I had thought to bring my stethoscope… Is it on my desk? Or in the pocket of my other jacket…'

'It is nothing… the damp. The cell is very damp.'

Rössler looked down at his shoes.

'Yes… quite right.'

The doctor walked into the centre of the room.

'We could use a room of this sort at the hospital. For the gymnastics…'

'Why have you brought me here?'

'Isn't it obvious?'

Rössler walked over to where Schreber's father had done his exercises, and above his head was the ladder—the space for it, anyway, since it had been taken away.

'We are here,' Rössler continued, 'to show you that this place is altogether normal.'

The old doctor gestured around at the hall.

'Nothing mystical. Nothing odd. Nothing out of the ordinary at all. Just a place.'

The doctor went on, but Schreber did not hear it all.

Above him, suspended from a climbing rope—one leg and one arm encircled by two sets of loops—was the Jew, Alexander Zilberschlag, as a boy.

'Just a room, like any other room.'

Alexander was silent and he swayed slowly from side to side like the pendulum on a clock that has almost entirely run down. In his hand was a bone-handled dinner knife, such as Schreber's mother had always laid out for the children, the silver cutlery being too good for everyday use.

'And we, standing here, are no different from any other men. And neither was your father…'

Alexander did not seem to see them. His eyes were fixed on the door and his head was never still—he was always craning left and right, and trying to make something out. And he listened, squinting when he did it, for some sound.

'I read his medical notes. Had them sent to me. A simple blow to the head, followed by chronic cephalalgia. An iron ladder, wasn't it?'

When Alexander was convinced no one was coming, he pulled himself close to the iron ladder and, with the knife, scraped at the plaster on which the fixture that held the ladder depended. He was very quiet, but, even so, each scratch made him nervous, and more than once he loosened his grip on the rope and began to slide down, eyes on the door, before climbing back up and scraping again.

'It is only that I cannot find a physical source of your illness, and I am not temperamentally inclined to attribute a spiritual cause, unlike some of my colleagues. It seems, then, that perhaps your confusions might be rooted in your own history.'

After a period of intense effort a piece fell from the wall— only about the size of a pebble, but it clattered onto the floor, and Alexander froze entirely for several seconds. Then he fell or slid down the rope—it was difficult to tell which, it happened so quickly—and, once he was down, he scampered away out of the room.

'It might be that confronting those causes and seeing them for what they are could itself be helpful to you.'

Rössler was under the ladder. If it had been induced to fall, by a failure of the bracket, by Alexander's sabotage of the bracket, it would have crushed the old man's skull.

'What are you staring at, Herr Schreber?'

He pointed up at the ladder.

'The wall? What do you see there?'

Schreber blinked and there was nothing—the ladder was gone and even the fixtures that had held it, and at that place where Alexander had scratched there was a patch about the size of a man's hand, of fresh, smooth plaster that had not been papered and so was a shade lighter than the wall around it.

'What do you see?'

The old doctor was staring at him intently.

'Nothing. Nothing at all.'

'Very good. So, you see, there is nothing supernatural… and your father just a man… and you just a son…'

'Am I cured?'

'Not at all, Herr Schreber. You do not seem cured at all. But I don't imagine there is anything much I can do to cure you. I can bring you here and you can see how it is that everything is quite sensible and ordinary. I can help you see that your anxieties are exaggerations of very simple and commonplace problems that a man might have. I can give you bromides to make you calm, and digitoxin for your heart, and these things will certainly help you. But I cannot make you see what is in front of you, or prevent you from seeing that which is not in front of you. So, perhaps, you do not really require my help as much as you require your home, and to be among those people that love you.'

Rössler pushed his glasses back up his nose and came over to Schreber, so that he stood in the middle of the room and the ladder could not possibly strike him, however it fell. The little old doctor took him by the shoulders.

'There is absolutely nothing, Herr Schreber, preventing you from returning home. Please think about what I have shown you today. I can do nothing else. Your wife and daughter have contacted me by telegram to say that they are coming to visit tomorrow, and when they arrive I will suggest that they should return to Dresden with you. As soon as the paperwork is signed, you may go home. Müller is already packing up your possessions. This is good news?'

Schreber said nothing.

'I am afraid you will need to remain in the secure chamber for one more night—there are no rooms available upstairs.'

Only one more night?

'Very well…' Rössler said. He took his hands away from Schreber's shoulders and led him back to the carriage. Schreber climbed into it entirely by himself, and it was only the old doctor that required assistance from the driver.

'I am sorry I could not be of more help, Herr Schreber.'

Schreber seemed to see him as if for the first time.

'Nonsense!' he said. 'The credit for my cure is entirely yours.'

Rössler smiled but said nothing. For the rest of the journey back to the asylum, neither man said a word: both kept to their own thoughts, and watched the trees and the fields.

Müller comes to Schreber's cell with too much liquor in his blood. There is talk of Karl, Müller's innocent brother, who was executed for his crimes. The Jew appears behind Schreber's closed eyes, and the attentive reader is left to wonder as to the ontological status of "Müller" and "the Jew" in a world overdetermined by a madman's delusions.

XXV

The door swung in so forcefully that it extended past its full opening and, hitting the wall, bounced back. It stopped suddenly, almost closing again, but not quite. By the light that came in through the crack, Schreber saw a hand. A fist.

It pushed the door again.

'Where is he? You can't hide from me, old man. He can't hide from me…'

Schreber turned away, and pulled his blanket up over his head.

There was the chink of glass knocking onto the wall, and then a dragging. A bottle scraped on the uneven bricks, chiming in the gaps between them.

'Judge?'

The bottle came away from the wall and slapped on flesh. His thigh?

Only a little liquor remained—it sloshed against the sides.

'Calm, brother! Do you see him?'

Acid, felt at the corners of Schreber's eyes and at the back of his throat—it made him swallow. Foul, drunken breath.

Hot air, pickled in gin, passing through the blanket as if it wasn't there.

'Judge! Wake up! I've got a case for you to hear.'

The back of a hand wiped across a stubbled face. Very near. Prickling and rasping. Two sniffs.

'Judge! Emergency session!'

A hand on his shoulder. Schreber turned, and there was Müller.

His coat gaped open to the waist. One side of it was pulled down and across, tucked into the ape's belt, so that the other side was bunched up. In silhouette he gave the impression of being a hunchback, but he was surrounded by white light, illuminated at the edges. He was clearly drunk, shimmering and swaying, and there was, just as Schreber had pictured it, a bottle glowing in his left hand.

He snorted and coughed and brought his sleeve across his lips. When Müller spoke, Schreber could see the light in the spray of spittle from the man's lips, but of his mouth and face almost nothing.

'Who's the judge now, Judge?'

He sniffed and laughed, but he hung his head joylessly.

Schreber held up his hand and peered from behind its shade, but he could make out no more of the man than if he left his hand where it had been, flat on his knees. Müller was a shadow, encroached on by light and whittled away at the edges, but a shadow nonetheless. The largest part of his presence was his odour and the weight of his mood. His anger and tension occupied the room.

'I can't see you,' Schreber said. 'The light… my eyes…'

'He can't see us, brother. The light. His eyes.'

Müller took two steps forward so that he blocked out the doorway. 'Can he see us now?'

'It is only you,' croaked Schreber.

'And Karl! Do not forget Karl!'

'I see no Karl.'

Müller turned and shut the door, and in the darkness Schreber found he could see, the excess light removed so that the grain of things, the differentiation in shades of grey and black, was visible again. There was only Müller.

'Karl is next to me,' Müller said. 'He is always next to me. He always was, and he always is.'

The orderly sat on the ground, next to Schreber. 'Always, always…'

Müller sighed and pursed his lips. He closed his eyes, and for a long time there was only the sound of his breathing.

Schreber watched him without moving, and the longer he watched, the more the man came into focus: the roundness of his shoulders—like a boulder, or a bison—his thick fingers with nails bitten down to the knuckle, almost. The jutting of his lower jaw. Under his breath he said something.

'I can't hear you,' Schreber said.

'We have come to…' the words trailed off.

'Come to?'

'Yes.'

'I don't understand.'

'Karl and me. For justice. But now…'

Müller took the stopper from the bottle and up-ended it, sucking the neck until it whistled. He kept on sucking, shaking it and sucking, and, even when it would have been obvious to a child that there was nothing inside, he wouldn't believe it. In the end he tossed the bottle into the corner of the room, spitting after it.

Then he turned to Schreber.

'I suppose you've got brothers and sisters, Judge?'

'My family is no concern of yours.'

'You've probably got brothers and sisters, too. Like I have… Had, I mean. Had. Did I ever tell you about my Karl? No. I suppose not. He's dead. You know that though? Guillotined. As a murderer. Isn't that right, Karl?'

Müller nodded in agreement with the silence.

'There is no one there.'

'He is always there. He looks after me, from heaven. He's an angel. A saint.'

'Who?'

'I've already told you. Don't you listen? You should listen...'

Schreber began to speak, but Müller reached over and placed his hand over the old man's mouth. He was gentle, at first, the hand barely making contact, but as Schreber moved his lips, he pushed harder.

'Don't speak...'

Schreber forced the hand away and started to say something—Sabine—but before the word could begin the hand was back and now the other one came with it, cupping the back of Schreber's head, so that the two worked together, pressing against both surfaces.

'You think he was a criminal? You're wrong. It's possible for an innocent man to get the chop. Agree?'

Schreber could make no sound and almost no movement of his head. Müller made him nod.

'Your lot will do it, won't they? To my lot? And charge them a fortune for the privilege! Ask my dad...'

Schreber was made to nod again.

Müller nodded too, and there was quiet for a long time. The orderly's eyes closed and nothing happened. After a while, the hands went from Schreber's face and he shuffled back into the corner of the room.

Müller didn't move. A long while passed.

Was he sleeping?

He was not sleeping. Müller lurched onto his knees and shuffled over until he sat with his legs splayed forming a square with the corner of the cell in which Schreber was contained. He spat in his hand, and smoothed Schreber's hair.

'Got to make you look neat...'

'Leave me alone!'

'It's not personal. It's just I won't get this chance again, what with you going home tomorrow. Rössler…'

'Call for him!'

'He doesn't think much of me. I can see he wants me gone. Then how long will it be before I return to my old ways? How long do you think?'

'Please! I am better. Send for my wife.'

'I haven't always been the upstanding type, Judge—not like Karl—that's the joke. He was the good one. Me? I've always been a rogue. Don't think twice about it. He was the gentleman.'

'I am old. I have been punished… every day…'

Müller picked up the bottle again and peered into it. Nothing. He put his index finger into the neck, and his knuckle was so thick that when he let go of the bottle, it dangled like a hanging man.

'The things I could tell you,' he said, barely letting the words trouble the air. 'It'd break your heart! Your precious Sabine… your precious Fridoline…'

Now it was Schreber's turn to close his eyes, and in the darkness he stopped up his ears, his fingertips forced so deep that the nails cut the skin.

'Revenge,' said the Jew, nowhere in the dark, 'is like all the appetites: one can only satisfy it temporarily.'

Müller sighed silently.

'Your brother, Karl, wasn't it?' the Jew went on. 'I can see the temptation. It is one I understand very well… Your father, he deserved better. Your birthright, lost…'

Müller let the bottle swing in the manner of a pendulum, and all the while the Jew spoke, quiet and certain.

'Killing this judge is something you will only be able to do once, and it will not be enough. Gustav will not return. Your father will not regain his health. You will still have no heir. You may feel some satisfaction tonight, but what about tomorrow?'

'I'll be for the chop… It doesn't matter.'

The Jew laughed, a particularly incongruous sound in that place, at that moment.

'No man has ever been killed for disposing of a lunatic. You must know that. There will be no murder here. Far too inconvenient. What family would send their people here, knowing that the staff were murderers? No. This will be marked down as pneumonia, or heart failure, or gangrene of the lungs—anything.'

Müller reached for Schreber's throat, as if he intended to adjust his necktie, delicately, but, at the last, he slipped his fingers around, and rested his thumbs where the cartilage made a natural hold.

'And what about tomorrow, Herr Müller? When you feel the lack of your brother again? Herr Schreber will be gone, but your hunger for revenge will not. Let me tell you, it gets worse. It will consume you, and you will attempt to satiate it, and in the end you will find yourself in a place like this. On the other side.'

He tightened his grip, and, after a little while, Schreber felt the life leaving him. It was a strange feeling, not at all uncomfortable. Not unpleasant. A relief! Like being lulled to sleep.

The world contracted before his eyes until he seemed to be observing it through the wrong end of a telescope.

He squeezed, and nothing mattered at all.

The next morning,
in response to Zilber-
schlag's letter, Sabine
comes at last.

XXVI

From down the hallway and up the stair: the rusty scrape of a key
turning in the lock. The bolts drawn across, first the top and then
the bottom. The twist of the handle, the metal bar rattling loosely
in its fitting, never mended because the function of this door was
to lock, clearly, and its opening was only an afterthought. Weak
candlelight, wavering in the crack beneath Schreber's own door. Dirt
and stones: a mountain range in miniature, the panorama stretched
thin between the wood and the floor. The sun rising behind it,
orange. Müller, whispering. Mind the steps? Speaking to her?

Then there was a man's weight on the creaking wood, the shrill
squeak of a board pulling against a nail that had lost its head—on the
third step down—and now, behind, a gentler tread. And another?
The light growing stronger. Yellow. A summer's day break.

Hesitation—the movement down the stair ceasing, the progress of the tiny sun toward the brightness of noon interrupted.
A child's voice. A girl!

'I don't like it.'

Fridoline? It was Fridoline! Her voice. Just her voice.

'He's in here.'

Boots under the door, blacking out the sunlight.

'Why is it so dark?'

Fridoline.

He could see her face—he ran his finger across her brow, smoothing away the sadness and fear.

'Quiet, child!'

Sabine? Behind the shut door. Locked.

'But it's so cold and dark.'

'Doctor's orders, little Fräulein.'

'Why would a doctor make it so cold? Why would he make it so dark?'

'Doctor's orders.'

'Enough questions, girl. What about his food? He always liked his food. Chops. Potatoes.'

'He won't take it now.'

'Nothing?'

'No, Frau Schreber, well… not by choice anyway. He says he doesn't have the stomach for it.'

'He takes nothing at all? How does he live?'

Sabine!

Schreber sat up on his mattress.

'I see to it that he has his porridge in the morning, and beef stock at night.'

'This is foul. There is a smell down here.'

'That'll be the drains—you quickly get used to it. I don't smell them at all.'

'The child… take her back upstairs.'

As soon as they were all home he would put it to Sabine that they must take the salts in Baden. He must always retire early despite the gay parties and young friends invited back from the theatre. Keep to his bed and sleep. Perhaps hire Cook's sister, as she was always suggesting.

No pipe in the drawing room.

Schreber licked his teeth and listened.

'You are sure you want to go in alone?'

Little round face. Smooth skin.

'I want to see him!'

Frida!

'Take her and show her the gardens.'

'I won't go!'

'Now, Fridoline, do this for your mother and we'll shop for dresses when it's all done.'

'I don't want dresses! I want to see Papa!'

'Fridoline! Is that you child?' the words echoed in the empty room and then silence.

'Papa!'

Quick steps and then banging on the door—two small fists! Hard knuckles.

'Take her upstairs!'

'I don't want to go! Papa!'

'Do what your mother says, Fräulein.'

'He is more of a mother to me than she ever was! Papa!'

'Fridoline!' Schreber at the door now, with his hands pressed against the wood, fingers spread, and his cheek flat.

'Should I take her?'

'You have my blessing.'

'Come on now, Fräulein; let's see the pretty flowers, eh?'

'Get off me!'

Fluttering, like a bird's wings. The knock of her shoe against the wood.

'Soon we will be away from here and then we can shop for a dress and take our lunch out. How does that sound?'

'Papa!'

'Fridoline!'

There was a struggle and then nothing.

Breathing? The rise and fall of thick cotton? The scarcely present friction between layers of *crêpe de Chine*?

'Paul?'

Sabine.

Schreber went as far from the door as he could and crouched until he was low enough to peer through the crack. Sabine's boots: black leather, four straps, her skirts wavering above them, held up away from the dirt, a white rose decoration, and a number seven heel.

'Sabine? Sabchen? I thought you were gone.'

'No. I am here. Are you decent? I have the key.'

Schreber straightened himself. He stood up on the damp floor and smoothed out his moustaches. He licked his fingers and ran them back through his hair. All at an end. Damned place. Foolish old man, paying attention to nonsense, letting Cook off early when there was an 'at home' the following afternoon, buying flowers for the skivvy on her birthday. Wearing her dresses. Pollutions.

'One moment. One moment please!'

Schreber coughed and drew the open sides of his shirt together, holding them tight in one fist at his chest. No smoking in the drawing room. Keep straight and your hands where I can see them. Lie straight, keep still. Don't shuffle. Don't fiddle. Don't cry. Stop crying. Fancy a man like him allowing himself to be f——d.

He wiped the back of his other hand across his lips. There was dirt under his nails, and he bit one back, the worst, tearing skin in his hurry. A drop of blood welled at the edge and he blotted it on the back of his shirt.

'Come!'

The door moved in.

Slowly, the shadow of a woman resolved on the wall, a silhouette, just like the one Sabine had done in the *Palais de Fantasie*, as a souvenir you understand—not vanity—and which she propped on her bedside table beside the blurred daguerreotype of her mother. Just the same.

The silhouette halted, with the door half open, and seemed to compose itself. It looked so young, so beautiful, hair piled high and pinned and a slight snub nose, a protrusion of the lower lip, just like Sabine, clear as day, outlined in candlelight.

'Please… come in.'

The silhouette stiffened but did not move, and Schreber did the same. Then, suddenly, the door came in again. The focus of the light became diffuse as the aperture through which it entered widened, and the silhouetted blurred away to nothing.

'Paul!'

Did she gasp it? Or was it a whisper? There was a restriction in her throat.

It was too bright.

'I want to see you, Sabchen. My eyes are accustomed to this darkness, but when light comes in… if light comes in… I can't see properly now. You are a shape?'

'Paul…'

'Speak up, old girl, I can barely hear you.'

She stepped forward, and now he could see her.

The left side of her face was dragged down, as if weights were suspended from the corner of her mouth. Her eyelid was heavy, giving the impression that one half of her was drowsy and the other half wide awake. The eye on the bad side was yellow—yolk where there should have been white—and the whole was specked with blood.

'What has happened to you?' Schreber cried.

'To me?'

'Your face… what has happened to your face?'

'My face? Nothing. Do you mean the palsy? I am told it is very slight. Nothing at all. Everyone says so. Barely noticeable.'

Sabine took a step back. Schreber came forward, pulling at his sleeves.

'Quite right, dear. Nothing at all! Silly of me…'

Sabine nodded, but for every step Schreber took forward, Sabine took one back, until they had made a circuit of the cell.

'Are you well, Paul? Your doctor…'

'My doctor tells me I must come home. I promised Fridoline…'

'Yes… she mentioned it. Some while ago. I was against her coming here, but she is such a disobedient little… Your doctor…'

'I thought I heard her. She is with you…?'

'She has gone with the man to look at some flowers.'

'In this cold? Does she have her scarf?'

'She is suitably dressed.'

Sabine looked around the cell.

'Sabine, please take me home,' Schreber said.

Sabine looked down at her feet. She was quiet for a long while.

'Your doctor…' she said.

'He says that I am utterly cured!'

'That is not…'

'He says I must return home.'

Sabine took a long look at him before speaking.

'Your doctor… he has not spoken to you today?'

'About what?'

'He has not told you?'

'About what, Sabine?'

Sabine turned away and stood, facing out of the door. She held her hands at the waist and was wringing them together, twisting one with the other, over and over.

'How are the preparations for Christmas progressing?' Schreber asked. 'Are we to have guests?'

'Christmas? In June?'

He reached for her hand, to stop the twisting, but she pulled away.

'The house is very difficult to manage. Your sisters are well meaning, but they are too much. They put everything into chaos.

They are worse than your mother. They each tell Cook a different thing. They want to control everything. Just like her, struck from the same mould. Who do they think I am? Some child, to be ordered around? To be made to do things against my will? You are all the same. Even the girl! She spends all her time running from them to me and back again. And this when I require my rest.'

'Your headaches?'

'They are not improved. I'm taking a cure, but it does not give any relief. It makes me worse, if anything.'

'I will put my foot down when I return. I know you prefer me to keep out of these matters, but I have some influence with the staff, and Anna will listen to me.'

'That, Paul, is the last thing I need: another voice, another confusion, someone else dictating what must happen in my own house.'

'Whatever you wish my love.'

'Fridoline is so difficult.'

'My girl? I don't believe it!'

Sabine almost spat. 'You doubt me? You prefer to take the child's side?'

'Not at all...'

'She is disobedient! She is wilful! She gets it from the father, that much I know.'

Schreber nodded, slowly. 'I apologise.'

'Why? It has nothing to do with you. That is the great joke, I suppose. That she should suffer on *your* account. That she should pine for *you*. She is very upset. About it all. The talk especially. On the street. At her school. She is very sensitive to it.'

'What talk?'

'Nothing. I should say nothing.'

'What talk?'

'Your sisters forbid me...' She laughed at this, but then her face fell. 'But then it is talk of you—why shouldn't you know? She is very sensitive to the things they say.'

'What do they say?'

'They say what they have always said. I, of course, shrug it off. It is nothing to me what these jumped up stuffed shirts have to say about anything. We theatre people are used to it. But Fridoline… I raised her differently, when you would allow it.'

'What precisely do they say?'

'Your illness…'

'What of it? Can't a man be ill? Please, Sabine. Let us go! Now! You have brought clothes for me, of course. I cannot be seen in public in this nightshirt—its buttons are gone. I have no trousers or shoes. Where are my clothes?'

'Things are difficult enough as they are. At home. Fridoline, the staff, your sisters, the gossip up and down the street, the way they look at us—even the Burgenthalers—the jumped-up little madam and her mouse of a husband!—it is very difficult. Not for me, of course. I am used to it. They talked about my father—you know this—they talked about him too. I am used to it. Water off a duck's back. It is Fridoline that I am concerned for.'

'She wants me to come home for Christmas.'

'Do you know what they call her?'

'It is nothing. Idle chatter. The Burgenthalers… who are they? A clerk and a wife who had the good fortune to be born to a man whose brother was rich and weak in the heart. Ignore them.'

'I do. I ignore it all. I ignore them when they sniff at me in the street, and when they hold their vulgar garden parties to which Fridoline and I are not invited. I ignored one of them today. It is nothing to me. Water off a duck's back. I ignore the Brahe boy and his mummery, the Merstenberg niece and her sniggering. I ignore it all. Pompous, straitlaced fools. I can stand the isolation. It is Fridoline for whom I am concerned. This is very hard on her.'

'We will move. Back to Leipzig perhaps. To my mother's house.'

'I will not set foot in that woman's house! And I will not be forced out of my home! I will not be driven away! I won't do it, Paul! I will not.'

She faced him as if she expected to be disagreed with. As if she expected a fight.

Schreber's hand went to his neck.

'Then we will stay.'

'Anna tells me that you have no intention of writing another book. Your doctor is of the same opinion. Are they right?'

'Yes.'

'Good. That would be the last straw.'

'You have brought with you a change of clothes?'

'I cannot look after you.'

'I will look after myself.'

'I am not in a position to look after an invalid. A lunatic. It is hard enough as it is. The headaches. I am weak down one side. Fridoline tells me I have changed. She weeps when I speak to her. She can be truly insufferable! Dannenberg advises three or four hours' sleep during the day. How can I be expected to run a house that way?'

'I will help. I will spend only afternoons at the courts.'

'Don't be ridiculous! How could you ever go back there? You were found gibbering in the doorway! Touching yourself! They call Fridoline the madman's daughter, and that is when they are being polite! They keep away from her. They pull faces at her. No. It is too much.'

'I am a respected man.'

'You are not.'

'I am!'

'No. And I am no longer a respectable woman.'

Sabine stepped away from him. Two steps now. Three.

'Wait! "*I remember nothing before today; all my memories are suddenly gone, and I only know that I lost all hope of ever seeing you again, of lifting my eyes to yours.*"'

'*Tannhäuser*. What of it?'

'Do you remember the performance in Leipzig? Just after we were married?'

'Of course I remember it, Paul.'

'Please, Sabchen, my dear. My love. Won't you stay? Won't you take me home?'

'No, Paul.'

'But Rössler!'

'Rössler tells me that he cannot cure you. I have asked that your care be put into the hands of another doctor—Kribben. He is much more sensible.'

Four steps. Five. Now she was in the doorway, silhouetted again. Beautiful again.

'Sabine!'

She turned, but she did not leave.

'Do you remember the other *Tannhäuser*, Paul? The last? When our boy was born... after the burial? Your mother bought the tickets and you demanded that I go? So that she would not be offended? The Dresden *Tannhäuser*? Do you remember that?'

'Please! I must go home!'

'In the scene from Elisabeth's aria?'

'I am almost well! I beg you!'

'You stood on the balcony of the box, in the middle of it all, and you bellowed out like an animal? So much that you were heard above the singers? And we were taken out? Everyone watching us? Do you remember that, too? Before they took you away, and left me alone?'

'Please, Sabine!'

'You left me, Paul. What was I to do? What if you never returned? They blame me, you know? For everything. For the end of the great Schreber line! Even Fridoline! That is the great joke. I was not to blame, Paul. It was never me. It was you. It was always you.'

'I know...'

'All you have to do is look at Fridoline, if you want proof.'

'I know…'

'Perhaps you wish she had been born a boy. Let me tell you something, Paul, when the midwife handed her to me and I saw she was a girl, I laughed! That'll do it, I said, let the whole sorry business end here!'

'Please, Sabine. I will rot here… I will die.'

'But Paul, I am not a doctor.'

'Please!'

'I am not a doctor.'

For a long time there was nothing, and then the door closed, and the key turned in the lock.

'Let me put my jacket down for you. Can't have you getting your knees dirty, now can we. Paul?'

'Is he in there?'

'Herr Schreber?'

'Papa?'

'He sometimes takes a little while to rouse, that's all.'

'Can't he hear me? Papa, it's me, Fridoline.'

'Come to the window, Paul!'

'Why isn't he coming?'

'Might I ask you to move over a little. I can sometimes… if I put my eye to the hole… yes! There he is! Paul! I can see you there! In the corner. Look toward the window please. It's Alexander Zilberschlag. The mysterious Jew. Your daughter wishes to see you—there isn't much time.'

'Papa, quickly! She'll find me, and she has said that I may not come again…'

'Keep away from me!'

'There! I told you he was there.'

'Papa, please, come to the window! Don't you want to see me?'

He turned his head, just a little, and looked up from the corner of his eye.

'Of course I want to see you.'

'Well, I am right here! Papa, you must come home!'

'I will keep a watch from the gate. If I see your mother I will clap my hands twice. Understood?'

'Papa, you must come home with me *now!* I am very firm on this matter. I will not leave without you.'

There was a glint of light at the window. It glistened in the water at the corners of his eyes. He wiped the tears away with his shirt.

'Papa!'

'Fridoline. Did I ever tell you how happy you have made me?'

'There is no time for that!'

'Your mother, too. Before you came it was very terrible. Do you understand?'

'Papa, please come home with me. Your friend says we can easily pull out this window. It seems it is loosened in the frame. The driver will attach a rope, and the horses will pull it.'

'Do not blame her, Fridoline. To have everything fall down. All her expectations turned to nothing. Like dust. That little girl and boy. Dead in her arms. She wouldn't believe it! She rocked them. Even when the nurse insisted. When the little girl was taken away… You must not imagine your mother does not love you. She had them entered on the family tree—our daughter and then our son. And those others that we never saw. Too young. Too small. Inside… terrible things go on inside, Frida. The way the world is… it is terrible.'

'Papa, there isn't much time!'

Through the gap in the window there came a worm—no, a finger—then another, slowly edging in, making no progress and then, suddenly, slipping forward an inch, perhaps less, until the whole hand was in, and then wriggling, seeking for something.

Schreber got to his feet and edged foot by foot to the window. He jumped up and looped his arm around the bars. The hand. It was warm and soft. He squeezed it. So solid! So firm!

'Fridoline! Listen to me! My papa—he knew how terrible the world was. The things inside: inside his head, inside the belly, everywhere. You must remain strong, Fridoline. Take your mother's example! You must take the world and write on it—make it obey *your* will. Do not obey its. Do you understand me? It is very important that you listen to what I have to say. I am a silly old man, just as your mother says. I am ill, just as she says, but I know some things better than either of you. The world cannot be allowed to dominate you. Other people cannot be allowed to dominate you. You must dominate them! Do you understand me, Frida? This is what my father knew, and he was punished for it. So too Gustav, in his way. But there is no choice. The world is chaos, there is no justice, you must enforce yourself on it. There is no other way.'

'She is coming!' said Zilberschlag. 'I've been clapping! I cannot stay here! Paul, I did my best.'

'Papa, please, let go of my hand! There isn't much time!'

'I am tired, Fridoline. The things I hear and see—they exhaust a man. Hope—it exhausts a man. I must make such effort just to remain alive. All I long to do is touch you and feel warmth.'

'Papa! You're hurting me! Let go!'

Schreber dropped the hand, and when she pulled it away she cut herself on the glass, very deeply, just above the wrist.

She squeaked like a little mouse and the hand hovered in the air, shaking and bleeding. He tried to stop the blood, but it came out regardless, dripping onto his shirt sleeves, splashing the wall. To find his hand again, she pulled away and cut the other side, just as bad.

There was screaming.

'Frida!'

'Hold still, you stupid child!'

Sabine!

'Papa!'

'Hold still! You'll cut off your hand, you silly girl! And you wonder why I tell you not to come!'

'I cannot leave him!'

The hand came in too far. It was smeared red and it grasped around desperately. The fingers opened and closed like a claw, until they reached him, gripping his face, but finding no purchase. Schreber pushed them away, but they found his hair and pulled it. He let himself drop from the window, leaving strands of his hair in her fist.

'Get away,' he muttered, too quietly for anyone to hear him. 'Go. Forget me. You are not mine.'

He went to the corner and curled.

'You are not mine, Fridoline. You are not mine.'

This he said to himself, over and over, and though for a while the room was filled with noise, soon Schreber forgot it.

Then there was a new doctor—not Rössler, but the same kind of man, with the same bearing. The same voice. He pushed his glasses up his nose.

'There will be a new regime, Herr Schreber. New medicines. A much more aggressive approach. I will demand your full co-operation.'

This new doctor wiped a damp cloth over the slate on the back of Schreber's door and scratched at it with a piece of chalk. When the prescription was finished he underlined it with a flourish and turned and moved on.

Behind him was Müller. He stood and watched, but he said nothing. He did not move or gesture, he merely stared.

'Müller!'

Before he left, the orderly smiled, sweetly. He let the tip of his tongue poke from between his lips.

Memories of a time before. Thoughts such as those that might fill the mind of a man who has lost everything, and who has withdrawn inside himself and found nothing of his own to cling to.

XXVII

In those final weeks he seemed to recover. They were happy, the family, first in that cautious excitement one feels on the regression of an illness, and then after, when one dares to take that regression for granted, a less acute but deeper happiness, redolent of all those days before, when there was nothing of import to be concerned over, but sweeter, knowing that something terrible has been overcome.

They went to the lakeside, to the place Pauline's family kept in Mecklenburg, and they blew the dust off the wooden chairs, and stamped back the weeds, and pulled up those boards on the jetty which had rotted and become heavy. Brittle and peppered with fungi, they added these to the pile of firewood, but at the far end, so that they might have time to dry out and not fill the little house with smoke and spluttering and that thick mushroomed earthiness that found its way into the lungs and could be tasted for days, even when they returned to the city.

When they walked the jetty, they hopscotched the gaps down to where the boat—overturned and slick with green—rested on its oars. They tipped it back into the water, their father laughing no less than the children when the cold water splashed Sidonie and made her shriek, and the ducks were set to flight.

The girls sat on the side and poked at the bottom of the boat with their feet, too nervous to put weight in it, while their father stripped off his shirt and trousers and, in only his underwear, dived into the cold water. The waves rippled back under where the children sat. When he came to the surface, impossibly far away, he shook like a dog shakes itself, and he roared. The peace of that lake had heard nothing like it for years, and neither had the children, and they roared too, and Paul and Gustav stripped naked and jumped in after their father.

Their mother smiled.

She went inside to the sound of laughter and water and flat oars inexpertly slapped down, and she pulled back the curtains. Dust filled the room. She opened the windows, stiff, so that she had to put her back into it, and, when they came in the end, the paint cracked away from the frames. The air was cold and fresh, and to breathe it in she felt she might never have breathed such purifying air, coming clean down the mountainside to rest in the valley.

She found she had to blink back tears. Silly!

Relief? It must have been: the relief of a heavy burden lifted, of locked doors opened, of unhappiness suppressed finding that suppression is no longer required. Of resentment finding no object. Of love returned.

She was grateful for the flimsy integrity of those buckling wooden walls. The rising emotion was too much for her to disguise, and she felt that to account for it would cause it to vanish—'Why are you crying, Mother?'—and so she hid herself in her work, in the search for pots for the evening meal, and in the scrubbing of potatoes: a ritual she had been taught by her mother's cook on sneaked visits to the kitchens, and which she secretly enjoyed, though she made the proper noises of annoyance and dismay when, *in extremis*, she was called upon to perform the tasks as a lady.

She slit a cut of the meat to remove a line of gristle. She pounded it with a mallet. She sifted flour. These things rendered her invisible to the world for long enough for the happiness to find its hold in her feelings—just a few minutes of peace—drawing strength from the misery that had gone before it.

All the while she could hear them—her husband and his boys, both now men—playing at fighting, and the girls—almost women—shrieking like children, bringing to mind the days before, collapsing the years of his illness suddenly, until she could almost believe that it had been nothing. She shut her eyes and listened, and made the milk mix with the flour smooth between her fingers. She took slow breaths, and when she pictured them the children were hip height, and her husband smoothed his wet hair straight and flat back behind his ears.

When the illusion was gone—as she cracked an egg—the return was not so disheartening because wasn't that the sound of her husband bellowing like a bull, and of Paul returning the call? Was a man laid low by an injury capable of such play? Was all hope gone, for a man like this? For all of them? No! There was hope. There was pleasure. She wiped her hands on her apron, slipped it from her shoulders and left the batter to thicken.

Outside, she took off her shoes and sat on the jetty so that her feet were in the water and she kicked and splashed, gently, like a gosling. She watched them out on the water, the girls shrieking in the boat, fending off the boys who made as if to capsize them, and Moritz supervising it all, a partisan for one side and then the other.

The sun passed from afternoon toward evening.

The dinner would be late, but the strict regimen of the clock had no place here: no place for the man her husband was today. If it was six, or six-fifteen, or seven o'clock, it made no difference at all. It was only when she tired of sitting that she decided to return to the kitchen, hot now with an oven that had burned through most of its wood, and she took more logs from the pile, and fed the fire, and put in the meat. The yellow-fleshed potatoes she left whole, and put some into the oven, and set others to boil, and soon the place was filled with the smells of her mother's kitchen and of her own childhood.

She felt the pang in the stomach felt on a Sunday afternoon when the desire is to play, but the appetite is stimulated by the smell of good things cooking. The stomach becomes ever more eager to eat, and the legs more tired, and the light begins to fade, and the colours of the garden deepen. Shadows fall long back toward the house, and suddenly, by some unspoken consensus, the children run back, and now it was her responsibility to take them and wash them and make them presentable. It seemed like this thought summoned them.

They came in, all of them—boys and girls—soaking. She rubbed them in towels, roughly, until they were tow-headed, stretching up, the boys bowing to her. Their father came behind, smiling, and shepherded them into the sitting room. She began to dish out the food, one plate for each, to be eaten on their laps, and, once grace was said, there was no pause and no formality: the food was taken and eaten, and all the while someone was talking—more than one—the room vibrating with conversation. Though she watched Moritz without letting him know, she did not see that characteristic flushing of his face, redness across the forehead and cheeks with a strip of bloodless white on the top lip. There was no tension in the muscles of his neck, no grinding of his jaw, no distraction in his eyes that told that he was elsewhere: in that place where pain could be countered, somewhere behind his face, somewhere inside. Instead he was everywhere, in his body, in the room, and if he was not laughing he was listening with great interest to the stories told by his children of the petty intrigues that filled their lives, of their amazement at this or that. The talk was never any clearer to her than that, because she was not interested in the play of the characters and stories, she was more aware of the tenor in which those stories were told, and even then not so much in that as in the spirit with which the words were received.

When eventually Paul saw her, he became aware of what was happening—of the significance of it—and she became aware of his understanding, and for a second, it seemed as if it would all collapse. In that second the father saw it, too. There was a moment in which everything could have changed—where self-consciousness could have undercut the living of life—but Paul's father took his wife by the hand and walked her out into the night. In the sky the stars shone and the new moon barely spoiled the darkness, and without saying a thing they realised that, for those final days, the world had changed.

That same moon saw him buried.

ACKNOWLEDGEMENTS

Thanks to Lavinia Greenlaw and Professor Lyndsey Stonebridge for their invaluable help during the drafting process. Thanks also to Paul Stanbridge, without whom this book might never have reached Simone Davies, Sam Jordison, and Eloise Millar at Galley Beggar, who took the brave step of publishing this difficult book (something that many of their contemporaries balked at).

I also acknowledge my debt to all the writers who have preceded me in the fields of Schreber studies and psychoanalysis, and in the unravelling of the psychological structure of fascism.